NIN

Born in Warsaw in 1960, Andrzej Stasiuk is the author of several major works of both fiction and non-fiction. He recently won the Nike, the most important literary award in Poland

ANDRZEJ STASIUK

Nine

TRANSLATED FROM THE POLISH BY
Bill Johnston

VINTAGE BOOKS
London

Published by Vintage 2008

2 4 6 8 10 9 7 5 3 1

Copyright © Andrzej Stasiuk 1999
Copyright © Suhrkamp Verlag Frankfurt am Main 2003
English translation copyright © Bill Johnston 2007

Andrzej Stasiuk has asserted his right under the Copyright, Designs
and Patents Act 1988 to be identified as the author of this work

First published with the title *Dziewic*

First published in Great Britain in 2007 by
Harvill Secker
Random House, 20 Vauxhall Bridge Road,
London SW1V 2SA

www.vintage-books.co.uk

Addresses for companies within The Random House Group Limited
can be found at: www.randomhouse.co.uk/offices.htm

The Random House Group Limited Reg. No. 954009

A CIP catalogue record for this book
is available from the British Library

©POLAND
This publication has been subsidised by Instytut Książki – the © POLAND
Translation programme

ISBN 9780099468622

The Random House Group Limited supports The Forest Stewardship
Council (FSC), the leading international forest certification
organisation. All our titles that are printed on Greenpeace approved
FSC certified paper carry the FSC logo. Our paper procurement
policy can be found at www.rbooks.co.uk/environment

Printed and bound in Great Britain by
CPI Bookmarque, Croydon CR0 4TD

To Jacek, also to Asia and Wojtek—they know what for.

NINE

9

SNOW HAD FALLEN IN THE NIGHT.

Paweł got out of bed and went into the bathroom. The light was on, the mirror was broken. Tubes and brushes and bottles had been swept off the shelf, were all over the floor. A stream of white toothpaste had shot out and dried on the willow-green wall. Disposable razors had been snapped in two and trodden into a torn box of soap powder. The cracked toilet seat lay in the corner. It occurred to him there was a lot of glass, so he went back to the hallway for his shoes.

He picked up one of the toothbrushes, rinsed it under the tap, scraped some toothpaste off the wall. Then he squatted and chose a razor with a cracked handle. He found the can of shaving cream under the bath. It was dented but something still swished inside it. He shaved in what was left of the mirror. He splashed water on his face. The Old Spice had been crushed, but there was still something left in the white plastic cover. He shook the crumpled container. It made a grating sound like a deaf-and-dumb version of a child's rattle. A few drops splashed onto his palm. He rubbed them on his cheeks. It hardly stung, so this time he must have managed not to cut himself. He used the toilet and went back into the living room.

Things were no better here. More smashed stuff. The cracked silver casing of the cassette player emptied its colourful guts onto the floor. He flicked the light switch. The lamp was in pieces. The light of early morning hung like dust in the air. Something white poked from the ripped upholstery of the sofa. He smoothed it with his hand and went to the pile of clothes spilling out of the wardrobe. He sniffed a few things to find something clean in the semi-darkness. He put on a shirt and sweater. By the bed he found his trousers; he dug out some socks from an untouched drawer and pulled them on, and at last stopped shivering.

He sipped at his coffee and gazed through the window. Snow lay on the roofs and on the pavement; the black trees were white now, and everything resembled a distant Christmas. A red bus cautiously made a turn. Sleepily and soundlessly it straightened, receded down the avenue of lime trees. The treetops faded into the low sky. He listened for the patter of drops in the gutters. There was no sound. "It'll lie for a while," he thought. He waited for the coffee to rouse him into a nervous flutter, into anything like fear or at least surprise. He drank the last mouthful, rinsed out the dregs, washed the mug, set it to dry, and went back into the living room. He shoved the pile of clothes back into the wardrobe to make room to walk—ten paces each way, from the door of the kitchen to the balcony window. He counted his steps, to a hundred and more, but in the end gave up, leaned his forehead against the cold pane, and closed his eyes. "Think, think," he muttered. "I should take something to help me sleep at night." Outside the window a gritter was passing, casting shavings of snow from the blue tarmac, but he did not see this, and when he opened his eyes, the white landscape had been scored by a horizontal line. He felt sorrow—the kind of sadness accompanying a memory that can't be summoned in its entirety.

He returned to the kitchen. The clock showed 5:32. Most of the poorest were now up and on their way to wherever they had to go. The long straight stretch of road to the bus terminal had been cleared. The dark band led to distance and the future. Two baby Fiats were approaching like toys the colour of cheerful fire and green metal. From the second floor, drivers' faces could not be made out, but he knew they were decent people: in less than nine hours they'd be coming back, in the same or reverse order. The bare tarmac echoed the growl of their two-cylinder engines. Two crows, indifferent to it all, remained in their chestnut tree, on branches that hung over the curve in the road like the spokes of a broken umbrella. The little cars accelerated and rumbled on, and Paweł felt a stab of envy in his heart.

He went into the living room to watch from the other window as the two patches of colour grew smaller, disappearing in the grey mist of early morning, where the trees blended with the pylons. The ribbon of road crawled onto the overpass across the train tracks, and for a moment it looked as if the little Fiats were climbing into the hazy sky.

He fetched the litter bin, set it in the middle of the room. But all this mess wouldn't fit in ten bins. He kicked the broken bottles under the bookcase, and did the same with the books. Now he could even walk with his eyes closed. He extended the path to the kitchen window between the remains of the crockery. Ten and five made fifteen paces each way.

At five to six he said to himself: "To hell with this." He put on his brown leather jacket in the hall, walked out, and slammed the door without even checking whether his keys were in his pocket.

On snowy mornings, when there's no wind, the air of the city outskirts tastes of coal smoke, and the scrape of spades on the pavement is metallic. He decided to go to the terminal and sit for a while in a warm bus. Sugary snow stuck to the red twigs of the hedge. He passed an old-fashioned villa with a four-column veranda that had a child's tricycle with an unmoving windmill stuck in a handlebar. On the path there were no prints except for a few cat's paws. He passed the next house and two others, grey and square-cornered. The occupants had already left, removing the snow with the soles of their shoes. Mud and sorry grass remained. Then the buildings came to a sudden end to make room for the tapered bulk of a church. The brickwork had the colour of congealed blood. Like a wound seeping through a bandage. At the far end of the street he saw a bus standing. There was no one around. Somewhere a dog barked. The yapping was drowned out by a distant clatter of railway carriages. It must have been an intercity or express train, because the sound quickly ended.

The warm purr of the bus made him feverish. In only a few minutes he had several dreams. People boarded and passed through his visions without dispelling them: the visions split, then fused again, because the stuff of the past from which they were woven still lived in the world. As alive as people. He dreamed several years, in episodes. He stopped at the night before, bounced back to his childhood, when no one yet imagined that commerce would save the world. He raised his shoulders, stuck his hands between his thighs. Leaning forward, his eyes closed, he looked like someone teetering on a cliff edge and about to jump, or to lose his nerve and fall safely on his back.

The buzzer sounded, doors hissed shut, and the bus moved. He kept his eyes closed. It was a game: to guess where on the route he was—he'd open his eyes quickly, "Just checking," and win or lose. Zawadzki's house, the screwed-up skip, the intersection with Bystrzycka, the stand of birch trees where the drunks hung out on a bench, and so on till the next stop. Listening to the engine, counting distances in the dark. He'd get it right or not. It's easier for the blind, because of the constant fear, and in the end they get used to it.

Feeling the bus turn, he looked out the window. The whiteness dazzled. The stop was coming up. A snow-covered square overgrown with bushes, then the tin wall of a warehouse and a path along which people approached from a small development of three barrack blocks where the weeks extended down long passageways: Monday at one end, at the other Saturday just beginning. The stop was deserted. The old-fashioned post was a red crayon stuck into dirty paper. Everywhere else they'd put up the new blue signs; not here. "Beirut," he thought. "What do they need a stop for? They're not going anywhere. They're fucked." And a sadness came, wretched self-pity, the kind of feeling you can get from memories, those unwanted images that crawl out from nowhere just when the mind needs to be cool, clear—as cool and clear as the present is.

The bus climbed the overpass. A milk float came the other way. The crates were the colour of rain, the caps glittered like cheap false teeth. That was how his imagination was working. The divider seemed thin, insubstantial. The openwork of the girders provided a hopelessly trite vision of infinity. The rails ran north and after three hundred kilometres fell into the sea like silver threads, while the power lines vanished in the sky, which at night was lit up by the fiery plumes of the refinery. A local train clattered away towards the city. It had emerged from the grey morning and plunged back into it at once. From the open driver's cabin a radio played for those already up. The music of Radio One had the taste of tedium; otherwise all those people would long ago have gone mad or died a violent death— you can't take five thousand mornings; there has to be a way out, some poison, something to fill the void between heaven and earth.

The overpass ended, the houses reappeared. Each stood alone, surrounded by a chain-link fence; the square links repeated into infinity the angular shape of the buildings, windows, and gardens. At the next stop three people got on. The bus lurched forwards; a fat woman with a ticket in her hand stumbled backwards and brushed his arm. He felt her soft backside, smelled her perfume.

To the right there'd once been fields. Clouds would gather over the river, rise and move across the sky, dragging their shadows over the autumn stubble where cows grazed. Cars would move slowly in the narrow street. The horizon was a decoration made from torn green paper. One day he rode his bike there. Yellow paths twisted among willows. He saw a teenage girl in a red bikini. She was pissing. He even saw the dark patch on the sand. When she saw him, she stood up slowly and pulled up her bikini bottom.

Now a row of billboards separated the road from the boundless grey grass that had taken over the vegetable gardens. On the horizon grey apartment complexes stood, or rather hung in the sky like ragged, dull curtains; the walls and the clouds were the same colour. "A blond pussy," he thought, remembering how the red cloth moved up, brushed her bright hair. Then it was gone with a snap as she pulled her thumbs from the elastic waistband and put her hands on her hips. He had pedalled harder, the hot wind in his face. The billboards separated him from all that now.

Someone came and stood by his seat.

"So you're taking the bus today?"

He looked up, recognized the guy, said:

"Yeah, sometimes you have to."

He stood by the window and stared at the brown building of the railway offices. Here there wasn't even a trace of snow. The road and pavement were wet. Wheels hissed on the tarmac. The façade behind the iron railings seemed to be sinking into the ground. "Tympanum"—he recalled the word from school, and then, also from long ago, "Brandenburg Gate," and other images and words. Three minutes passed. He raised his eyes to the Orthodox church, its black spheres wreathed with a network of bare branches. "Who the fuck needs it?" he thought. "Russkies here, Germans there, Germans here, Russkies there." An electric train pulled into Wileński station, and the crowd filed over the pedestrian crossing while the light was red, entered the maw of the underpass, and emerged on the other side, by the post office. The trams took bites from the churning mass of people, swallowed some and whisked them off to the four corners of the city. The ones travelling to the WZT television plant had it worst, they had to walk to Ząbkowska Street and catch a crowded, sagging 138 to the huge gas tank that he dreamed about at night. He dreamed that it exploded, that the fire moved across the ground, stripping it of everything, of the brush and grass and the unkempt skips in Olszynka, and it poured into the railway tunnels on Kozia Góra, till all that was left were the frames of buildings and cars, naked skin with the raw veins of rails. Kamczatka Prison burned like a house of cards, and all the women thieves and the murderesses, beautiful and unattainable, melted into the metal skeletons of their own beds. He had dreamed this many times.

At the corner by the post office and Władysław IV Grammar School were three Gypsy women, brightly coloured and motionless. The light of early morning could not deal with them. They waited for the crowd to thin, went underground. He looked for them, but they did not resurface. A number 21 tram scattered sparks, hurrying south. The air parted before it with a groan. A woman carrying a large red and blue striped bag barely managed to jump out of the way. He tried to remember whether there were trams in Moscow. He drew a curlicue on the window, a blurred, greasy smear on the dry pane. He went to the other end of the apartment. The hardwood floor creaked under the grey carpet. He went into the kitchen. Here the floor was broad varnished boards. On the table were the remains of breakfast—two egg cups, two stoneware bowls, and a basket with brown bread. One of the eggs had barely been touched. The yolk showed through the white like an eye with cataracts. A cornflake, stuck to the rim of one of the bowls, was wet and cold. He took it and tasted it. No sugar. He tried a little milk from the other bowl. It was sweet as syrup. Back in the hallway, he pushed open a yellow door, but shut it again right away. He returned to the kitchen and opened a dark wooden cabinet. Plates and bowls were in two stacks; the rest of the space was taken up by a coffeepot and a soup tureen, both covered with dust. Three teacups from different sets. The smell of damp wood and food. The smell of old bread lingering, as it always does in cupboards rarely used. He looked out of the window but saw nothing moving. Lifeless windowpanes glistened on the wall of the building next door.

In the main room he circled around the spot where once a table would have stood. He broke away at the fourth lap, drawn to a white bookcase. His hands in his pockets, he studied the objects on it. They reminded him of nothing and served no purpose. A china ballerina, glass receptacles filled with knick-knacks, an Egyptian dreambook, a Chinese I-Ching, a phonebook, four volumes of an encyclopaedia, a row of cassette tapes: Marillion, the Pet Shop Boys, English for Beginners, Smoleń and Laskowik, Kora with Maanam. A hairbrush, a shoehorn. He looked in the drinks cabinet and found an opened bottle of cabernet, wine glasses, an ashtray, and a reflection of his stomach in the mirror. He closed the flap; the glassware rattled, a tram sounded its bell, and the floor shook.

The cupboard was locked. He couldn't get the key to turn. He pressed on one side, tried again.

The sheets and quilt cases lay close together, ironed flat. To slip his hand between them he had to wiggle his fingers as if separating the pages of a heavy book lying on its side. "From the cleaner's," he realized. It wasn't so tight between the bedding and towels, so he put his hand in further, almost to the elbow, and felt in a semicircle the cold, rough darkness, but there was nothing there. On the shelf below was an iron. He moved it aside so he could reach behind a stack of tablecloths and linen curtains. The iron was slightly warm. It was set to cotton. He examined the clothes. The T-shirts had the softness of things worn and washed a hundred times. Green, black, red, two white, another black, at the very bottom turquoise. Four pairs of jeans: white and light blue Levi's, dark green cords, and faded, frayed khakis lay next to thick tracksuit tops. Labels and logos could be seen on the edge of some. He could feel the embroidery or sticky rubber lettering against the back of his hand. Higher up were blouses and skirts. He ran his thumbs over them like two packs of large, flimsy playing cards, pushed them aside, and looked behind them. The little bundle was wrapped in newspaper. He took it out carefully, squatted, set it on the floor. He whistled a dirty song. "Fuck, oh fuck, he made a fucking mess," as the yellowed page from *Życie Warszawy* crumbled like a wafer and Jaroszewicz's face cracked in two. In the chocolate box he found a lock of light hair, a dry rose dark with age, and a stack of index cards with writing on them. He stopped whistling, wrapped the box roughly, and thrust it back where it belonged. The scraps of newspaper he kicked under the rug.

The shelf with underwear was at face level, brassiere cups stuck into one another: black, white, black, flesh, ridiculous and disembodied, pairs of hats side by side, cycling caps without peaks. He stopped and went to the window. The crowd had thinned; the clock on the tower was frozen at a quarter past three on some unknown day. His eyes swept the pavements and pedestrian crossings, Świerczewskiego and Wileńska, Targowa. The pane was cool against his forehead. A 101 bus dragged its belly across the tram tracks and pulled up by the Orthodox church. A man in marbled jeans left the queue at the kiosk and jumped through the doors as they were closing. Three characters came around the corner, turned into Cyryla, and marched towards the park, the wind from the river lifting their nylon jackets like wings—black, brown, navy blue. They'd been drinking already and did not feel the cold. He would have liked to have been in their place. Another hundred metres, and they'd be among the tangled paths, hidden by the bare bushes, still visible but safe. The trees would close over them like a ceiling. They'd find a bench next to the old men playing draughts. They'd relax, and the smoky sky would provide light all the way till dusk and the moment when, freed of pain and fear, they would head back into a darkness filled with electric stars strewn by the pantographs of the trams moving down 11 Listopada and Stalowa towards the Bethlehem night of Szmulki and Targówek, and they would wait and wait an ocean of time, while time was exactly what he didn't have.

They crossed Jagiellońska by the petrol station. A 509 hurried them with its horn, but he no longer saw this. He had returned to the open cupboard. He touched the knickers. They were like a stack of colourful children's books. Fairy tales in pastel shades, read to me Mummy, a yellow Donald Duck, a green Funny Ducky, the Adventures of Fiki-Miki, the Tricky Monkey . . . He passed his fingers over them, from top to bottom, back again, then pushed gently between the white and the black ones. He felt himself getting hard.

A moment later he sensed that he was not alone. He froze, listened. The tapping repeated. It was barely audible but definitely came from the apartment. He took a breath and closed his lips tightly. He took a step; the floor creaked. He stopped, and there was an even clearer knock. He approached the sofa covered with a white furry throw. He lifted the edge.

The tortoise stared at him, motionless and cold as a camera. Matte brown, like something very old and leathery. It moved, and the empty cup in which its leg was stuck tapped the floor. "Fucking reptile," he said softly, and started to breathe again.

Just as he closed the wardrobe door, he heard the click of the bolt in the hallway.

She was wearing a long grey woollen overcoat. He went to help her off with it, but she slipped it from her shoulders with a quick, deft movement and hung it on a hook. She removed her shoes, put on slippers, and went to the kitchen. She started clearing the table, putting the dishes in the sink, scraping the leftovers into the bin, the half-eaten egg on the draining board. She didn't look at him once; her hands shook.

In the grey light, in the silence, the clatter was hard to bear. Then she said finally, "Sorry I left you like that. I had to get there on time. The director is a dragon, and I owe them from last month." She glanced at the green plastic clock on the wall. It read 8:22. "What do you want? Coffee or tea? I have to leave in a minute."

"When does the kid start school?"

"Next year. I'll make you coffee."

He sat on a chair and looked at her legs. Her feet, in their blue slippers with raised heels, pattered between sink and stove. She liked to look smart, even at home. She never wore her tattered slippers. Pat, pat, pat, and a cup and spoon, pat, pat, the coffee jar, the whistle of the kettle. "With cream?" "Whatever," he answered, and stared at her arse under her beige dress. Not a crease, so she must have got up at some ungodly hour to see to herself and the child. And do the ironing—he remembered the warm iron. Her dark hair was tied at the back.

"What's going on with you?" she asked.

"Nothing."

"You come here after all these years, at the crack of dawn, and you say nothing's going on?"

"I was passing by. I thought I'd just check to see if you still live here."

"Where did you think I'd be living? California?"

She put a brown cup with a green stripe in front of him. He caught the scent of her perfume and the warmth of her body and suddenly noticed that it was cold in the apartment. When she leaned forwards, he glanced at her breasts. That was where the scent was coming from. Little bits of heat stole out from under her dress, rising from her pussy to her stomach and flowing out between her tits like water from a fountain. He thought of putting his hand there after all these years, to see what would happen, if something could be done with time, curious. But this lasted only a moment. She straightened and moved away. Again he found himself in the cold, empty air of a home that rarely has visitors.

"How's Jolka?" he asked. "And the rest?"

"She married a Greek guy and emigrated. Bolek . . ."

"Yes? I met him on the street one time. He was in a hurry."

"He's making money. Actually, it seems to make itself for him. He sells, buys—I don't know what." She set her cup down on the sill. Grey dust dropped from the window, the ceiling, the wall; a dog barked in the courtyard; beneath the radiator lay a wounded soft toy.

"I go and see him sometimes." She took the cup to the sink, came back for his. "I really have to go now."

"He's still living in the same place?"

"Yes."

An almost empty number 26 took her into the distance due west, by the putrid branch of the river—a minute in space when from the other bank the city looks like a model of something that hasn't been built yet. Little towers try to touch the sky—they are always too short.

Without thinking he followed the tram. He cut across Jagiellońska, turned into the park to think. The brown tree trunks shone with a moist gleam that made things even darker. He passed a tramp on a bench, who looked like an old mannequin. The man didn't look up. He was smoking a cigarette in a dark holder, his hands thrust into the pockets of an army coat. "This April's like autumn," Paweł thought. He reached a broad avenue that led to the zoo. But he had no time for monkeys or penguins. He turned left, went back to the street. Seeing a kiosk reminded him he was out of cigarettes. He rummaged through his pockets, adding note to note. A hundred and twenty thousand, not a penny more. A Zippo imitation, keys, a used-up phone card, no ID, two tokens. He bought a pack of Mars; he lit up, and his head spun. The spires of St Florian's aimed skywards like old-fashioned rockets. Old women were filing in, their outlines small and black. Rolling along like beads. A 162 left the stop. People looked straight ahead, or into the future. A red-headed girl glanced at him with vacant eyes. He waited for the green light and crossed. He decided to give himself a bit more time and have another cigarette, and as he was looking for a place to shelter for a moment, to shield himself from the wind off the river, he realized he'd been born here. A few yards away was the hospital. Amid a tangle of bushes in the little square, in the mud, beneath a swollen sky, the white ambulances by the entrance looked as unreal and shameless as death. In the doorway were the scrubs of the orderlies, because when shit happens, people get jumpy and try to put a bungled life to rights in fifteen minutes. "I ought to go in," he thought, "and have myself sewn back up into some pussy. A Caesarean in reverse."

The tramp in the coat passed him. Everyone was passing him, though there weren't many. At nine thirty the city hides, halts, gives time to those who have nothing to do. He flicked the butt away. It landed on yellow grass. A thread of smoke rose vertically, then the wind caught it. He stopped thinking, turned, and went towards Floriańska, where since time immemorial men loitered at the kerb in bouclé sweaters and flared trousers whose creases had been ironed in twenty years ago and had stayed that way ever since. Above their heads, over their whispered chatter, brick walls rose to the sky, but no one would bet there was anything behind them—apartments, a room with a kitchen, old furniture with peeling veneer. Teenagers copied their fathers, though their outfits were more garish, Ford, Bulls, or Nikes with tongues licking the pavement. They huddled in tight circles discussing how to handle the world that day, the angle to take. No women. A black and white mongrel ran from group to group, looking for its master. Someone threw a firecracker. "Oh, right," he thought. "Easter's here."

In front of the Pedet department store a memory came: he once went to a puppet theatre with his mother. Cigarettes glowed in the dark. Men stood in entranceways talking in a language he didn't understand, though some words were familiar. It was November, December. The white light of the street lamps couldn't reach the pavement, remained trembling and hissing above. The bare branches were metallic. His mother quickened her pace; through her cold hand he could feel her fear.

On the stage, in a flood of gold, in the silver dust of the spotlights, a prince was rescuing a princess or something like that, a story he cared about only because it was the first time he'd been in a place like this. He wanted to walk once more down that street scooped out of the darkness, a few steps from the brightly lit Targowa, once more see the red sparks wandering up and down. When the show was over, his mother took him firmly by the hand and slipped into a large group of children and adults. He was disappointed. Pedet resembled a glass cabinet. Somewhere inside was the plaster woman with large breasts squatting over a basket of food, her arse like two cushions. He often thought about her.

As he crossed the deserted, glistening Okrzei, on which a single distant car was coming from the river, he remembered it was there, behind the department store, that he was with his father. Low, single-storey buildings you entered through a gate in the wall. In a dingy room, men in rubber boots threw entrails into metal containers. A concrete cylinder filled with glistening pieces of liver—a mountain of slippery, shining red, with blood splashing underfoot. His father knew someone there.

A car passed him with a wet hiss. Carrying with it the smell of mist from the port. He turned left. At this hour the buses were empty.

He walked by an endless line of cars, noted the makes. A mustard apartment building protected him from the wind. The trees had grown, and the field of rubble had become a playground. He reached the end of the building, and the cold hit him in the face, but then came the next building. He counted the stairways. Intercoms had been installed everywhere. Block 4, stairway 6. It was supposed to add up to ten. He could never remember the numbers. His finger roamed the buttons. Someone asked questions, stopped, then someone else, then finally the buzzer sounded. He pushed open the door, caught the smell of wet concrete, and to save time took the stairs.

The man who opened was tall, big.

"I'm not buying anything," he said, and was about to close the door. "Lot of good that goddamn intercom did," he muttered.

"Bolek?"

The door stopped closing.

"Oh? Who are you? Listen, pal . . ." The man raised his voice. In the apartment a dog barked. A moment later a rottweiler poked its head between the man's jeans and the door frame.

"Easy, Sheikh. What's this about?"

"Bolek, it's me, Pawel."

"Pawel who?" He frowned. The ball in his memory started to spin and clatter till in the end it found its slot.

"Kicior's friend?"

"Bogna's, from way back . . ."

The man relaxed. A faint smile of disbelief. He opened the door wider and grabbed the dog by its collar.

"And here I thought you were a door-to-door salesman . . ."

"I bought the place next door and took the wall out. It makes thirteen hundred square feet in all." His gold chain slipped from his wrist onto his forearm. He shook it back when he reached for the bottle. Each time he raised his glass or cigarette, the bracelet fell halfway to his elbow. The dog lay on a red mat dozing. Paweł said he was picking up his car from the shop in the afternoon, and he only drank every other round. Fire blazed in his empty stomach and rose to his throat, but his head was clear, cold. The day was filling out, rising; an umbrella of clouds hung over downtown, but the light gradually cleared a path for itself, and the sky kept getting higher. Over a hotel fluttered a blue flag. It probably wouldn't get warmer, but as it got brighter, he looked around the apartment. It was like a copy of something that doesn't exist. Heavy black furniture with yellow fittings on the corners. A huge cabinet went all the way to the ceiling, may have continued to the floor above. China lay behind frosted glass decorated with golden flourishes. He was sitting in a black leather armchair, drinking from a glass with a silver pattern. Bolek let his belly spill out of his T-shirt. A palm in a glazed pot threw a shadow on them. Above the palm a brass chandelier burned. His thoughts were calm, exact, but had nothing to hold on to. He felt hunger, so he smoked cigarette after cigarette. An aeroplane moved across the window from right to left: a twinkling green firefly on a tattered strip of cloud-free sky.

"Paweł, you remember when those soldiers went for us at the Caprice?"

He remembered. The drunken corporal got a chair over his head, so the cloakroom attendant locked the door and they used the chair to climb out of a big window and ran towards the station, down the steps into the park, to hide in the dark. Out of breath, they fell on the snow and howled with laughter as the trains on the bridge tore through the sky like yellow lightning.

"You couldn't run now, you bastard," he thought. Bolek took another drink, pouring from glass to throat. The vodka arced through the air, fell between the parted lips. Time was playing tricks, hurrying, slowing, making almost invisible things almost visible. He couldn't remember if two strikes meant the quarter-hour or the half-hour. The sun had come out, but it shone only on the back of the building. Another plane flew past, this time from left to right, its nose up, bright as a speck of fire, heading north, Stockholm, Oslo, Helsinki, maybe even Greenland, where it would be extinguished with a hiss in the snow. His left boot was cold, he cigarette his toes, the sock was wet. Bolek crushed his cigarette end in the ashtray with a soft clink of gold, hiccuped, got up, walked to the back of the apartment.

Now alone, Paweł could take everything in. To his left was the sea. Boundless, blue, with white horses and a yacht halfway between the armchair and the horizon. The potted palm stood where the land should have been. He turned even more to the left. The photo mural did not end with the wall but bent at the corner and continued on the next wall, the one with the window, and if not for the window frame it would have blended with the sky.

He turned back. He'd already seen the cabinet, so only the right side remained. The wall was covered with flesh roses on brown fabric. A green-flower lamp bracket jutted out. Below it, a bronze bar tray on lion paws and wheels. Jack Daniel's and Johnny Walker shoulder to shoulder, hardly touched. The Smirnoff wasn't so flush, but the brandy hid both label and level in shadow. "Son of a bitch," he thought, the white fever of rye in his mouth. The dead body of a television gleamed in the far corner and had everything needed under it, VCR, video-cassettes, CD player, radio. Three remotes poked from the shelf like the tips of polished shoes. His gaze returned to the cabinet.

His thoughts circled the room, sometimes keeping up with his eyes, sometimes not. He reached for a cigarette, a Marlboro, but put it back. He could have hidden the writing under his finger, but there was no gold band like on his Mars. He got up.

Bolek returned just in time, zipping himself up while the flush sounded behind. Paweł felt his hair stand on end. He froze, tried to look behind him.

"Don't move. Not another step."

"I've been meaning to get rid of this stuff. I could have chucked half these things and got new." He adjusted the picture on its hook. The frame knocked the wall. Somewhere in the building a lift moved. Bolek looked once more at the boy in the white suit with a Candlemas candle in his hand; he sat on the sofa and poured another drink. "You'd have lost your balls, you know."

"I wanted to look up close," said Paweł.

"Yeah, well you wouldn't have. I forgot to tell you not to move. He's like that. You know what I paid to have him trained? It probably would have been cheaper to get a new one."

They drank; time passed. Paweł felt himself moving through the room like a draught, speeding up, down the stairs, pouring out into the street, sweeping everyone up like a flood, carrying them. The people would try to stay on the surface but would sink, only the restless and the single would manage, so he set his glass aside but didn't reach for a cigarette.

"Bolek, I need money."

The other man looked at him with eyes as empty as the bottle on the table, completely sober. He folded his hands on his belly.

"Don't we all . . ."

"Bolek, I'm serious."

"Me too. Everyone's serious about money."

"Bogna told me to see you."

Bolek leaned forward, pulled the sleeves of his jacket back a little as if preparing to make an important shape in the air.

"What's she got to do with it? If she's so smart, let her lend you the money."

"She just said . . ."

"How much?"

"Two hundred."

Bolek unclasped his hands, straightened his leg, reached into a trouser pocket. He took out a roll of notes, peeled off two, and threw them on the glass tabletop. They looked like unfinished paper flowers.

"Bolek, I need two hundred million old zlotys."

Bolek rested his elbows on his knees and looked at Paweł as if for the first time.

"Are you nuts? I hardly fucking know you."

The bus was almost empty. They were riding beneath the concrete rainbows of the overpass. Two teenagers were spitting on the traffic from above. An old game that all boys play: hit the moving target. At their feet, a beer bottle waited quietly. To the left and right the apartment buildings took deeper root. They were old. They brought to mind steep riverbanks where birds nest. The people in them had had time to age; some died, and new people moved in and were now stuck with the lingering smell of others. A person must sweat a lot in a room for the stink to get into the walls. He tried to remember which building he threw up in once, how then he tried to get home in the middle of the night but had nothing, not one cigarette, or money for a ticket. In those days he didn't smoke as much, so he walked for two or three hours, the city at night as huge and still as a thing from a dream. "She had a bra but no tits"—but he couldn't recall the building or her name. The vegetable gardens appeared. The cumulus sky flattened the land, the fences, sheds, and trees were like toys, a country of tiny folk, dolls. A naked tangle of branches along the horizon like a stiff web and not a soul, only the little vanes on the roofs of summer houses with their faces to the wind and spinning in endless air. That too went by. Again they found themselves in the shadow of apartment buildings. The daylight congealed; the cross-street traffic thinned it for a moment, then the sun put the car in its cement, while he tried to recall another distant thing to escape the present, to catch his breath and stay in the past, where there is never danger.

But there was no time, they were on the bridge. The chimneys of the Siekerki power plant smoked, the wind pulling their white braids west. They drifted over the Sadyba River and Paluch, over the dogs howling day and night in the animal shelter cages, though no one came. Something whizzed by in the left lane; he saw a red rear with Berlin plates. "If it went from west to east, it'd be easier," he thought. "Some could go with the current, some could use sails." He remembered a schoolbook picture: ragged, bearded men pulling a barge along a bank. It would be easier, but now it was all fucking train, car, plane. The yellow river crept its oily way. Slow eddies made swirls of foam, straightened, and moved north under the bridges: five here, then in Nowy Dwór, Wyszogród, Płock, two in Włocławek, one in Toruń, another in Fordon, which stuck in his mind ever since he learned there was a women's prison there—the name had been familiar only from the labels on jars of jam. A long time ago, but the river always woke the memory: red, sweet strawberry jam, with the delicate crack of those things not seeds or chewy bits but like bumps on the skin of a fruit. And the cool, dim corridors where silent women move in solitude, more untouchable than the queens of old and a thousand times more physical. He imagined their fingers on the jars, and he sought the taste of their skin, no doubt smooth and white under that dull prison cloth, delicate as plants that grow in darkness. But that was long ago; he remembered it but felt nothing now. The tavern ship gleamed on the bank like a gnawed bone. The bus was moving at speed. The day was taking a deep breath before the afternoon crap when the route would clog and come to a standstill. In the distance, the black maw of Rozdroże. Then a guy in a bomber jacket, sheepskin, asked for his ticket.

He went through his pockets with the lethargy of a hopeless cause. In his jacket two inside pockets and two low, then the back pockets of his trousers, the front, the rubber pouch, the jacket again, watching the dark tunnel come dizzyingly. The conductor stood holding the overhead bar with both hands. Out of the corner of Paweł's eye, a white trainer tapping the black floor. A woman in a red coat stood at the exit. "So what now—keep playing stupid or do we get off and talk like people?" The bus slowed and rolled into a stop. He waited for the hiss and jumped. He felt a hand on his hair, ducked, the woman jumped too, pushing the crowd aside, clearing a path, stumbling. He jumped over her, hit someone with his shoulder, and made it to the steps. Running up, he knew he didn't have much of a chance, but didn't stop, went right, to the open gate of the park. The place was empty, damp, quiet. He tried to go faster but tripped, and his knees barely kept him up. He'd had enough, thought of stopping, then was tackled. Head first, his hands in the gravel. Now he could catch his breath. He tried to get up, but a foot was on his neck pushing his face into the ground. He got two kicks; he curled up, turned on his side, and saw there were three of them. The one in leather was doubled over and gasping for breath, the others too, though less so. On his knees, he waited in the middle of the triangle.

"What good did that do you?" asked the short one in jeans and a baseball cap. "Fucking sprinter," said the third. From his panting, his words were tattered, faint.

Paweł got up slowly and sat on a bench. The men surrounded him and waited for their hearts and lungs to manage the air and blood. Their anger gradually left them, and his fear left him. Red lights from the buses on the Aleje, through the gloom of the park; drops of silver on the branches. The drops fell, losing their gleam in the air.

"All right, your papers," said the one in leather.

"I don't have any," he replied.

"Then out with the money."

"No money either."

The one in leather nodded, and the other two pulled Paweł to his feet. They found some change, less than a hundred, looked at his lighter, then gave it all back.

"Crap," said the one in the baseball cap. "We should take this joker in. If we tell the cops he resisted, they'll keep him for a bit."

"Why bother?" said the third.

"He pissed me off. I got all sweaty."

They tried to push him towards the exit on Piękna, but he wouldn't move. They grabbed him by the shoulders, and one of them whacked him on the back of the head. "Move it, you piece of shit, or you stay here for good."

"Please, I can't go to the cops—I don't have time."

He tried to break away. They pulled him; the gravel crunched. A woman with a pushchair appeared, and feverishly he remembered the black grip of the gun he saw in Bolek's hall, it had been sticking out between the clothes in the cabinet by the front door. Just a glimpse, but Bolek had been behind him and knew he saw it. The woman with the pushchair was getting closer; she had on a grey coat. In the mist the glasses she wore were like discs of ice. She slowed, then took a side path and broke into a run. The child started crying.

"Listen," he said, "I have a wedding ring—take it. It's worth something." He pulled at the ring, but it was stuck. With spit, the ring came off.

In the meantime Bolek was pacing from room to room in his apartment. From the room where they sat before, black and gold, to the blue room with silver trinkets, to the red one. The kitchen was white and gleaming. Coming back, there were two more rooms—one the colour of sea water with an empty aquarium, then a silver-grey room with a swivel chair in the middle and a mirror full of sky but brighter and prettier than the sky. The dog stayed in its corner. Bolek opened the last door—this room was pink. Dark inside, but smelling like a powder compact. He went to the window and parted the curtains. A woman lay under a white sheet, the thin fabric on her body like a second, looser skin. Her legs, backside—everything visible, just a little blurred. He sat on the edge of the bed and patted the backside. She murmured and stuck her head out, a peroxide blonde. She turned over, her breasts pointing straight at the ceiling. He covered her left nipple with his hand.

"Come on, Porkie, I'm not even awake yet."

"Then sleep. Who's stopping you." He kicked off his slippers and lay next to her. He tried to roll on top, but she slipped a hand out and pinched his roll of belly flesh.

"Give over, Porkie. Tell me who that was. I heard. Or was I dreaming?"

He put his hand between her legs. The sheet made rays like drapery representing the sun.

"Just a guy. Paweł."

"What did he want?"

"Money. They all want money."

"And?"

"I gave him Mr Max's phone number."

"You're heartless, Porkie."

"I could have set Sheikh on him." He moved closer, kissed her neck. Tried to throw his left thigh over her leg.

"Give it up," she said.

"Please . . ."

"Did you shave?"

"Yes. And I showered."

"Then you can do the thing I like."

Bolek slid off the bedding and crawled to the foot of the bed. He lifted the hem of the sheet and pulled it over his head. He looked like an old-fashioned photographer. Three fire engines raced down Ostrobramska. The blue magnesium of their lights tore the river of traffic in two. An old woman in a baby Fiat, afraid, rode up onto the pavement. Syl's eyes were wide open. It was a game she played: to keep them open as long as she could, till they shut on their own.

Paweł stepped out of the lift, adjusting his eyes. In the semi-darkness he thought about how he was safe as long as it was quiet and the lift was still going down. No one would see him, no one would hear him. This floor was empty. Some Chinese had rented it, but all they did was put new locks on the doors. Below, life murmured and clattered. He could even smell people. The kitchens in those apartments were cramped; at dinnertime the women put the chain on and opened the door a crack. He took out a cigarette, lit a match. A gloom hung at the end of the hall, as if dust were rising from the floor, though the air was still. Old walls do that. The match was reflected in the pane of the door leading to the outside gallery, but there were no windows there, only a wall and the black overhang of the roof. The flame died. He put the cigarette back in the pack. He moved down the hall almost by touch. The sound of his steps carried far in the building. Six steps, a landing, six more, and a speck of light. He felt for the door with his hand and knocked softly.

The owner wasn't in—sweating somewhere else. An hour ago he had closed the door behind him and taken the stairs down. Afraid of the lift, its closed space pressing in on the body and brain from all six sides, crushing them into a hot cube from which blood would spurt. This was how his imagination worked. He had run down six floors to feel the rush of cool air on his face, pushed open the steel door, which slammed behind him as if the whole goddamn building would collapse, but no one on the street noticed. He was dressed in grey. Jacket, sweater, trousers; only his shoes were black. They had not been polished for a long time. On Marszałkowska he was swept by the wind into the underground passage near the hotel. Here the fretful neon equalized everyone, the ugly and the beautiful, rich and poor. The dead glow covered the skin like powder, getting into body and clothing like a bad smell or old age. No shadow, no pity. Everyone swimming like upright fish. Jacek (that's right, I remember now, his name was Jacek) turned left, passed the tram stop for Żoliborz, passed the exit for the Metropol Hotel and the Aleje Jerozolimskie, passed the trams for Praga, pushed through the human carpet rolling down the steps from the Domy Centrum department store, passed the tram stops for Ochota, and began the circle again. Because it was safe here, and what was left of the blood in his veins moved him in the safe orbit of his madness. Besides, he knew he looked awful, so it was better to stay underground. Scraggly beard, greasy hair, skin as if the winter had gone on for ever and the sun was stupid scenery, used up long ago like an old battery. "Fucking nuts," he thought. "One more lap, and I'll go up." But he did three, because the plain, dead faces meant he could imagine himself one of many. He put his hand under his sweater and felt for his cigarettes. Some cops had pushed a drunk into a dark corner. Four guys with caps on backwards were walking side by side. Headed for him, so he turned off and came out on a street next to a Vietnamese kiosk that smelled strange, while the palace cast its great shadow across the bare branches of the maples. Half the city could have fitted into that shadow standing shoulder to shoulder. It wasn't the shelter he was after. He moved west, along the row of stalls, where in the five minutes before they left town Russians were going through the clutter of displays in search of pornography, high-end cigarettes, and presents. In the distance was the railway station: angular, massive, driven into the ground as if it had fallen from a height. He made for it but got no closer. When thoughts pass too quickly through a person's head, they're always ragged, absurd. They detach themselves, are a weight on the chest, as in one of those dreams where running takes you no further from your pursuers. "Shit, I'll never get there," he thought. His body was dry, but he felt covered with cold sweat. Like wind going through him, like being empty inside, filled with nothing but pieces of the city—like a silent film speeded up inside him. "Shit," he repeated, the beginning of a prayer but he didn't know what came next. The sky above made huge geometry, but he couldn't figure out the shape. Afraid to look up. No better than in the lift, this. He lit a cigarette, took three short drags, three long ones, three short ones again, then reached the steps that led into the bowels of the station. "In Leviathan your stomach plays a march"—a name came to him from somewhere. Cold again, yet he felt warmer.

In red glow, kids were trying to beat arcade games: bells, electronic gurgling, shots, and the dismal, sensual sound of tokens swallowed. Jacek approached the boys, but they all shook their heads, eyes glued to the screen, hands gripping the machine tight, because this was their only protection from the world outside. He left, turned right, turned right again, a warm prickling still in his body. He glanced at a clock, quickened his pace. This passage was the busiest in the station. It linked two bus stops, the main hall, the platforms, and the two longest corridors. Plenty of light here, and the crowd was animated, as happens in a place where some come to in hope while others are glad to leave. He began to look for familiar faces. A short, scrawny, mop-haired kid with blank eyes shook his head. The kid was standing by the sliding doors—the only motionless figure in an unbroken stream of bodies. Jacek went towards him, but the kid looked away. By the escalator to the platforms stood a girl in flared brown trousers and a stained sheepskin jacket. Below, the rust-coloured roof of a railway carriage was passing, the train headed for the other side of the river—Białystok, Moscow, maybe even further. He couldn't tell whether she recognized him, because her eyes were fathomless. Unable to remember her name, he just asked:

"What's going on? Is there any?"

She shrugged, regarded him. He saw a blackened tooth, and she was also missing a tooth. Her hands were covered by the sleeves of her jacket.

"Is there any?" he repeated, then placed her.

Last summer he'd been looking for a hit, and it was like today—not a gram to be found. They took her with them in the car because she knew a guy and so on. The hot seats burned; everyone was sweaty and dirty. At red lights at deserted intersections, the glare of the day poured from the sky like molten metal. They drank water, cursed, and drove in circles between two bars and the playground of an elementary school (yes, it was mid-June), she and three guys, and the pitiless sun filled their skulls and spilled from their eyes and noses, and in another minute they'd go crazy, their guts would catch fire, the car would explode, and white flame would engulf them for ever. In the end she got out at the corner of Jana Pawła and Nowolipie, took the money, and was gone. They sat in the blaze and counted the red minutes on the dashboard clock, and the Broom reassured them: "She'll come back, I know her"—but they doubted he believed it himself. But she emerged from between the buildings, skinny, in oversized jeans and a blouse of yellow and green parrots. She got in the car and said she had two grams. They were mad, because the deal was three. "She took it," said the driver. "She took a gram for herself." Then they were even madder, because the stuff was crap, sticky yellow. "I never saw shit this bad," said the Broom, and he told her to give back the money or what she'd taken. She just sat there on the back seat with her arms hanging almost to the floor and said she took nothing, the guy knew how things were in the city and took advantage. If they wanted, they could go and talk to him themselves, but it would be better if they didn't, because he could handle all three of them. While the other two were trying to divide the crap into lines, the driver took off like a madman and turned on Solidarności. They had a string of green lights, went down Wolska, and under the viaduct turned at Prymasa and found a quiet spot at the edge of the park, then the driver turned and told the girl to empty all her pockets and bag. There was nothing, a used-up tube of lipstick, a pack of cheap Klubowy cigarettes, an old piece of foil licked clean, thirty thousand zlotys, bloodstained tissues, so he pulled her from the car and patted her down. Nothing in her pockets either—lint, the smell of sweat, a clipping from a magazine. He got personal, but there wasn't anything in her knickers either. She didn't even resist. She just kept asking them to leave her a hit. "All right," said the driver, "but you have to blow us."

Back in the car, the driver said more than once, "You should all know that she used to be a nice-looking girl."

"No," she answered. "Don't you watch TV?"

"No."

"Then buy yesterday's paper."

"You don't know someone?"

"I'm into different things now."

Her eyes closed from the heroin, and that was the end of the conversation. Another train—this time the colour of black velvet—rolled into the station. He left her, headed to the passage under the roundabout, and found a phone that took tokens. It was midday, and the crowd had thinned out. In the receiver, a long signal. Trams rumbled overhead. He changed phones and tried a different number. Again, nothing but the long signal, calm, filling his head, then the labyrinth of the passageway, then the entire city. He hung up, and there was silence, only the rustle of people who walk quickly. He chose the Aleje Jerozolimskie exit and went up to the street. From the Poniatowski Bridge the wind blew, driving the occasional frigid cloud over the huge Coca-Cola billboards. The cold bore him towards unimaginably vast space, and this calmed him, for he was only a tiny figure in all this, his pulsing fear only a drop in the ocean of air. A small red plane flew east, towing an ad for Fenix life insurance. He decided on Saska Kępa: he knew someone there, though didn't have a phone number.

Paweł simply pressed down on the door handle and found himself inside the apartment. The air was only a little brighter than on the stairs. The smell of old clothes and shoes, the taste of dust. A door with a frosted glass pane led to the living room. A grey, powdery light filtered through the closed curtains and settled on the furniture. He opened the curtains. In the space of ten years, the apartment had faded, approaching invisibility. Nothing destroys colour like time; nothing wears away edges like the passage of the hours. The red bookcase was now the colour of brick, and the spines of the books had thinned out like teeth in old age. A glass of strong tea stood on the table growing cloudy. He looked for signs of life but found nothing. A clock ticked. He went into the dark kitchen, cocked an ear, said, "Jacek." He was answered by an echo to the side, a rumbling, a knock on the wall, noise in the pipes. In the ashtray, the butts were short and all of one cheap brand. He sat down and tried to recall, but all he could summon was a slim blond man in jeans and a denim jacket. Once they spent time together. But not a word was left in the memory, just scraps of feeling. He held them for a moment, to decipher them. "Life runs away from you," he thought, "and leaves shit behind." His shoulder hurt, and he was hungry. He turned on the kitchen light. No refrigerator. He looked in the cupboard and found some cream cheese. He scraped up a few stale bits and swallowed them. There was also tea. He turned the knob on the stove, but the burner was dead. In the living room, on a windowsill, was a prison-style heating element made from two razor blades. Afraid to plug it in, he drank some water from the tap. He lay on the narrow bed. The bedding was coarse, dirty, but in this filth he felt safe. A forgotten place suspended over the city; life went on elsewhere. At their last meeting three years ago, some-one touched his arm on Marszałkowska. The guy was tall, gaunt, unkempt. His grey suit hung on him, with things stuffed in the bulging pockets.

"Sir," the man said. "I need a few pennies. If you could help . . . just fifty thousand . . ."

Paweł quickened his pace, muttered, "No change, pal, and I'm in a hurry." But then he slowed down, turned, and asked, "Jacek?"

Only now it occurred to him that it could have been a set-up, that the guy knew whom he was stopping, though at the time Jacek seemed surprised, pleased. They spent the afternoon in the bar at the Metropol.

"So? Are things really that bad, man?"

"Things are fine," Jacek had answered with a smile.

"Right, going up to people in the street and asking for fifty thousand . . ."

"You mean begging."

"I guess."

"Sometimes I need a couple of thousand. I can see you're doing nicely for yourself. The suit has to be worth a couple of big ones."

"A man has to look decent."

"Business . . ."

"Yes." For the rest of the evening he did most of the talking, told the long and boring story how he started out with a few hundred but in the end came out on top, so he couldn't complain, things were moving and in a few years it would be quite something. Only once did he stop and ask if he could help, get Jacek some work, something to start him off, but in Jacek's eyes there was only amusement, so Paweł dropped the subject and felt a surge of anger. Finally he put two million on the table. Jacek shook his head.

"No, man. I wanted fifty thousand."

And now, lying on the dirty sheets, Paweł thought, "He conned me, the bastard." He got up, paced, knocked a copy of *Captain Blood* from the shelf, kicked it into the corner under the seventies coffee table on which stood a Jubilat radio. He turned the knob through the stations. Nothing but talk, static, music he didn't know. On some fast-talking cackle of a programme they gave the time, almost two.

"So many things we did together," he thought, staring out of the window. Blue sky, apartment buildings like cutouts made of grey paper, a grown-up version of those cardboard fairy tales with little windows that held princesses or Hansel and Gretel or shepherd boys. In the narrow gap between walls the Palace of Culture jutted its freshly gilded spire. A red plane passed it, towing a condom labelled *Fenix*. Then he sensed someone's presence and turned. She was maybe eighteen and wanting to be older. Dull sweater, green jacket, rolled-up blue jeans, Doc Martens. A string bag over her arm. She looked at him without surprise.

"I brought him some food," she said, and went into the kitchen.

"He's not here."

"When will he be back?"

"I don't know. When I got here, he was gone."

"What do you want from him?"

"I was just passing by."

"He shouldn't go out."

"Why not?"

"Because he doesn't come back for a long time."

"You're his girlfriend?"

"I bring him food. Vegetables. He needs to eat more vegetables. He always wants meat. He shouldn't eat meat."

"He's sick?"

"No. But meat is bad. It's like eating suffering and death. It isn't normal."

"And eating lettuce is? What are you talking about, kid?"

She came out of the kitchen and draped her jacket over the arm of a chair. She had large breasts. Something loud was going on in the next apartment. The plane had swung over Wola and now headed east. She rolled up her sleeves, brass and copper jangling on her wrists, and returned to the kitchen, where she got a pot from under the sink, removed leeks, carrots, cauliflower, and parsnip from her bag, and began chopping everything up.

"They shut off the gas," he said.

"I know. I'll take the seal off, then put it back again."

Her breasts bounced under her sweater to the rhythm of the knife.

"He has to eat vegetables. When he goes out, he eats crap at those stalls."

Watching her focused him. It was two; he had an hour yet.

He practically told her his life story as he stood in the doorway of the kitchen. The pot bubbled. His forehead was wet. It could have been from the heat and steam, or from nerves as he spoke and as she listened with half an ear, busy scrubbing the sink to remove the sticky filth of the week. "Fuck it, I'll never see her again, and she doesn't care anyway," he thought. From time to time she glanced at him as if to check that he wasn't the radio but a real person. She had acne. She took her sweater off. Had on a black cotton blouse.

"I don't see why you need so much money. Me, I minimize. Minimize your needs, and you are independent. If only people realized they could do without all this . . . You have to live in harmony with your nature, not with what everyone tries to talk you into. Of course you don't eat enough vegetables, of course you prefer meat, you think it'll make you tough and all that. But eating vegetables changes your consciousness, and then you're living in harmony with yourself, not by some chauvinistic Christian ideology that lets people kill and eat innocent creatures, that leads to chaos in the cosmos, because humans are a part of it just like plants and animals, and the plants and animals don't do harm. Cauliflower, cabbage, Brussels sprouts without salt are good for the upper loins, and blocking the energy there makes a person worry too much about material things. The right kind of massage could also work . . ."

"The problem is, I borrowed money and now I have to pay it back. But I don't have it. Brussels sprouts won't help."

"If you started right, you never would have ended up in a situation like this. Me, I divided my body into seven zones, and every day I nourish myself with vegetables from one of the seven groups. In this way I live in total harmony. I mean, we're cosmic beings, aren't we?"

"Gagarin?"

"What?"

"The cosmonaut."

"Oh, you mean those fascist technocrats. You know what Lao-tzu said?"

"Yeah. You can't jump higher than your prick."

"What?"

It occurred to him that in ten minutes the plane from Prague would be landing at Okęcie. Long ago, he recalled, in the main hall of the airport, when the crowd thinned, they'd hunt for empty packs of foreign cigarettes. They'd look in the rubbish bins or see the little coloured boxes in ashtrays. Finders keepers, and they didn't care who was watching. Green and white Suezes, white and red Winstons, brown plastic Philip Morris boxes, yellow, gold, and dark blue 555s, the kind that Mao smoked. If they'd only known then that the price would shoot up and for one pack you could get a green LM box with the carriage on it plus a dark blue Dunhill. The black and silver Desires and the brown Kazbeks no one wanted. Tall men in dark suits and blue shirts watched them with a smile. Once, when he was picking through an ashtray, a dark-skinned guy gave him half a pack of

Marlboros, but they were the red ones, nothing special. Out on the concrete viewing terrace, a fine rain fell, and the planes emerged from the fog—silver, smooth, glistening—and disappeared back into it. Perhaps it all began then. They would take out the crumpled packets in the 175 bus, examine them, and pronounce their names.

"Nothing," he said, and went to the living room. In the next apartment someone was hammering, or knocking someone's head against the wall. He read the spines of the books. There was a large black Jack London, a dark red Buster, a white Suchecki. The minutes hit the ground at his feet like droplets of mercury, quivering, rolling into the corner under the coffee table with the radio. "The floor's crooked," he thought.

She stuck her head out of the kitchen and asked if he wanted some chicory coffee.

"It's made of thickly ground grains, so the structure hasn't been destroyed and—"

"I'll take the massage," he said.

"All right, but go to the toilet first. You need an empty bladder to reduce the tension. Then the energy can flow freely. In general, fluids have a negative effect . . ."

"OK."

The bottom of the bath was rust red, the toilet as yellow as an old bone. He pissed into the sink, pulled the chain, washed his dick. The water was cold. A green tracksuit hung on a line. Next to the toilet was a pile of magazines. He squatted to look at them: *Razem, Perspektywy, ITD, Panorama*. Whoever lived here was freeing himself from the passage of time. There was no mirror to show change.

"A perfect spot," he thought. Now safety had the smell of wet concrete and chlorine.

She told him to take his clothes off and lie on his stomach. From her bag she took a small bottle.

"This is a special oil," she said.

She rubbed the yellow liquid on her hands, poured a little on his back. It felt cold, but when she touched him, he didn't mind. She started from his sides, kneaded firmly, almost roughly. Short fingernails. Then she moved lower, to his buttocks, and up again. She pinched his flesh as if handling fabric or the rubber of a shop dummy. He grew warm. Again thought about safety, which now had the acrid smell of her sweat. She did not use a deodorant. He closed his eyes, pressed his face into his arm, imagined her pulling out his flesh in handfuls and moulding it into balls, cubes, shapeless and novel objects, tossing them around the room, into corners, under the kitchen sink, behind the radiator, on the windowsill. The stuff would be covered with dust, forgotten like children's clay, and no one would ask about him any more. It didn't hurt. He was heavy, sticky dough, his nerves, blood, eyes all folded into putty meat. Then there was a chill on his ribs. Her slender hand slipped inside, felt for his lungs, bit by bit removed the spongy matter, making pink balls the size of doughnuts. He could survive in this disjointed state, his mind dimmed but not dead, and someone eventually would piece him back together. Except that the apartment was too small for him now, there weren't enough places to hide all the shapes, pieces, pellets. He didn't want to be thrown into the rubbish bin at the far end of the dark courtyard with high walls on all sides and where white shirts flashed in windows—some offices, though the main occupant was gloom and still air. And the cats, constantly fighting for food in the dustbins. At night their yowls were louder than the traffic. He was barely living stuff now, but those insatiable animals would tear at him. He felt her touch his heart.

"There," she said, "you're relaxed."

Now she slapped with open hands, tenderizing meat. He felt good. He imagined her large breasts bouncing under her black blouse and knocking together with the same wet sound of the hands on his back. He told her to stop a moment.

"All right," she said.

He turned on his back, showing his hard-on. But she was sideways and paid no attention. Her forehead was covered with sweat. He noticed that she wore a silver earring.

"Where do you live?" he asked.

"In Praga."

"What do you feel when you're doing it?"

"Nothing."

"It doesn't turn you on?"

"What?"

"You know, massaging me?"

"It's supposed to relax you, not turn you on."

"What turns you on?"

She shrugged. He reached out and touched a breast. She didn't move, didn't look. He took advantage of the reality of it, that there were no secrets, and slipped his other hand under her skirt.

"It'll all be wasted," she said. "No benefit, just more tension and blocked energy channels."

He found a nipple, pinched it lightly, gently twisted, but nothing. The other breast seemed heavier. He knelt on the bedding, put his arms around her from behind, squeezed both breasts. He and she made a strange pair. She leaned forward, not to defend herself, only to rest her elbows on her knees. He brushed her hair with his lips. It hadn't been washed. He could see the white part at the top of her head.

"I also know Thai massage," she said.

"What's that like?" he asked, holding her even tighter. He passed his hand over her stomach and found three small rolls of flesh and her navel among them.

"It's done with the feet. You lie on the floor, and I walk on you."

"But you take your shoes off?"

"Yes. The energy mustn't be blocked."

He liked this too, though at times he couldn't catch his breath. He was on his stomach next to the bookcase—she had to hold on to it so she wouldn't slip off his oiled back. He could feel her feet up to the ankles sinking into his body. She waded through his innards, which were warm and slippery, but there was no pain. Earlier had asked her to take off her jeans. She did it indifferently, as she had allowed him to lick the sweat from her forehead. "She doesn't have to be lively, as long as she's warm," he thought, and knew exactly what he was doing as her fingers kneaded his hot mud. He was drawn to an old and formless thing, an inconspicuous, unmoved, and passive thing.

When he explained to her what he wanted and she got down on her knees by the chair, she asked him to turn on the radio, because the silence would bother her. He went and turned the knob, and remembered the time.

The voice at the other end was low, sleepy.

"He's not here. He'll be at this number at three."

"Is there another number where I can reach him?"

There was laughter before the line went dead. The receiver

in his hand, he stared at the scratched-up case of the phone. The concrete ceiling of the booth was so low, he could touch it. Overhead trams dispersed rumbling to the four corners of the world. Where he stood was the centre, and he felt like crying but didn't know how, he couldn't remember. Someone had left the smell of perfume. He pressed his cheek to the black plastic, but the touch was cold, gummy, sad.

"It broke?" he heard behind him.

"It broke," he replied, and a Vietnamese in a dark blue cagoule smiled and went to look for another phone. He stayed a little longer in the booth, to use the phone to give sense to himself, dialling random numbers, breaking off imaginary conversations, seven two one three zero zero, and again, and once connected with a woman's voice, but heard only hello. He tried to reconstruct the sequence of numbers, but an angry man in an overcoat said in a loud voice:

"Tokens! You need to put a token in to talk!"

He went out into the passage and noticed that his flies were open. He zipped up and lit a cigarette. He headed north between the glass walls. Hardly any wind. Two chicks passed with their arses practically exposed. They wore knee-length black boots but must have been cold. He'd never understand tights, stockings. Never got a straight answer when he asked if they kept one warm. As far back as he could remember. He could always return to the apartment and finish what he started. The crowd jostled him, moved him along, so he took advantage of that and decided to forget. Not far from here was a hamburger joint, the first in the city, twenty years ago. A woman in white overalls would lean out of a window in a bare wall. A little roll containing a flattened burger for two zloty fifty or five. And it was good. A multicoloured stream poured as always from Rutkowskiego. Once, long ago, when he still had time for such things, he turned off Nowy Świat to count the stuff in the windows. Sunglasses, vanity bags, shoes, belts, socks, porcelain figures, watches, sachets, suitcases. After a thousand, he lost count, his head swelled like a watermelon, so he never tried that again. Now he looked towards Bracka and felt desire. It hung in the air. Everything gave off a scent that penetrated the panes of the displays and showcases, drifted like smoke or fog or heavy gas. It filled the narrow street and rose over the roofs; the wind spread it across the sky over all the neighbourhoods. Filthy Wola got its share, drowsy Mokotów, cunning Praga too though it had its Różycki Bazaar. The glow, aura, smell flowed from the artery of downtown like blood, attracting flies. People are not drawn to new things, only to what they've already seen. The glum outskirts, the shacks out in Wygoda. The pathetic workmanship of recycled bricks and insulating board in Białołęka, the merciful green of Siekierki, hiding all those houses where in winter people piss in a bucket on the porch. The crooked wooden structures of Grochów, Koło and Młynów with walls in abstract patterns grimy from the smoke of filterless cigarettes, Mazurs, Sports, Wawels, and filter tips like Silesias and Zeniths, and women's flat cigarettes with a mouthpiece. All this had to yield, because the smell came from the sky and filled their dreams, and life without dreams is useless, a shoe without a heel. Nor any thing that is thy neighbour's. Maybe that's when it began . . . But nothing has changed. People walked shoulder to shoulder like vigilant deer. They looked right, left, and straight ahead. No one looked back.

The cigarette had a foul taste. The men were fast, self-assured, walking to their cars. Some of the cars had been taken by thieves. It was a game of sorts. The cops were on Widok.

Large sheets of glass doubled the world like a window to the other side. That's what infinity looks like. Enter, and you wander till you're shitfaced. The ways through the city are without number. It's always possible to find a door, because any hope is good.

He reached Kniewskiego and turned at the Palladium to stand for a while in the recess by the entrance. Cars plunged into the tunnel with a screech. The view to the right was blocked by a furniture shop where dummies fucked on leather sofas, because everything has to look real. A minute was enough, so he crossed and passed the Relax Cinema, remembering twenty-zloty tickets and the men with crafty and blank faces. They were always crowded in that dark walkway, their white T-shirts glowing like phosphorescent fish. They had cold blood and quick, self-possessed fingers. He feared them as he would dogs that don't move.

Then there was the building by the public toilet and the big Sezam department store. He recalled the smell that filled its floors, with the food down below and all the other stuff upstairs. A steamy aroma, neither pleasant nor unpleasant, simply strong. He recalled the dark, rough surface of the stairs, where your shoes stuck as if glued. It made walking difficult, because teenagers like to shuffle. To the side was a place where sausage and pasta were served for under ten zlotys. One day when it was raining he went there and dropped a plate.

He waited for the green light, hopped on a number 18, and, eyes darting, rode for two stops.

He looked to either side before he went in. It was dark inside and warmer, the radio played Wolność with Szczota on drums, and the girl got up when she saw him.

"Good afternoon, boss," she said.

He returned her greeting and carefully looked around.

"Was anyone here?" he asked.

"Just customers."

"Have there been many?"

"The usual."

Rain was slanting outside. The cloud would move on soon. His things lay on the shelves, worthless. He hadn't yet paid for most of them. He went behind the counter, opened the till, counted the notes.

"Is this all?" he asked.

"All."

"It's not much."

"At noon Mr Zalewski came to collect what was owed him. A week ago you said he was first in line."

"All right, Zosia," he said quietly, though he felt like grabbing the metal box and hurling it at the mirror on the wall, then dropping into an armchair and covering his face with his hands.

"How much did you give him?"

"Ten million."

He counted the notes once more: a thin bundle. As thin as death. He shuffled them, arranged them into pairs, threes, fours, but it didn't change anything. He slammed the drawer and sat in a chair. When it creaked, he realized how still the place was. Just the radio playing; no sound of breathing.

"Zosia, I know I owe you for last month, but I'm taking this money. I need it now."

"There has to be something in the till for the morning. I don't have much of my own," she said as if she were the one apologizing. Outside, the rain was almost over. Cars pulled the dust of drops behind them. A yellow Polonez passed a white Ford. The trees on the other side of the street glistened brown.

She wore a grey skirt and a green blouse fastened at the neck with a silver brooch. He told her several times to wear less—"You understand, Zosia, for the clients"—but the next day she'd turn up the same. At the most there'd be no brooch and the top button of her blouse would be undone. Or her hair would be down, like today. He asked for coffee. When she went into the little back room, he saw her slender calves, her feet in their dark flat shoes. She was never late and never made the least miscalculation; she spoke little, spoke sensibly and softly; she had brown hair and did not wear lipstick. He found her through an ad in *Gazeta Wyborcza*.

The cup she handed him contained one level spoonful of sugar. The sight of the coffee made him sick, but he wanted to be nice and ask her for something. She smelled faintly of flower water; her fingernails were trimmed short and she wore a modest ring on the third finger of her left hand. She returned to her place behind the counter.

"No," he said. "Close today at seven, Zosia, and don't open tomorrow. We'll take a short break. If something more comes in today, it's an advance on what I owe you."

Someone passed by the window. It was growing dark. Lights came on in the apartment building opposite. A black man, bent, crossed the street. A tram whined as it braked. A cold wind blew and gradually uncovered the stars.

"I forgot to turn on the light," she said, flustered. The mirror reflected her figure distinctly, indifferently. His mind was a blank. He had a little more coffee before he left, looking out of the window. In a first-floor apartment they were preparing a late dinner. He noticed the candy lamb.

"You brought the little sheep?"

"I did, but it can come down . . ."

"No. It's fine there. Looks nice."

It occurred to him that he could spend the night at her place. Somewhere in Ursynów in a two-room apartment: pine furniture, a fringed runner in the hallway, a kitchen with a collection of wooden spoons, a portable television on the bookcase. He had known her for several months. A coffee table with red and white checked tablecloth, a pink fluffy mat by the bathtub.

"Are you in trouble, boss?" she asked softly.

He smiled, put the cup and saucer back on the counter.

"Nothing much. Business."

"If there's any way I can help . . ."

He got up, went to the door.

"Thanks, Zosia. You don't need to stay to seven. You can close sooner."

He crossed the street and zipped up his jacket because of the wind. The stars silver, sharp as needles. From Dobrzańskiego a car stopped at the store and two men got out. One had something in his hand. She stood in the window, and he could practically see her assuming a polite expression. He walked slowly, turned on Biała, and ran to Elektoralna.

Meanwhile Bolek was eating meat and Syl was drinking grape juice. They sat in the black and gold room, the TV on, he wearing what he wore that morning and she in a white T-shirt. The pork chop on salad leaves surrounded by fries; beside it a glass of beer. Syl, bored, sipped her juice, watched the people on television, let them talk a while, then killed them with the remote and went to other people, in some story or other, but they were all men, so she kept searching, a German commentator saying the names of Japanese motorcyclists, amusing for a moment, then a music channel, but they were songs from before she was born, so she tried a black-and-white Arabic channel where the same film had been on for three hours.

"Porkie, let's go out."

"You made dinner," said Bolek, pointing at the plate with his fork.

"Not to a restaurant. Just out. To the movies, or dancing."

"I can't. I'm expecting a call."

"You can take your mobile with you."

"I can't. I might have to leave and take something from here."

"I'm bored, Porkie."

"Watch a video."

"I've seen them all."

"Call the store and have them bring new ones."

"I don't like videos. I like the cinema."

"Not today."

"And not yesterday, not the day before yesterday, not tomorrow, not the day after tomorrow . . ."

Syl's glass banged on the glass tabletop.

"You keep me here like it was prison, and you only have one thing on your mind."

"Lucynka, today I really can't."

The phone tinkled, Bolek reached for it. He didn't speak, just listened. "OK," he said finally.

"You see, I told you."

"At least lock Sheikh up. I don't like the way he stares. You can't move."

"He's a good dog."

"I know. But lock him up."

Bolek went out into the hallway and dressed. When he was done, he looked in the mirror. Everything was right.

"I'm locking from the outside," he said.

"Fuck, Porkie! You keep me here like—"

"Lucia, either I lock the door or I don't lock Sheikh."

She picked up the remote and went back to her search. In the window, purple clouds.

Still running, like a few hours before. He didn't slow down till Marchlewskiego, at a bus stop where two old women were waiting and now him. There were no trams to be seen coming from Żoliborz. He considered a 17: it went directly south into the neighbourhoods between Konstruktorska and Domaniewska, which would be deserted this time of day, with the terminus at the bottom of Marynarska where cars climb the overpass, close to heaven for a moment before they drop in defeat among the vegetable gardens. He could take refuge by the Cemia plant, on those creepy, windswept streets with not a soul around, a few caretakers at most, and nothing of interest for thieves. The cube warehouses and office buildings of Unitra with their dark, dirty windows, haunted at night by phantom robots. No one in his right mind had any business there. He'd go there if a 17 came. By the time it reached Woronicza it would be like an empty aquarium, cold as ice. He'd been there once. An early Sunday morning. Everything looked abandoned as soon as it was built. He'd heard about towns like that in America. No 17 showed, so he waited for a 29 to take him to Okęcie. A tram terminal in the early evening always circled a void. Shelters made of glass and tin over shadows and the glowing tips of cigarettes. Notes are riffled by fingers in pockets, to shorten the wait. Okęcie, he thought, where the city stops at Mineralna, then darkness from there all the way to Grójec. To the left, drab grass and the giant X of the two runways; inky lights behind a chain-link fence summon the planes, and the distant control towers are like the tops of sinking ships. The roar in the sky makes the earth seem twice as large, and uninhabited. Three stops before he once slept with a woman. But no 29 showed.

In the end, out in Muranów a single swinging light came into view. Then he remembered he didn't have a ticket. From Hala Mirowska wafted the white stink of dead poultry. He went up to a woman in a light-coloured coat and asked if she had a ticket she could sell him.

"Leave me alone!" she barked.

A number 19 finally.

He didn't find a kiosk till Świętokrzyska. He bought tickets and two soft packs of Marlboro. He looked around for a large, dark car. He'd already counted five. They passed indifferently or sped by at the roundabout. A Vento, a Vectra, an old Scorpio, and Christ knows what the other two were. He was gradually losing his fear, because he was losing hope. A glow spread from the right. Wola was almost extinguished; it was a little brighter in Poznań. A fringe of light over the skyscrapers near Central Station. A narrow black cloud, its sharp edge pointing down. The land was fading, the stars were coming out, and people were taking cover from the wind at bus stops. The pavements still wet. He guessed that in the night there'd be a frost and the puddles would ice over. He had a little over a million now, but it was too little to hide out somewhere until morning. He considered going home, but the fear returned, though he still had three days. Counting from this morning, so really only two. "Fucking wind," he muttered. The collar of his jacket didn't protect his neck. He thought of going to the Centrum to buy a hat, but decided on Central Station, because it was warm there for free.

The passageway was filled with the stink of dustbins set on fire. A teenage girl on roller skates passed him. She was dressed in tight-fitting black and wore a helmet. He caught the smell of sweat and perfume. His legs hurt. The girl was way ahead. Warm air came from the far end of the station. He turned right and went up the escalator to the main hall.

The brown light of the cafeteria barely hulled the faces from the dark. People ate, sat, slept like rag dolls, as if they'd been there for ever. He couldn't finish his second helping: the burger swam in overcooked cabbage, the cold potatoes were like salty custard. Below, a stream of cars flowed along the Aleje, their roofs like glimmering lights on the surface of dark water. He tried to focus on one particular person, for example the man in the red Honda, but couldn't stay with him beyond the intersection with Krucza, terrified by the chasm of the Poniatowskiego Bridge, which at night was always a huge mouth, and you never knew for sure you'd come out whole on the other side. So he chose a white baby Fiat, which a moment later turned into Nowy Świat, drove down the Aleje Uzajdowskie, and reached the developments near Jałtańska, Batumi, Soczi. A man of fifty with a briefcase on the back seat. The briefcase smelled of sandwiches— slightly sour because the bread had sat too long in foil in a hot place. Under the rear-view mirror hung a small medallion of Our Lady of Częstochowa. Those people can never get their hands clean. His brown jacket was fastened to the neck, and he wore a brown hat. He parked outside an apartment building and took the lift to the sixth floor. His wife opened the door.

———

He turned from the window and saw a scruffy man in a green coat. From the man's sleeves poked out another pair of sleeves, and from them a third pair. The man leaned forward a little and asked:

"Excuse me, sir, are you going to finish that?"

"I'm not," he replied automatically.

"In that case I will," said the man, sitting down. He ate calmly, not hurrying, a bite of burger, a little cabbage, a forkful of potatoes. Tattered dark-red wool at his wrists like rays.

"Pity it's cold," he said, swallowing. "Sometimes it's hard to tell. You were sitting far from the door. I always look through the window first, and I only go in when I'm certain."

"I bought two and couldn't finish the second."

"One person has two, another has a half. Not so bad, is it?" A red face, blue eyes. He didn't stink. Maybe a little, like an unaired closet. When he finished, he said, "Thank you." Some of his teeth discoloured.

"You live here?"

"I've been here for some time. It'll get warmer soon. This isn't a good place." The man looked around the room. "The witch is working here today. If you buy me tea, I can sit a while longer. She chucks people out if they don't order."

He took out a note and put it in front of the man.

"Should I bring you some? Food's awful greasy." He nodded. The clock said 7:42. The man came back with two glasses of tea and change. They dropped the teabags in, watched the toffee streaks spread in the water.

"This place isn't good, but at this time of day there's little choice. East Station is worse—that's the worst place on earth." The man said it softly, as if someone were listening. "I lived there once. It was hell."

"Why was it hell?" he asked, dropping the slice of lemon into his tea.

"Do you believe in the devil?" The man leaned across the table; he smelled his foul breath. "You know," he whispered.

"I don't." He shrugged. "The devil?"

"See, if you don't believe, then why should I tell you? It's a story for believers."

"And here?"

"It's awful here too but bearable."

"Like purgatory?"

The man chuckled.

"Something like that. Penance. You keep doing penance, but shit comes of it. You could do it your whole life, and nothing."

The tea had stopped steaming in the half-empty glasses; it was almost eight. Two guards in black uniforms entered.

"Where there's business, there must be a routine."

"What business?"

"Give me a hundred, and I'll do whatever you want, sir. When you don't know anyone and you need something, a hundred for a middle man is nothing. A bottle, some powder, H, coke, a women, a boy, little girl, all of the above, eat in or carry out, at your place or in your car. Or maybe you need someone to take care of something? A straight hundred, boss."

"Thanks. Maybe another time."

"I'm here every two hours. Closer to the odd-numbered hours. Give me fifty at least."

He set the money in front of the man and walked out onto the mezzanine. The man continued behind him: "But this isn't an advance. If you need something, it's a whole hundred."

He leaned on the railing and looked down. The tramp descended, crossed the hall, and joined the queue at the kiosk.

Before he reached the window, the tramp changed his mind and set off towards the concourse. Two burly guys in bomber jackets leaned at him. He said something to them and pointed at the clock over the stairway that led to the platforms. One of them clapped him on the shoulder, then both men went down the steps.

The station light lent a corpselike pallor to all the faces. Every figure cast many weak shadows.

When the sliding doors clicked shut behind him, Emilii Plater was dark as usual, because even at night the Palace cast a shadow. The large block of sky moving over the neighbourhood was cut off by the Domy Centrum department store and gnawed at the right by the notched edge of the buildings on the Aleje. People hid in the lighted buses. The 501, 505, and 510 were small caves hollowed out of black rock. The driver of the 505 went to get something to eat at a Vietnamese stall while the passengers wiggled their frozen toes in their shoes. He watched a 510 with a drooping belly pull away from the stop. One cigarette, two, separated him from the next bus. He could get in, ride to the end, and tidy up his place, sweep, put things in order, as usual, but more carefully. Just half an hour sitting with indifferent people with a single bridge between two voids, the colossus of the power station to the left, the chimneys with their red lights like an electric crown of thorns. So he lit a cigarette to measure time. The wind blew from around the corner, making sparks. He cupped the cigarette in his hand. A man in an unfamiliar uniform tried to light up, gave up, asked for a light from his cigarette.

Then, through the dirty panes of the sliding door he saw Jacek. The same suit, the same long mousy hair. Running towards the closed door. Two steps and on the moving part. The doors opened, and the grey figure flew past. Then a man in a bomber jacket came running. When he was half outside, Paweł kicked a metal litter bin in front of him.

A red neon light at fifteen-second intervals. Also a night-light atop the radio in the apartment. They sat opposite each other at the table, their shadows on the bare wall blowing smoke. Faint old music from the radio.

"He had a gun," said Paweł.

"Who?" Jacek turned to him like someone waking up.

"The guy chasing you. When he went down, it fell out. Maybe he had it under his jacket. It slid across the ground. Black . . ."

"Why didn't you take it?"

"I was running."

"It would only have taken a moment. You could have."

"Yes."

"Then shown it to me now."

"You don't believe me? That I stopped him?"

Jacek got up, went to the radio, changed the station. It was Wolność with Wiesiek Orłowski, but they didn't know that. He turned the red dial to the left, found something classical.

"She told me everything," he said.

"You don't believe me," said Paweł, following his own thought. He regarded the other man's face in the dim light.

"That's not the point. We could have had a gun."

"What do we need a gun for?"

"Better to have something than not to have it," he said with a smile.

It was violins, lots of them. The sound couldn't get out of the room. It buzzed high, then dropped suddenly, to the dark double basses stumbling in the poor-quality speaker. He upped the volume to a rasp, listened intently to the noise, and turned it down again.

"You say something?" he asked.

"No. What did she tell you?"

"Everything. They were at your place, smashed it up, said they'd do the same to you. Who was it?"

"I don't know, never saw them before. Hired. One did the talking, the others didn't say anything."

"Who you borrow from?"

"This guy from Falenica. We were sort of friends."

"And now he's after your blood."

"I'm six months behind."

"Even so, he's not asking for that much interest."

"We knew each other. I met him at the pool."

"You swim?"

"Then we went to a bar. That was how it began."

"You could use a gun."

"He was into all kinds of business. We talked about stuff. You know how it is. I visited his home; he had dogs and cats . . ."

"A 92 Beretta, fifteen rounds in the clip. Or you can get a bigger clip—holds twenty."

"I was doing this and that, getting a loan, getting a ride; business was going to save the world. Then later, when things took off . . . I needed money from one day to the next, and I'd make it back right away. But with the bank things always drag on . . ."

"Why did you go to a pool if you don't know how to swim?"

"I was with someone."

"The clip with twenty rounds sticks out of the grip."

"He told me there was no problem, to him it was nothing. I thought it was nothing to me as well . . ."

"What is it you actually do? You told me, but I forgot."

"I sell."

"What?"

"It varies. Used to be wool, now it's cotton."

"Knickers?"

"Among other things."

"Long johns?"

"Everything."

"You spent five hundred million on underwear?"

"It's not that much. Do you know how much the shipping alone is?"

"Pity you didn't take the gun. Black?"

"Yes. I tried getting another loan to pay it, but they all knew there was something not right about me. Besides, I didn't really have anyone to borrow from."

"Maybe it's still there on the ground?"

"No, it's bright as day there. Why was he after you?"

"I don't know. He started running, so I did."

"How did you know he was chasing you?"

"One knows."

The red neon calmed, stopped flashing, filled the room with an even light. Jacek said, "It's broken again," and the two fell silent, listening to the street noise—the momentary quiet of Nowogrodzka, the murmur from Krucza, and the incessant bubble of the roundabout, which never sleeps, except perhaps briefly before dawn, when it wheezes like a sick windpipe. The sounds are a reminder that space is infinite, it'll swallow everything, that no Russki long-haul lorry, no convoy from the Reich can smuggle through a human sound, there are only echoes on the stones, the rumble of dustbin lorries, shouts, the whistle of the wind in the overhead tram cables, the underground groan of trains, cars wailing, screeching around bends as they try to catch one another on the fog-slick curve of the Solec ramp then disappear in the darkness of the Wisłostrada, while the Vistula reflects sound and light as if it were quivering metal, as if this was what caused insomnia, the infinite nature of the world, in which any piece of shit can grow beyond the boundary of the visible.

So they smoked and listened to it all, because it's always a consolation to be here and not elsewhere, in an endless number of other places, which makes you nuts to think about.

Jacek went to the window and closed the curtains. The red grew pale. He put his hands in his trouser pockets and circled the table. The air moved. On the table, a plate with leftovers looked like a big ashtray. He went to the Gents, came back right away. From the shelf he took a candle stuck to a saucer. "The bulb is out," he said, and left again. A glow filtered through the glass door into the living room. Paweł thought someone was standing there. He went to check but didn't find anyone. For a moment the darkness had taken on human form. He went back to his chair and lit up again. The pack was almost empty. It was quiet in the next-door apartments. Garlic in the air. The smell of her sweat lingering in the apartment. Jacek returned, blew out the candle, and put it back in its place.

"That girl," Paweł began.

"Beata."

"Have you known her long?"

"Six months, a year. She comes here sometimes. You like her?"

"She talked nonsense, but I guess."

"I taught her."

"What?"

"What she says. All that crap about energy and everything."

Paweł looked at him intently, though it was too dark.

"You're kidding. You believe all that?"

"No."

"Then why?"

Jacek laughed, went to the window, parted the curtain, looked down into the street.

"What matters is that she believes it. Half a loaf is better. Am I right?"

"I don't get it."

"It doesn't matter. You will. And you should get yourself a gun."

Paweł jumped up from his chair and shouted:

"Fuck that gun! What do I need a goddamn gun for? I'm a normal guy."

The neon went out, came on again, resumed its fifteen-second rhythm.

"You see? Sometimes a shout does it." Jacek moved away from the window, continued: "Listen, I don't have any money to give you. All I can offer is advice. That's it. Theoretically I could sell something, but you see for yourself there can be problems with the buyer."

"Then at least let me stay here tonight," murmured Paweł.

Meanwhile Beata was sleeping. In Praga. In the darkness, her body like the moon. Kijowska was quiet now. Cars entered Tysiąclecia, some never to return, a one-way trip. First to the viaduct at the Radzymińska intersection, then to Zabraniecka and on to Utrata, between the willow trees and the dustbins out under the starless sky, where the lads did what they had to quickly and dawn found only the gutted chassis. The sheet covered her to the waist. The great sarcophagus of East Station in a dirty glow. The light rubbed the window but could not get in, because her body was too young, no thought of death yet, not even in a dream. Her mother slept in the other room. There was also a kitchen. That was it. On the floor, plastic tiles and rugs; in the shiny credenza, crystal. Her room was cramped, cluttered, unlike her mother's, where words thinned like cigarette smoke. Things all piled up, overlapping, squeezing together, embracing. Sometimes she would wake at night, sit on the bed with closed eyes, recognize them by touch: the grey teddy bear that ten years ago she medicated using a dropper with a light blue rubber bulb; the small guitar, or ukulele, that no one could ever tune, so occasionally she'd play a song on a single string; a vase for keeping things that were not supposed to get lost, an accumulation of forgotten stories, errands to run, things to examine, finger—buttons, loose rosary beads, ticket mementoes, old lighters, change, earrings without backs, green notes with the picture of a general, empty oil bottles, half a nail clipper with a gold fish embedded in green enamel, a postcard with faded lettering in Arabic. By the sofa bed, a bookcase with a bedside lamp and a few books on diet, philosophy, the philosophy unopened. It was enough that they were there, that she could touch the spines and covers showing gods or the faces of men with half-closed eyes and orange flowers around their necks. A clay ashtray she made herself, now empty, clean, because a month ago she gave up smoking. A china ballerina missing an arm. A glass heart with a hold for two ballpoint pens, red and green. Her possessions. And the tape player, and the cassettes in a neat row on a shelf of the wall unit that held her wardrobe, and the woven basket filled with cheap cosmetics that she hadn't used for weeks, and the hand mirror, and the three cacti on the windowsill. All hers. Also the walls, or actually just the one above the bed, free of shelves, and the one by the window and door, where she had painted a huge yellow sun. Her mother came home from work and was furious, but nothing happened—it was too expensive to call a painter. Two years ago the sun, and a year later, across it, a jagged green cannabis leaf. This time her mother said nothing; she may not even have noticed. Then the Kurt Cobain picture. She cried all night when he died, took the tape player to bed with her, hugged it and played "Never Mind" all night. In the early morning she fell asleep bathed in tears. Her mother came into the room, saw the wire snaking from the socket into the sheets, and shouted, "You little idiot, you'll electrocute yourself!" Beata waited for her mother to go to work, took the Sacred Heart in its gilt frame down from the wall, pulled out the backing and the picture, and put in Cobain instead.

Some time later Jacek gave her a picture torn from a book: Krishna with a blue body, in garlands. From that time on she stopped dreaming of Cobain. At first she missed the dreams, because she would wake from them in tears, a little sad and a little happy. But then it occurred to her that screwing with a guy was one thing, screwing with a god another. Even in the daytime, in the city, or at school she imagined the blue body. "It would be like doing it with the sky," she thought with a smile. When she told her girlfriend once, her girlfriend gave her a look and said, "I'd prefer Cobain, though he was so messed up, he probably couldn't do it." They sat in the playground and watched the boys gather and talk about the man found hanging from the swings that morning with twelve stab wounds. The discussion was whether he'd been stuck before or after. Those close to him knew that it was a warning, and they said little.

Now she lay on her stomach, and her body filled with blue like moonlight. It was hard to imagine anything bigger than the city night and anything smaller than her in it, because the night moved in all directions to join with the darkness of the universe. A cold fire burned inside East Station. A man in a light suit came out unscathed and tried to get into a cab, but the driver locked the door. The next driver did the same, and the next. Then several men ran up and dragged him off down into the dark concrete yard where during the day deliveries by train are dropped off. From the port the wind brought the stench of foul water mixed with the nervousness of downtown. Among the lights on Zieleniecka a group of Russians drove in an overloaded Lada, towing a trailer, heading east. In the next room her mother stirred.

Paweł lay on the floor, Jacek on the bed. They spoke softly, trying to remember old times, but everything they recalled was flat, as if trapped behind glass. Paweł listened for the clanking of the first trams. They were supposed to come before four. He imagined them leaving the depot in Mokotów and the one near Huta; they would speed up, move slower, then finally, as in a dream, move yet stand in place, and the day would never begin.

Meanwhile Zosia was talking to her cat, but it had had enough. It jumped from her lap and, tail stiff, went into the kitchen to sit by the refrigerator. This was how it spent most of its time—staring at the white enamel and licking one paw, then another. Then staring again. Always the same. At such times Zosia was left on her own. Like now. The desk lamp was on, and she sat in the armchair opposite. The small apartment was just the right size. She only wished it wasn't so high up. The trees didn't reach the fifth floor. Once she dreamed of waking up and seeing her carpet dappled by sun through leaves. Or in rain, branches whipped by the wind tapping the window and leaving wet marks. But the fifth floor wasn't bad, especially in spring and summer, when kids hung out till late on the benches with their boom boxes. The foul language and dirty jokes were muffled when they reached this high. You could open a window and look out at the apartment buildings on Pięciolinii. In the evening, a fascinating view. She imagined that the far apartments were toy houses and the people sitting down to supper living dolls in perfectly stitched little clothes. They would visit one another, invite one another in for coffee in tiny cups or tea in glasses the size of fingernails, while their books were printed in pinprick letters.

But now her curtains were drawn, the bedding crumpled. She had tried to sleep, but couldn't put the light out, things are too clear in the dark. She had taken the cat on her lap and talked to it, but cats have no interest in human stories. As if they just arrived and are on the point of leaving.

When she came out of the Stokłosy metro station, she called. No reply at Paweł's place. The sky over Stegny and Wilanów was the colour of the public telephone and as cold as the receiver in her hand. Nearby, a red letterbox mounted on the wall, an empty Królewskie beer bottle on top. The wind blew; from the phone, from somewhere deep in the city, an electronic beeping. The number began with a twelve, probably Praga. She hung up, and the machine with polite boredom returned her card. She didn't shop on the way home. Now she was reading but couldn't understand the simplest sentence, because they all left the book, went into the past, and said what happened a few hours ago. She also had a radio, but the sounds did the same. She had made herself some muesli and tea, but both remained untouched. She paced between the hallway and the kitchen. She ran a bath but was afraid to undress. She couldn't stand the mirror in the bathroom. She thought about her girlfriend on Wiolinowa, her sister in Gdańsk, her acquaintances in Rembertów who had the house with the garden where in summers she drank jasmine tea under a white parasol, but it was always the moment when the men entered the store, when the first one gave her a broad smile and placed his hands on the counter. He was so big, she could barely see the other, who stood with his back to them looking out at the street.

"You have something for us, kid?" asked the big one. "Something special."

She asked what it was supposed to be.

"For me." He laughed, pushed back, turned around, lifting the tails of his jacket.

"Like this!"

She set a few of the largest in front of him. He took each in turn, spreading it as he lifted it, looking inside.

"You understand, they have to be airy, that's important, otherwise—ha—you know yourself what can happen."

He put each pair down on the counter and looked at the shelves. On his right hand, a gold signet ring; in his eyes, nothing.

"No, these are no good, honey. What about something a bit more"—he pointed to a pile of women's knickers wrapped in plastic. "Those."

She brought him a few items. He flipped through as if they were old magazines. He tore open one or two.

"Sir, please . . ." But she didn't finish, because his smile was lifeless. "All right, sweetie, let's see what you have."

He swept away several pairs to make room. She took the opened ones, spread them out slowly in a row: three, white lace.

He chose the middle pair. Touched it with his finger. Looked from it to her, stroking the fabric. The other man stood by the door, his face to the street. She wanted to scream, but the scream would only bounce back off that huge body and die before it left her throat. She tried to look at him, his close-cropped blond hair and pink forehead, but lowered her eyes, because of his smile. His hand groping the material, his breathing. The hand crumpled the crotch of the knickers. She backed up against the shelves.

Then the big man told the other to lock the door. Hearing the click of the bolt, she ran for the back room, but he blocked her with his hip, caught her, as if he had been waiting. The knickers hooked on the long, manicured little finger held out to her.

"Shall we try them on?" he asked.

She pressed against the shelves; things fell. Wide-eyed, shaking her head no, because words wouldn't come.

"If that's how you want it," he said. He spun like a dancer, put down the underwear, barked, "Turn around."

She turned, pressed her face into green cotton blouses, for a moment happy not to know what was going on. As in childhood—you close your eyes, and the bad disappears.

But he shouted at her to turn back. She saw and screamed. The other man came and grabbed her by the blouse and pulled, his face white and featureless. In his free hand was a truncheon. She felt it on her cheek, a delicate touch, like a caress almost. She fell silent. The black rubber went over her closed eyes, her nose, then her mouth.

As they were closing the door after them, a howl rose in her, so she crammed a red cotton T-shirt in her mouth, but she had to take it out again to throw up.

Now too she ran to the kitchen sink.

On the off ramp from Łazienkowska onto the Wisłostrada a blue Polonez hit the guard rail. The radiator was smashed; the car couldn't be driven. A woman had been driving. Sober. The man in the car with her stopped a taxi and asked the driver to call roadside assistance on his two-way. The woman wept. Several lights were on in the apartments on Górnośląska. One person saw the accident. In the bushes by the pier an old drunk slept, warm. He would wake at dawn covered with frost but alive. He used to live on Przybyszewskiego, where at this very moment the wind was blowing a crumpled newspaper across the tarmac and under the wheels of a green Ford Capri. The car's engine was still warm. A stray cat sat on the bonnet. It was dark grey, striped, tail-less, a sly old thing, the king of the alley, but today someone had closed the cellar window it usually used. On the entire street there were lights in only two attic windows. The owner of the Ford was making himself a late supper. He had once lived in Grochów, then downtown and a few other places. He moved about, like everyone. This was nothing new. Before morning, nothing was going to happen. Most people sleep till morning. Dawn reaches the city first in the neighbourhood of Stara Miłosna. There had been a greasy spoon there called the Szafa Gra. Paweł hadn't been there in a long time, but he remembered its green door and windows. Many years ago. On the little square in front stood dying lorries, Stars and Jelczes—drab, rusty, with broken springs, and inside their cabs were naked women cut from magazines and medallions dangling from the rear-view mirrors. The drivers would eat in the place then continue on. The Russians to Białystok, or the other way, to Lublin. Paweł had borrowed his folks' baby Fiat. The dusk thickened along the tree-lined highway; in the fields it was still light. Jacek sat next to him drinking one Królewskie after another, because in those days they sold them in the small 0.33-litre bottles, inkpots people called them. Getting drunk, he asked again:

"What the fuck do you need down for?"

"I sell it," he answered, sorry that he'd taken him along.

"What the fuck does anyone need down for," Jacek mused. "They pluck it when the birds are still alive, I saw it once. Afterwards the birds walk around all pink."

They turned off towards Kołbiel. It got dark. Gardens, fences, wooden cottages, and the smell of manure. They found the farmer after sunset, his two sons standing behind him scratching their balls. The father wore rubber boots, but the other two were barefoot. Paweł gave a long explanation, while they stared, not understanding, so he started over again—who had told him, who he got the whole story from, all the details. In the end the farmer shook his head. "I don't have anything," he said, and waited for him to leave the yard and the yellow circle of lamplight. Paweł began at the beginning again: who, why, that it was definitely here, no mistake, it wasn't possible, he'd pay good money, but the farmer stepped towards him and waved a hand, which meant fuck off, because the farmer didn't feel like standing guard so some moron from the city wouldn't help himself to a souvenir, though there really wasn't anything there, dirt, an empty kennel, nappies on a clothesline. Paweł backed away, furious at Jacek for sleeping peacefully in the car, but when he was at the gate, one of the sons said, "Maybe it's Stach he's after." The old man gestured again, but this time meaning, "Wait." He asked, "Who is it you're looking for?" Paweł gave the name then, and it was the right one, a brother who lived somewhere else, dealt in the stuff, younger, Stanisław.

The old man went to the fence and drew a complicated map that the dusk erased.

They drove around for half an hour before they found the right farm. Beyond it, nothing but night, not a single light. Jacek woke up and complained they were out of beer.

The dog choked itself on its chain, as if it had never seen a stranger before. A light went on, and they heard, "Who's there?" He had to shout to make himself heard over the dog, the same story, who, why, how, and the man somehow heard, waved them in, and threw something at the beast to make it quiet.

A yellow dresser with blue knobs, a plastic tablecloth, a radio that no one turned down. The table, chairs, a stove— nothing else. They sat and watched a woman in a grey apron kneel on a canvas sheet on the cement floor and transfer the down from one bag to another. Particles in the warm air like snowflakes that refuse to fall. She was helped by her daughter. When the daughter bent over, they could see her white thighs. A sour smell. The farmer smoked. They felt like smoking too, but there was no ashtray on the table, so they just sweated and watched the packing. Paweł said something was wrong, he could see feathers in the down. "You can pick 'em out," muttered the farmer, the girl laughed, and a white cloud rose, as in a dream. The women were strangely slow, sweat trickled, flies buzzed. A pot on the range bubbled. Finally the two bags were full, and they began to weigh them on a rusty old porcelain scale. A bag slid off; commotion, white stuff flying about the room. No weights: the man used a sack of sugar from the dresser. Paweł said the weight of the bag should be subtracted. The guy said a kilo was a kilo. Paweł said the hell with this sort of deal, but when they opened the door, they saw that the dog, big, pale brown, was free in the yard, so they asked the farmer to tie the bastard up. Stach said they hadn't finished their business, hard-assed about it. No fucking way was he going to put that crap in another bag, he didn't want it floating around the whole house, he was already running at a loss. Three bulging bags side by side, and no way out. They sat down.

They left after midnight, Jacek staggering. Paweł wasn't, because he'd passed on the bottle though he'd paid for it. That was the custom, Stach had said, and his wife nodded. As they were going, Stach invited them to buy from him again. The dog accompanied them to the gate. It wanted to play. The cops stopped them in Wawer beyond the viaduct. Paweł took out his wallet, but Jacek gave them an earful. They had second thoughts and refused the money. They took his driver's licence.

In the dark, neither could put the story together.

"When was that?" asked Jacek.

"Eighty-three? In eighty-four I got my licence back."

"What did you need the down for?

"To sell it to this guy."

"We didn't go anywhere together after that?"

"No."

"I could have sworn I went back there a few times."

"No. After that I went on my own."

The first tram: a high-pitched whine from the north filled Marszałkowska, lowered, landed, then soared again and sped off towards Mokotów.

"The 36," said Jacek.

"How do you know?"

"It's always the first, and usually empty."

"How do you know?"

"Sometimes, instead of lying here I get up and sit by the window. I learned it all. In a moment there'll be an 18 from Żerań."

"Will it have passengers?"

"A few people in the first car."

The building stirred. Someone entered or left, the thud of the iron door passing through the walls like rain. Huge lorries from Russia circled the roundabout. The rubbish bins at the stops had been emptied.

"You know," said Paweł, "I sometimes think that if all these people didn't get up, if they stayed in their beds, the day would never begin. It would be dark the whole time."

"Why don't you just get the fuck out of here."

"Where to?"

They fell silent for the 18. It started at Konstytucji Square and skipped the stop at Wilcza. Its rumble opened up at Wspólna, tightened between the apartment buildings, eased off in the pass of Żurawia, but then the light must have turned green, because the noise rose again like a great wing over Defilad Square, till it reached the Palace and broke against its walls.

"What was the point rebuilding it if there's nowhere to hide," said Jacek.

"What?"

"The city. The whole place stinks of dead bodies."

"They removed the bodies."

"Sure. Suppose today at noon is Judgment Day and the resurrection of the flesh . . ."

"What judgment?"

"OK, that won't happen. But the resurrection, everywhere. On Marszałkowska the tarmac cracks and they crawl out; on the Aleje the pavements open and it's the same. You're sitting in

McDonald's on Świętokrzyska, with your Big Mac, and wham, the flooring, concrete, everything crumbles, and there's a dead body, and another, everywhere, at the traffic circle, in the Passageway, the lawn at Saski Garden peels and they pop up like mushrooms or those German garden gnomes, on Powstańców Square, Defilad Square, across the parade ground, on Widok the cops are giving some crackhead a hard time when up jumps an even better specimen from the ground, then Mirów and Muranów, hordes of them . . . It won't be all nice and genteel like before, like in the cemeteries out in Wólka and Bródno and Wola, where it's deserted, no one's around, plus they're all in tidy rows with their arms crossed the way they were left . . . Here it will be different."

"You've flipped, Jacek."

"I haven't. I sometimes think different things. Like this. Don't you?"

"I never had the time. And I'm not religious."

"Did you see Michael Jackson's *Thriller*?"

"Yeah."

"Something like that, except here. You're buying smokes at a kiosk, and you get sucked into a hole."

"I can't get excited about that," said Paweł, reaching for a cigarette.

"No one gets excited any more about the end of days," said Jacek, and laughed softly.

"Today some head case at Central Station asked me if I believe in the devil."

"What did you tell him?"

"What was I supposed to tell him? Nothing."

———

They fell asleep finally, on their backs with their mouths open, dreaming their own lives but not knowing it, so their bodies didn't struggle. Daybreak came in over the windowsill and went slowly across the floor like dishwater. It rose higher, submerging them, then reached the tabletop and finally the ceiling.

Sheikh rose from his mat, stretched out his front paws, arched his back, yawned. He went to the kitchen, but there was nothing in his bowl. His master and Syl were asleep, so he had a drink of water. He lapped three times for something to do. He felt uneasy. His black nails tapping the dark red tiles, a dry but clear sound, he went into the hallway, sniffed his master's shoes, came back. He put his front paws on the windowsill and looked out. A strange thing: from somewhere in Rembertów or Wesoła, fire rising. Not visible yet, but over the Olszynka woods hovered a smoky red. Like a dark fire inside the earth, a fire that is blind. The higher the glow rose, the brighter it got, as if fed by the air—orange, then gold, more and more diluted, hotter, till at the highest point of the sky it became a silvery white. A black braid from the chimney of the Kawęczyn power station was a straight line, but near the fiery disc it tore, broke, as if from a gust of wind, but instead of dissolving, the smoke formed a huge figure, half human, half animal. The cloud moved, thickened, thinned, let light through, looked like a person or thing trying to jump from the earth, take a step, another, head towards the river, to cross it awkwardly. Sheikh lifted his snout and whined. He sniffed the air, barked, took his paws off the windowsill, and went to the other end of the apartment.

In the train depot in Olszynka women were cleaning the red and green cars of a EuroCity. One woman, older, grey, a scarf tied under her chin, went out onto the low platform and crossed herself hurriedly.

The two men woke too late to see it. They finished the cold soup, smoked a cigarette each. They did not speak. Jacek opened the curtains to a blue, clear sky. The red latticework of the crane on the other side of the street was like the leg of a giant insect. In the kitchen Paweł drank water from a white mug. He put on his shoes, turned on the radio.

"It's after ten," said Jacek, so he turned it off again and they went out.

Jacek had to go to Praga. Paweł asked if he could join him. Jacek nodded unenthusiastically. They ran across the street and hopped over the barrier just as a 2 was coming. Jacek got in first. He found a seat and did not look around once. Paweł stamped his ticket and sat two rows behind him. The tram was uncrowded, transparent, cold. The air pale gold. Dust floated in diagonal streaks. He had slept a few hours, did not feel hungry, and his shoulder hurt less. In his mind he went over the events of the day before. They fitted. All events fit when they're over. He felt no fear but was bothered by his dirty socks, itchy feet. At Świętokrzyska the tram emptied even more. No one got in. He saw a piece of paper on the floor and picked it up: a page torn from a notebook, folded in four. Nothing written on it. He put it in his pocket, checked that no one was looking at him. Three women stared out of the window. "But they could turn around," he thought. The Saski Gardens on the right glowed brown, the trunks of the trees vivid. Prams like large moving flowers. In the distance, a lifeless fountain came briefly into view. "Fountains are turned on May first," he thought. At what used to be Dzierżyńskiego Square the light was green, so they sped past the gold skyscraper, which in the empty square looked about to collapse. The iron structure dizzy from all the air. His stomach stirred. They came to that cheerless neighbourhood where nothing had changed for decades, not counting the Mostowski Palace on the left. Then a double wall of drab apartments. Whenever he came out this way, he wondered who could live in this place of constant shadow, where it's dark when people leave in the morning, dark when they return in the evening. He closed his eyes, slept, opened them again, saw Jacek's grey back out the door. He leaped. The door closed, but he grabbed the handle, yanked the door open again, jumped out.

"You were going to leave me," he said.

Jacek paused, turned, looked at him in surprise.

"No . . ." A vague smile. "I completely forgot about you. Thinking."

"You were trying to get rid of me."

"I forgot. It happens." He headed towards Stalingradzka, taking a short cut past a stall selling beer and chicken. At Leńskiego he stopped and said:

"Listen. You can't go with me. Hang out here, have a beer, I'll be back in an hour tops." He turned at Skoczylasa, looked left, right, vanished into Brechta.

Paweł walked to the Filipinka like a robot and went in. These were places where time dies. He ordered a beer and asked the man behind the counter:

"So who was Haller?"

"What Haller?"

"You know, the general they renamed the Leński for."

"How would I know? I didn't know who Leński was either."

"Leński was Leński."

"So Haller must have been Haller."

"But out of the blue like that."

He took his beer and sat at an old table with iron legs. He wondered if Jacek really had tried to lose him. "Maybe," he said softly. "The prick." He raised his head quickly to make sure the man hadn't heard. The digital clock over the bar said 12:07. He took a long drink to forget all that and get back to his memories, which were safe.

Twenty years ago he lived in an apartment two blocks from here. There'd been Cuba libres in their glasses—him, another guy, and two women. He'd never had rum and Coke before and was feeling shy. The women were good-looking; their jewellery jangled, and their jeans were tight. The older one had big breasts, but he was with the younger one.

The apartment was reached via a filthy stairwell; one flight, then a door lined with metal and soundproofed inside. The smell of things beyond his experience. Wood, leather, thick colour catalogues of furniture and clothing, and the first time ever he saw a photo mural. It depicted an autumn park or forest. Behind him, but he kept turning to look at it. He was afraid to touch it, though he wanted to, almost as much as the other woman's breasts. They were watching television and listening to records brought from the West a week before. Then the women served food. He didn't know how to eat it. Never saw anything like it: toasted, fragrant, and covered with red sauce; in small, long glass dishes. The older woman was the owner of the place. The glasses had foreign words: White Horse, Johnnie Walker, Malibu, Stock. It was all exciting, stirred up a sweet pain. On his feet, dull trainers. Worried that they smelled, he kept his feet under the low table and pressed them together. When the food was finished and they started drinking again, he got up and went to the bathroom. The pink interior and the smell of lavender made him dizzy. He locked the door, checked the handle, examined the tiled shelves, the strange, chunky tap, and before he figured out how it worked, he scalded his hand. Holding his breath, careful to put everything back in its place, he removed his trainers and socks and put his feet in the bath. He watched with alarm as the water turned grey and dirtied the pink enamel. The towels were blue and white and fresh, so he wiped his feet with toilet paper. With a can of plain-looking deodorant he sprayed his socks and the insides of his trainers. He threw the paper into the toilet and flushed it. When he went back into the room, the man guffawed and said, "Upset stomach? Not used to it? Would have been fine with black pudding?"

He laughed till he was red in the face and his girl said, "Maniek, knock it off."

Paweł sat on the edge of the sofa and heard the leather creak beneath him. He downed his drink, felt his face burning; but the other two were busy whispering, giggling, pinching each other. The woman with the breasts guffawed, throwing her head back; her thick fair hair lay across the top of her armchair. The one he'd come with sat staring at her glass. Finally the other two got up and disappeared in the next room.

Afterwards, in his dreams, he often killed the man and fucked the woman. While he was awake too, and taking his sweet time, and always in the room with the white pile carpet and the autumn park on the wall.

Jacek pulled up a chair opposite him, smiling.

"How did you know where I'd be?"

"Where else could you have been?"

"Before three I have to make a call."

"There's a post office on the other side of the square."

"The same one?"

"I guess."

"I haven't been here in a while."

It wasn't one yet. Empty trams moving along Stalingradzka. Between the bare bushes you could see the pony enclosure. They stood there, dark brown, almost black, heads lowered, sideways to the sun; their long manes reached to the ground. There was no one at the zoo except a few kids playing hookey. Looking for the elephants, because elephants are easiest to find. But the elephants were inside.

So for a second Bolek watched the ponies: two sun-soaked patches. A white Passat tried to pass on the right, so he stepped on the accelerator and cut the guy off. Then lost interest in him. Went back to thinking about how it would be good to have a son one day and take him to the zoo, sit him on a pony, take his picture. Bolek had lots of photographs in his album, but they were mostly of adults, all buddies and people he knew, apart from the pictures of himself from thirty years ago in a ridiculous plywood pram reminiscent of a Citroën 2CV. Or naked on a blanket in a tiny white hat with a turned-up brim.

A 176 bus came out of Leńskiego while he still had a green light. He honked, stepped on the accelerator, slipped in front of it, on the count of sixteen entered the roundabout with a squeal of tyres, then into the continuation of Stalingradzka, leaving behind him the dismal police barracks at Golędzinów and that last solitary red-brick building where people kept stubbornly living. For the next five kilometres nothing, depots, hangars, the vastnesses of the FSO auto plant locked in high steel, factory scape to the horizon, with overhead cables and the straight vein of tram tracks along which chassis are brought three times a day and three times taken away.

Now he was doing a hundred in the left lane, gazing at all he had managed to avoid. The lot next to the test track glittered with a thousand coloured roofs in the sun like a Pop Art version of ocean waves. He sneered at an Opel he passed; he was doing a hundred and twenty now, and his Beamer was barely purring. He sneered at all the people—at the moment only a few here and there—waiting for him to go by so they could cross the road and, raising their pass, enter the main gate, or the one by the body shops.

Kids kicking a football around on a cold court, their bodies helplessly white against the tarmac. In a few minutes they'd get dressed and go to their next lesson in the trade, because their fathers were getting older and more tired.

He passed the school building. In the distance, the Toruńska overpass. A few seconds, and he was in the cement shade, parking outside the iron gate of a church. He locked the car, straightened his belt over his gut, and ran across the divided highway.

Three Ikarus buses at the terminus, their drivers waiting for replacements. Bolek went into a brown shack where a few men stood with Królewskie beers thinking about a cigarette, because inside it was no smoking and outside it was cold. A small-boned guy drinking wore black gloves with ripped seams and a red anorak with a Porsche logo. His two-day stubble stopped just below his eyes.

"What's the matter, Iron Man—cold?" asked Bolek.

"No, it's just that the water was off this morning and I didn't wash."

"Couldn't you have done it somewhere on the way?"

"In the bus?"

"Fair enough," said Bolek, and waited for the man to finish his drink. This the man did quickly, then nodded towards the bar.

"Stand me one, Boluś?"

"Later, Iron Man, I'll buy you as many as you like."

"What's the job?"

"No job. I just want you to go with me to a place and be there."

"What do I do there?"

"Nothing. Keep your eyes open."

"Oh," said Iron Man. He looked left, right, said, "Let's go then."

Bolek shook his head, tapped his Rolex. "In a minute. I don't want to wait there."

Iron Man took hold of Bolek's wrist.

"Nice. Gold. Does it keep good time?"

"You're still in the business?"

"You have to do something. But it gets worse and worse. Pieces of crap at two hundred a pop. And anyone who wears anything better doesn't ride the bus."

"Do you ever think about giving it up?"

"Then what? Go work at the plant? I'd come back from the late shift, fall asleep, and they'd steal my watch . . . That's not for me."

"There are options."

"I got set in my ways. Maybe things will change. People can't go on being so poor."

"Would you like to be rich?"

Iron Man spread his elbows on the counter and looked up at Bolek. "No, Boluś. That's not for me. I'm too delicate."

"You never did like fighting. I had to watch out for you. Remember?"

"On the other hand I was fast. You had to fight because they always caught you."

"One or the other, Iron Man. Those were the days, eh?"

In the end Bolek stood Iron Man that second one. He gave him a five and didn't blink when Iron Man brought back a mulled beer but no change. They stood and reminisced about the terminus buses and trams hidden behind lilac bushes, in green evenings, about the yellow street lamps so low you could break them without effort.

"And that beer shack," Iron Man went on. "On pay day they'd just lie there like in some war film, but I was too young then."

"Right," Bolek said, glancing at his watch so he wouldn't get sentimental.

Meanwhile, across the highway a priest was standing at the side door of a church, looking at the black Beamer, surprised that someone had parked right outside the place of worship. People only drove by. The big rigs from Russia going to Gdańsk went past ten steps from the entrance. Overhead, at the height of the cement cross, wound the ribbon of the overpass, from which cars trickled from the other side of the river, from Żoliborz, or sped straight on towards Bródno, leaving in the air a hanging carpet of exhaust and a constant vibration that forever blocked the church from the sky like a quivering sheet of metal. The rumble eased a little only at night, but the walls could never entirely shake off the tremors of the day, because before dawn new vehicles came around the looping ramps, calling like tugboats in the fog. More, the brick mass of the power station would sometimes blow steam, and then the air would fill with a cracking roar as from a time before there were people or any creature that had the power of hearing. Not a living soul in the neighbourhood. Nothing but work, haste, coal, the bells of trams, and the endless procession of shifts, and at night red rosettes on the soaring chimneys—to warn the planes, but they looked like electric crowns of thorns.

So the priest stood and considered the Beamer, which was almost touching the gate with its bonnet. The two men were now picking their way across. Bolek beeped with his remote, and Iron Man slowed to take a look at the majestic rear of the black machine.

"Are you here to see me, gentlemen?" called the priest, but his voice was swallowed up in the growl of diesel engines starting at the light. He tried to speak louder but then saw their faces, so he came down the steps to say something else, but Iron Man bared his teeth in a smile:

"There's still time, Father."

"Please don't block the gate. There's no parking here."

Bolek, the door half open, looked at the priest as if seeing him only now, and shouted:

"Hey, Iron Man, see the attendant." Then to the man in the cassock: "So how's business?"

The priest opened his mouth. Two lorries thundered across the overpass. The two men got in the car and merged with the traffic. Slipping into the left-hand lane, they disappeared behind the curtain of red that stopped the cavalcade behind them.

Three minutes later they left the car between two Ukrainian buses and walked slowly across the square. An attendant stood in their way and said it would be two zlotys. Bolek nodded to Iron Man, and Iron Man took the change from his pocket. They stopped at terrazzo stairs between plastic pillars.

"We go up," said Bolek. "You stay in the hallway and make sure no one's coming."

"Who might come?"

"If they show, you'll know. But they're not supposed to."

"What if they do?"

"Knock and come in, or give me a shout, I don't know. To buy me time."

"And then?"

"Then beat it."

"OK," said Iron Man, and drew on an unlit cigarette.

Inside, the smell of stale smoke, dust, toilets. A large, dark room with pictures of Switzerland on the walls, fake palm trees, red tablecloths. No windows, three chandeliers with weak bulbs, and a fan. At the far end, beneath the Matterhorn, a few people sat and ate. No one looked up, so Iron Man stuck his hands into his pockets and said, "Nice place." Bolek went to the bar and spoke with a platinum blonde who sometimes nodded, sometimes shook her head. When Bolek left her, she turned up the radio: the Fireflies. She half-closed her eyes.

They went upstairs. The hallway was long, doors on either side. At the end Bolek gestured with a finger. Iron Man leaned against the wall and finally lit his cigarette. Bolek knocked on a brown door with a painted 15.

The woman stood at the window. She was big. He closed the door behind him and slid the bolt shut. She was eating from a small Styrofoam tray.

"What's the smell?" asked Bolek.

"Fish and chips," she answered.

"You're eating fish?"

"I'm Catholic."

He came closer and looked at the tray: only bones and the last French fry on a plastic fork. She stuck it under his nose. He opened his mouth and took it.

"I'd never have thought."

"That I'm a Catholic?"

"No, I mean in general, where you're from . . ."

"Where I'm from, a lot has changed."

"I know, but."

"You're a fool, and all you think about is food."

"Irina . . ."

She wore a dark dress with silver thread, and her perfume was even darker, coming from her cleavage, into which a gold chain fell. Her high heels made little holes in the carpet. Bolek looked at the holes and thought about her heavy flesh. She took a hand mirror from the bedside table, a crimson lipstick, and touched up her lips.

"You have it?" he asked.

She turned her back to him, spread her legs, reached under her dress, and handed him a packet wrapped in plastic. It was warm. He placed it against his cheek, took a deep breath, chuckled.

"You wear perfume there too."

"Poles are perverts."

He put the parcel in his pocket. "I'm not checking it. If it's not right, I'll be back."

"You'll be back anyway," she said.

He went up to her and put his hands on her breasts. She

didn't move, just grew heavier. She slipped her thigh between his legs and pushed.

"You'd better go if you want to come here again."

In the parking lot two men were standing next to the Beamer. One on one side, one on the other. Peering in. When they saw Bolek and Iron Man, they stepped back and watched them get in. The men wore blue and red tracksuits. When the black car left, they went up to a rusty Lada and started unloading checked bags. They dragged them to the hotel.

On the short straight stretch, Bolek got up to eighty. At the intersection he braked, and Iron Man pitched forwards.

"Put your seat belt on, arsehole!" Bolek snapped. He glanced left at the unbroken line of cars and in the rear-view mirror at the empty alleyway where dust was still rising into the air. His foot twitched on the accelerator, and the speedometer needle jerked like the tail of a restless cat. When the traffic eased up, they moved—but straight ahead, onto the dull grass strip between the two sides of the highway. The Beamer bounced over the kerb and came to a stop angled left, sniffing for a gap in the traffic, but it was half-past two now and the lorries kept coming like a moving wall of words: Sovtransavto, Kruger, Kleeber, Mariola Cat Eyes, Faith Hope Charity, Olech, Your Baltic Your Herring—the last empty, because they were returning north. Iron Man put his seat belt on and asked what they were doing.

"Look and see if they're coming."

"They're coming and coming—there's no gap."

"Not the cars, idiot, the guys! From outside the hotel."

"I can't see; they're all blocking my view," complained Iron Man.

The traffic thinned, Bolek let up on the clutch, the Beamer

jerked forwards, stopped, shook as if overcome by lust and needing to rub against something.

"Damn cop!" roared Bolek, and punched the steering wheel. Iron Man tried to slide down in his seat, but the belt held him in place and all he could do was nervously squint left and right. No blue cop car in sight.

"Damn cop," repeated Bolek, a stream of yellow mud and last year's grass sprayed from under the Beamer's rear wheels, and a baby Fiat behind them turned on its wipers and smeared grey across its windscreen. Bolek put the car in reverse, first, reverse, second. The Beamer inched forwards as in a dream, and from the right Bolek could see a new wave of vehicles. Finally a bump over the kerb, and they were off to the left, urged on by a bleating of horns.

Three kilometres later, by the cement works, Iron Man's neck grew stiff. He turned and asked:

"Where are we going, Bolek? We were supposed to go to the city."

"Change of plans. We're visiting the old neighbourhood."

"Why the hell for, Boluś?"

Patches of shadow on the long empty street. Leafless poplars and chestnut trees cast a tangled pattern across the tarmac. They passed the little brick church on the hill, the acacia wood as well, and the clump of pines. Now slowly, as if moving against the current of time. To the right, on a square that looked like a forest clearing, was an old wooden building like the prewar houses on the Otwock line. Not many of its kind around here—in fact it was the only one. Two stories, a steep roof, a porch added later, and verandas clearly trying to separate from the rest of the building. The old crossbeams like Venetian blinds. Sawdust and dry leaves spilled from the crevices. Bolek said it used to be bigger, and Iron Man explained:

"The other half fell, so the folks in the first half had firewood for the winter."

"What about the people in the second half?"

Iron Man shrugged. "I guess they moved."

Further on, set back from the roadway, surrounded by chain-link fences and half hidden by the bare stalks of raspberries and lilacs, a row of colourless cube buildings with flat tar-paper roofs. Ferns and geraniums behind windowpanes, so someone lived there, though not necessarily—maybe someone just came to water the plants. Driving slowly, they watched an old film in which men in polyester suits stroll at a self-satisfied pace towards a station of the suburban train, and in the afternoon they return by the same route, on a path through wild grass between stands of birch and willow, tired but calm, because time stands still, and food prices rarely change, and when they do, it's only a twitch, not the daily betrayal of modern times. Women carry groceries in open-weave bags that served their mothers and would be passed on to their daughters, along with heavy glass siphons with a plastic trigger lever, empty, carefully folded sugar bags, jam jars, milk bottles, coloured confectionery boxes, plastic sacks, tin containers for sauerkraut from the private shop with the barrel in the corner, and a hundred other things whose quiet pulse slowed the turning of the world so much that between Saturday afternoon and Sunday you had the most matter-of-fact eternity filled with the fluttering of pigeons in a still blue sky.

"What did your old man make?" asked Bolek.

"When he was alive? About twenty-six hundred. As far back as I can remember, always about that."

They slowed even more.

The bushes to the right thinned to an open area of trampled earth and a two-storey apartment building. Pepper-and-salt brick beneath crumbling plaster. A red Fiat 125 stood with its nose down like a dog sniffing at something. Smoke from some of the chimneys. The bench by the wall on the sunny side was empty. Sixty degrees in the sun and no one drinking wine. In the windows upstairs no women leaning out, elbows on pillows, because there was no one now to look at. Those who hang around are the first to go in times like these. It's not easy for young people to gather in those small groups that can sit in one place all day, and if some leave, others appear in their place so the eye sees no change.

At an intersection Bolek asked:

"Where do you want to go?"

"Maybe to the store."

Paweł stood at the corner of Dąbrowszczaków and thought about the voice that just told him to call a completely different number that evening. When he asked for Mr Max, a woman answered, but it could also have been a man, a boy, a recorded message. A dead, flat voice. Though he did hear the person breathing. It gave seven numbers that Paweł was now trying to commit to memory.

Jacek approached with a large bottle of mineral water but nothing to write with.

"I'm good at remembering phone numbers," he said, so Paweł repeated it, then asked what the mineral water was for.

"To drink."

"But it's cold."

"So?"

"I don't know. It seems odd."

"Water is for drinking. Are you OK?"

"I wouldn't mind something to eat."

They walked through the square and turned into Skoczy-lasa, where there were fewer people, hardly anyone—an occasional parked car, no shop windows or displays, nothing but stubby apartment buildings from the 1950s, all yellow and grey, made for a hardworking life with no frills. The Albatross and the Seagull were gone. The young hoodlums gathered elsewhere. Paweł and Jacek both looked at the great iron doors that once led to two cinemas, the left blue, the right red, with gilded balustrades and rooms as long and narrow as sausages, seating no more than fifty or sixty people.

Jacek stopped to say something. Paweł muttered, "I don't remember," and walked on quickly towards Borowskiego, a stretch of brick huts, warehouses, garages, and the telecommunications depot with a row of orange vans in the yard. The cheerful Żuks and Nysas—no trace of them. It occurred to Paweł that apart from bills he had only received three or four letters in his life, hadn't sent more than that himself, and this would never change. Then Ratuszowa, a 6 tram was turning carefully at Targowa. Jacek caught up with him and asked:

"Have you been to see your folks?"

"They don't have anything," was the answer.

They followed the tram. Outside the school stood a bunch of kids in wide trousers and their caps on backwards. They were passing something from hand to hand with furtive glances. Paweł and Jacek walked through the group, and Paweł said:

"I was here yesterday. Remember Bogna?"

"Not really."

"She didn't have anything either."

"Does anyone have anything?"

"I already tried the people who do, and they don't have anything either."

They cut across 11 Listopada and were swept up by the main current of Targowa. From the bus stop by the Four Sleepers monument a mass of men moved diagonally across the intersection and into the open doors of local trains: Ząbki, Drewnica, Zielonka, Kobyłka, and Tłuszcz were reclaiming their citizens after the first shift at the FSO plant. The lights were red, but the men walked like the old-fashioned working class, shoulder to shoulder, with the heroic feeling that the world still belonged to them and that the permanently smiling Koreans from Daewoo were a phantom only or a joke that would end before it turned ugly. Colourful Gypsy women stepped out of their way, while the pickpockets had no interest in the men's wallets, which contained nothing but pictures of wives and children and loose change for cigarettes. It was an age till pay day. Everything smelled of sweat, metal, and a hurried wash after the factory whistle, and even at night in their beds lingered the stink of the factory, because fathers had passed it down to their sons, the way talents and traits are passed down. The stink of hot aluminum, steel, enamel, rubber, of air burned by arcs.

"Where are we going?" asked Paweł when they found themselves on the other side of the human wave.

"You wanted something to eat."

They went down into the underpass, where the neon was like fog, blurring everything. In this place people regained their shape only when they emerged again by the post office and went to catch a 4 tram or a 26 or a 34 and found themselves across the river, where the world was completely different. For decades they'd been getting out of trains and suburban buses at Wileński station dressed in garish clothing to invade, to conquer

89

downtown with its wonders, glitz, and glamour. From Łochów, Małkinia, Pustelnik, Radzymin, Poświętne, Guzowacizna, and Ciemne, from all those little backwaters with their cockerels crowing at five in the morning, their fire stations and flat, ploughed horizons, where instead of the sun the great city rises like a mirage magnified by the tales of those who have been there, seen it, touched it, or heard the legend. It was to tempt them that the Różyckiego bazaar appeared two streets on. By Brzeska, the smell of the country. White pyramids of heart-shaped cheeses, eggs, pickled cucumbers, bundles of dead chickens, their pale, plucked bodies, live birds in shit-stained cages, carrots, parsnips, cream in metal cans, black rapeseed oil in old vodka bottles, sacks of wheat, linseed, poppy seed, dried peas and beans, barrels of sauerkraut, pigs' heads, cows' udders, flies, the stink of burned feathers, the dry smell of burlap sacks, old women's armpits, honey in bottles, lard in jars, buckwheat, rhubarb, blueberries measured out in a half-litre mug, and the sour stench of cottages in which the air hasn't changed for generations.

But a moment later, the smell of shiny plastic, celluloid, and non-iron fabric. Beatles boots with stacked heels and turned-up tips, Plexiglas cuff links with naked women inside, neckties on elastic bands pre-tied and labelled "de Paris," gold chains, crimson lipstick, Dacron, nylon raincoats with silver buttons, Cossack boots with zips, baggy trousers with a permanent crease, blouses tight as diving suits, badges, belts, buckles, bags, and beads—all made of bright psychedelic polymers as in a child's kaleidoscope. From the reek of cabbage you entered a world of glistening, sterile colour, everyone did, those too who had hardly anything, who had seen these man-made hues only in their churches during May services. And that was the real revolution, because it took place in their hearts and eyes, and from that time they were destined and nothing could stop them in their march from the eastern plains of Sokołów Podlaski all the way to Ostrów Mazowiecka, from Kałuszyn to Wyszków, from Mińsk Mazowiecki to Ciechanowiec. First they sent spies, then an advance guard, and eventually captured bridgeheads in Ząbki, Zielonka, Rembertów, on the Otwock line, in places where at sunset you could see the tattered line of the downtown skyscrapers, with the Palace of Culture and Science against the disc of a sun as red as the Sacred Heart.

While Jacek phoned, Paweł stared at a youngster in a leather jacket who held black-strapped Casios on the fingers of both hands and twirled them like a juggler. Next to the kid stood an old man selling fluffy slippers, and a pisshead in a light jacket held out a pile of LPs with the band Christie on top. But mainly there were the Vietnamese, selling tracksuits, T-shirts, Puma and Adidas imitations. Their small, frail figures like theatre puppets, or immaculate dolls whom someone had locked in the cellar but who kept their good humour and elegance.

Paweł went to a stall and touched a black tracksuit.

"How much?" he asked.

The girl in the quilted jacket smiled and said:

"Sis hundre."

"Good deal," he said. She looked him in the eyes and nodded.

"You buy thuree, one million fi hundre."

He turned the packet in his hands and tried to feel the material through the plastic.

"You want see?" she asked.

"Yes. This one."

She took out a turquoise blouse with an eagle on the breast. He rubbed the fabric between his fingers.

"Chinese."

"*Not China*," she said in English, shaking her head. "Hong Kong."

"It's really cheap," he said. "What about those T-shirts?"

She fanned out a pile of white Ts bearing a comic-book drawing of a man's face.

"Che Guevara one hundre."

"What?"

"One hundre thousan. For thuree, two hundre fitty."

He couldn't tear his eyes from her long, dark, delicate fingers. Her nails had a pearly sheen and were convex.

"What about for five?"

"Fou hundre."

She wore no jewellery. Fine sinews moving under brown skin. The cadaverous light of the underground passage did not affect her hands: he was certain they were warm. He asked her to show him a dark green dressing gown patterned with brown and gold flowers. She held it up to her own body. Too big for her, it almost reached the ground. He leaned over the table and saw her feet in small, shining white trainers.

"Million," she said. "Look good. For wife?"

"No, not wife." He was about to say something nice to her but felt someone touch his arm.

And Bolek and Iron Man were sitting in the Beamer drinking beer. To the left, a little store on the first floor of a crumbling apartment building. To the right, another building like it. On the dirt courtyard a kid bounced a ball and took shots at an iron ring fastened to a tree. Two others appeared. He passed the ball to them. One had bandages on his arms. They tried a few times more but kept missing, so they began kicking the ball about.

The other houses on the alley were single storey. Some with bullet holes. Jars of food on windowsills. Someone went into the store and immediately came out again. An elderly woman with a walking stick carried bottles in a bag. The sky was blue. The view down the street was blocked by a railroad embankment.

They drove slowly. The black roof flashed in the sun. From a window over the store a forty-year-old woman wearing make-up and a housecoat was watching them. She took a drag on her cigarette. She had red nails. Her name was Bożena. She turned around and shouted into the apartment. In the building opposite, on the second floor, a boy and girl lay on an imitation leather sofa and watched *Walker, Texas Ranger.* The boy slipped his hand under the girl's dress.

A left turn. A narrow cinder road led through a stand of pines. Beyond, a small green patch of winter crop. Houses reappeared—small dwellings assembled from brick, asbestos tiles, and reed mats roughly plastered over. A man cut firewood in one of the yards. His son digging in a vegetable patch. The mother baking a cake in the kitchen.

A right turn, stopping at the tarmac to let a bus go by. The doors of a church open. A little girl walking up the steps with a bouquet of white flowers. Her silhouette disappeared inside as if into dark water. A cat lay in the road, flattened, dry. By a kiosk a full rubbish bin smouldered. A kid rode up on a bicycle and without getting off asked for a carton of Klubowys. There was no wind. Bare poplars cast graceful shadows. The air soft and sickly.

Iron Man popped another beer and passed it to Bolek. He opened one for himself too. They passed an overgrown villa with a veranda and columns. In the yard someone tinkering with a red Zastava, but they couldn't tell if it was a man or a woman because of the raised hood. Smoke rose from the chimney of a small bakery. On the square, once a playing field, was now an unfinished house. A woman in a pink sweater taking a short cut through the bushes, smoking and talking to herself. Her high heels sinking into the earth. A green Laguna with a CD dangling from the rear-view mirror moved towards them. Behind it a lumbering orange Kamaz lorry carrying a full load of rubble. Young birches, a golden haze, two teenagers playing with a condom, blowing it up and releasing the air with a shrill farting sound.

The Beamer moved heavily, sensuously. At the tracks the silver razor of the rails lay on the high embankment, so bright that they couldn't see which signal light was on. The brown woods in the distance as if cut in two. They reminisced about when trolleys with old Warszawa chassis travelled the rails and the ties were made of wood and smelled of dynamite, urine, and grease. Waiters in the buffet cars of long-distance trains would toss out sacks of rubbish. The boys would find them torn open and scattered along the embankment. Sanitary towels, glass, filthy stuff, nothing special, but occasionally Coca-Cola bottle caps and empty packs of foreign smokes. Once they found the queen of spades from a pornographic pack of cards, a woman spreading her legs. They followed her trail and found the ten of hearts with an ingenious threesome. They continued to the last houses but were unable to complete the pack to play any sort of game. They rooted in the ditch, scoured the bushes, walked in the middle of the tracks, then turned and searched the slopes. It was autumn, the grass turning brown and yellow, taking on the colour of human bodies. The jack of diamonds was such a tangle of flesh, they couldn't figure out which side was up. Scraps of paper, bottles, cans. An express train drove them off the tracks. The king of clubs lay on the path that ran alongside the ditch, distinct but incomprehensible. At dusk, an October chill rising from the earth. They hopped like sparrows from one piece of litter to the next. Bolek had three cards, Iron Man only one. Desire kept them hoping. An occasional glance at what they held, as if sneaking a look at a crib sheet. Zigzagging along the track, embankment, ditch, and path. Iron Man found half of the ace of clubs, the top half of a blonde with eyes closed and mouth open. Then smaller pieces, quarters, that showed nothing. Night was falling, and they didn't even show each other what they found, just stuffed the cards into their pockets and ran faster, further, covered with sweat. Finally picking up anything that was visible, flat, and felt like stiff paper. They stopped only when they saw the lights of the next station. They returned breathless, silent, with their fingers trying to feel what they had in their pockets.

Now, adults, they slowed to a walking pace because the Beamer was lurching over potholes and scraping its belly on the cinders. To their right, a long building roofed with felt. Several of the chimneys smoking. Life was going on in ten one-room apartments. People sitting together and watching television. Women opened doors and let out kitchen smells. Men pottering about in small sheds behind chain-link fences, fixing mopeds or cars that would never drive again. Between chicken coops, old discoloured refrigerators, things still kept in them. Objects rarely used or completely unnecessary, but even when thrown out they remained in reach and were property. A crow perched on a satellite dish.

"They probably still eat rabbits."

"Rabbit is good," said Iron Man. "But I hated it when the old man killed them. You start to be fond of the thing, then it's the holidays so grab it by the ears and no more bunny."

"Are we going to stop?" asked Bolek.

"Why? I don't know anyone around here now. They're all new."

"You sound like the old folks."

"Beirut, Bolek; this place is Beirut."

"We could take a piss on it, then torch it."

"Come on. You'd torch your family home?" Iron Man reached for his beer.

"I have one more job for you," said Bolek.

"I just hope it's not a big one," said Iron Man, and they moved off in the direction of the city.

"She'll be out in a minute," said Jacek, and flicked his butt into space.

They were sitting on a bench and staring at the longest complex in the city. Like a wall with holes, or a precision-made cliff face. Jacek and Paweł were small, almost invisible; no one took notice of them. People hurrying to eat something or buy food. Only the children weren't hungry: on roller blades and skateboards they did stunts in amateur imitation of their black brothers across the ocean. Freckled, pink, chubby-cheeked, in wide trousers and tracksuits, they whizzed through the labyrinth of the yard beneath spray-painted graffiti that read *Harlem, Bronx, Luśka gives head.*

"She said we couldn't because of her mother," said Jacek, and lit up another. Plastic clattering on concrete, an echo skyward, resembling gunfire—probably the point. A young kid sped past them backwards. He crouched, ducked under the carpet-beating frame, circled the sandpit, and vanished.

"You see? In curves," said Jacek. "And if they fall, they get up and start over."

"So?"

"I'm just saying. They don't go in a straight line. Kids used to. These guys turn."

"It's not like they have anywhere to go."

"Right."

Then they saw her. She was walking towards them in her green army jacket, carrying a plastic bag. She came up, stood in front of Jacek, lifted the sack:

"Lots of goodies. We're going to my girlfriend's."

Again he was watching the rapid kitchen knife. The blade clicking on the cutting board. Pieces of leek scattered in thin rings, mixing with the slices of carrot, cubes of celery. From time to time she would push the pile to one side; the rhythm would be broken, and her breasts would fall still under her black blouse.

"You didn't bring any meat?" he asked.

"No. My mother keeps it in the freezer, but she's got it all earmarked."

Somewhere behind him, from the other side of the dark hallway, music. Jacek came out of the bathroom, went to the girl, stroked her hair.

"The usual?"

"Yes," she answered, "but different proportions."

"Proportions are important," he said, and stared out the window. The music grew louder. A door slammed, and a girl in a miniskirt and black tights poked her head into the kitchen. Large gold earrings glittered in her dark blue hair. High heels with a leopardskin pattern. Paweł said hello, didn't hear a reply, maybe he had missed it. Jacek, back turned, tapped out a rhythm on the windowsill.

"You have everything?"

"Yes," said Beata. "Except I couldn't find any oil."

"There's butter."

"Yeah, but . . ."

"I know. But there isn't any. Yesterday we made French fries, and the oil got so dirty, I had to throw it out."

She almost brushed against Paweł and started rooting in the cupboard. Musk mingled with coffee, cinnamon, and pepper. Tiny freckles on her arms. He figured she was a redhead. She slammed the last door shut.

"There isn't any. Send one of them to the store. And by the way, why are they standing around like that?" She turned to Paweł. "Sit down, or you'll get tired. Or come into the living room and let them run the show here."

Against the window she was a sharp shadow. Moving her hips slightly. The rhythm made her exquisite, mechanical. At first he thought it was for his benefit, but then he realized that she'd simply returned to her music, permanently linked to it, moving as long as it was on. When the song ended, she turned and rested her backside on the windowsill. He thought she would say something now, but the next song began and her knee took up the pulse. The Lycra like a reflected sunbeam. Now planting her feet wider, she was a guy perched on a fence waiting for a bus. His gaze strayed about the room but kept returning to the darkness between her thighs.

"What is it?" He nodded at the hi-fi.

"Don't know. Got it yesterday. Cool, huh?"

"Is there singing?"

"No, it's just music."

Now tapping with the tip of her shoe. First straight, then to the sides, pivoting on the heel. Her right thigh shifted and let through a little light.

"That guy of hers is a little wacko, right?" she asked.

He shrugged.

"He looks like rubbish. Must have got that suit from his father. You known him long?"

"On and off."

"Does he wash?"

"How should I know?"

The blue behind her was immaculate and distant, as in a movie. The sun over the apartment building, over the black thicket of antennas. He couldn't remember which floor they were on, but from the ceiling he felt heat laced with glue and asphalt. The girl herself glistened like tar. The ball of the sun at its zenith, shadows re-entering their objects. He thought about slipping off the leather sofa and kneeling before her. She indifferent to everything except herself. Her body one with her underwear, her clothing, the music-soaked air. If he slipped a hand under her dress, he would find no crevice, only a faint electric warmth, smooth sheath, no trace of sweat, no unevenness, as if she were all one piece.

She pushed off the sill, crossed the room, and stopped in front of him, her hips at the level of his face. He watched them sway, their black repeatedly blocking out the blue of the sky.

Jacek had his hand on the back of Beata's neck. The vegetables in the pot smelled stifling, sickly. Ikaruses drove down brightly lit Kijowska.

"That's where we met," she said.

Even in the most glaring light East Station looked dingy with age.

"I remember." He held her closer.

"You looked like a beggar."

"I was older than you."

"You still are, but I don't feel it so much now."

He sought out her ear and gently took the warm lobe between his fingers. He remembered that she'd been buying something at the station kiosk and as she walked away she dropped a hundred thousand. He picked it up, crumpled it in his hand. She turned around, searched her pockets, and their eyes met. She stood confused, helpless, small. People passed by them and between them. She wore the same faded army jacket as today. She took him with her. Her mother was out.

"You don't wear earrings any more."

"No," she said. "Not for a while."

"The holes will close."

"They won't." She raised her head, laughed, pressed her whole body against his side.

A white 13 tram set off from the stop. A brown ad stretched across both cars read "Mane Tekel Ares" and showed a pack of smokes. Everyone got off at the station. It entered Szmulki empty, then from the terminal at Kawęczyńska it picked up a woman with a small baby. She was going to Koło, the last stop, where her mother lived. Running away from her husband. But her mother was growing less lucid; she moved about almost by touch among imitation crystal, pottery seals, dogs made of coloured glass, prints of Our Lady, hunters in little green hats, and as she made weak tea she kept repeating, "My, how you've grown, Dawidek. Going to school already? Granny will give you a cookie," and she would take out an old tin decorated with arabesques and half-naked ladies, but inside there was nothing but buttons and scraps of cloth.

Condensation covered the pane, and the white tram disappeared. Beata drew on the glass. They looked at the fragments of world that appeared at the touch of her fingers like a puzzle ready to be assembled. A man stood in the doorway of the kitchen, but they didn't notice him.

"If you want, I can start wearing them again," she said.

"No. They're nice like that," said Jacek. He listened to her breathing, matched his own to it.

He was trying to catch up, but whenever he got close, she'd slip away, as if she had eyes in the back of her head. He thought to trap her in the corner between the battered gold lamp and the leopardskin sofa, or in the narrow space between the stand with the plastic flowers and the hi-fi cabinet, or in the gap between the table and the bookcase; but she got away without effort, indifferently, as if she were dancing alone in an empty room. He bumped into furniture and tripped on the rug like a blind man or a cripple. A few times he touched her hips, her backside. It was a clumsy conga. Perhaps the record would come to an end. He reached out and touched her shoulder. She stopped, turned, and he saw she was smiling, but the smile was blank. "That's how it should be, that's the best way," he thought, and went to touch her breast.

Then the guy came into the room. He was wearing a purple tracksuit and a leather jacket. Paweł stepped back; the guy grinned; the girl didn't move a muscle.

"Party time again, Luśka?" He made himself comfortable on the sofa, his white Nikes shining as if polished, the skin on his head bright under his buzz cut. Keys on a silver carabiner attached to his belt next to a pouch. He tapped a foot though the music had stopped when he came in.

"Who's that with Beata in the kitchen?"

"A friend."

"She won't come to anything. She might have once." A questioning look at Paweł.

"Another friend. They came to make themselves dinner."

"To make what?"

"Dinner. I just said. Her mother's home today."

The guy slapped his knee and said:

"There you go, Luśka—you see how good it is to be an orphan. You don't have to go visit other people." In the silence, he took out a cigarette, lit up, inhaled, blew out smoke, and watched it hang in the air. Either waiting for something or just sitting there in the knowledge that they had to sit there too. He was tall, broad, young. He liked it when things fell into place. He finished his cigarette, crushed out the butt, stood up, went to the window, and beckoned Luśka. He took something from the pouch and gave it to the girl, then said, not too loud and not too quietly:

"There's a hundred big ones in here. I'll be back this evening. I don't want to carry it around town."

She took it, weighed it in her hand, then opened a cupboard and stuffed it between white bedsheets.

"All right," he said. Hands in his pockets, tipping his head as if thinking something over.

"Good. Now tell them to get the fuck out of here."

The girl shrugged, leaned against the cupboard.

"Tell them yourself. I have nothing against them."

"I don't either, but they need to get the fuck out."

A 26 passed Kijowska and went under the viaduct. A young soldier with a backpack, head shaved, was looking around nervously, mentally counting the stops. It was only at the Powszechny Theatre that he got up the courage to ask an elderly lady in a mohair beret. "Oh, you missed it," she said. "But if you get out at the next stop, you can walk. Left on Lubelska." He got out at Rogatki, smelled the chocolate from the Wedel factory, and felt like crying.

An electric train set off from Powiśle station. It took the iron spans like a sleepy rollercoaster. A blonde with a green pack on her lap tried to look into the windows of an apartment building on 3 Maja, but they were black mirrors. Then water underneath, so she closed her eyes, and, as every day, her gorge rose. In a whisper she counted the thuds of the wheels. At forty-three she knew she was over the hill.

"It's up to you," said the guy, and closed the door behind him. Paweł listened, but the girl turned the music back on and began moving her hips, looking out of the window. His eyes moved between her arse and the cupboard door. Musk from her armpits, perhaps, but stronger was the smell of stiff sheets starched at the laundry and lying in a tight stack. Something was going on outside the door: a vibration, a thumping, a kind of unease. Then some actual noise over the music, but he couldn't identify it before it dissolved back into the music. He refocused on the cupboard door and the arse. Then a sudden movement, the air in the apartment quivered, then silence.

The guy came in and sat in his former place, and the girl turned the music off.

"You'll have to clean up," he said. "The crap got spilled. New tracksuit." He stretched out the fabric on his thigh and looked at a small stain. "Just as well it's a loose fit, or I would have been scalded."

Then he turned to Paweł as if only just noticing him. Narrowed his eyes, stared with his pale blue gaze, and gave a broad smile.

"So how are things? You OK? What are you up to now?"

Paweł felt a hot tongue on his back licking upward from feet and across shoulders; on his neck and in his hair it burned.

"I keep busy," he answered.

"You have to, pal. You have to keep moving." A nod, still the same smile.

"Luśka, bring something to drink." Issuing the order to the girl but not looking away. Paweł started to dig in his pockets. Out of the corner of his eye he saw the girl go and open the flap of a cabinet.

"Here, have one of mine." The guy took out some Camels. He had to shake one loose because Paweł couldn't get it.

She put a bottle of Wyborowa and two glasses in front of them.

"Pour some for him. I have to go in a minute."

She did as he said and put the other glass away.

"Come on, just the one. Don't be shy," the guy urged. "Tastes good, does you good. I'd have one with you, but I can't."

Paweł raised the glass, felt the vodka dripping over his fingers, poured it down his throat, and in his mind the words *I better leave* rattled.

"Just as well. You know how it is, right?"

Paweł waited for the vodka to drop and said:

"Yeah."

"You see what I'm saying. Luśka, give our buddy here another."

The girl refilled the glass. Paweł was trying to understand what the guy was saying, but he heard only the volume. The words were strangely detached, as if someone were speaking from inside a well or calling in the darkness. He concentrated on the man's mouth, watched it move. When it stopped, Paweł would nod. He saw uneven white teeth, one of them broken; a pink tongue appeared, disappeared. Sometimes the mouth opened to laugh, so he laughed too, careful to finish at the same moment, not wanting his own voice to remain alone in the silence afterwards. He tried to count the drinks but soon lost track. He couldn't focus: the girl, her arse, the cupboard door, the guy's mouth, his own hand with a cigarette trying to hit the ashtray. All of them like separate machines. Space had slipped between them, so even if they wanted, they wouldn't have been able to touch one another. The guy's watch glittered on his wrist, but the hands were in constant motion and Paweł was unable to see the time. Finally, when the watch hand slapped down to rest on a knee, he saw that it was after three.

The guy got up, went to the door, put his hand on the handle. Paweł sighed with relief. The girl had turned away, looking through the LPs. The guy opened the door. He nodded at Paweł in farewell. Paweł smiled, winked. But the guy stood where he was and finally said:

"Well?"

"Nothing."

"Then let's go. Were you thinking I'd leave you here, wise guy?"

———

105

"I was never here before," said Iron Man when Bolek pulled the Beamer off onto the edge of a cinder track. They'd driven halfway across the city. Now it lay far behind them, black against a red sky. The railway embankment above them. A litter-strewn field, solitary bushes casting long shadows. The sun about to set. Near a clump of pines, the wind was making something flap in the grass: a piece of plastic, paper, hard to say.

"You stay here," said Bolek.

"Where?" Iron Man looked around, at a loss. "There's nothing here."

"Wait over there." Bolek pointed to a small hut next to the pines. It looked like an old outhouse. "You can't go with me."

Iron Man shook his head, pulled the zipper of his jacket up to his chin.

"At least leave me some smokes."

Bolek reached into the glove compartment and took out a pack of Marlboros.

"I won't be more than an hour," he said, and turned the key in the ignition.

Dusk already in the trees. He drove slowly across mud, deep puddles. At a corrugated iron fence, he got out and knocked on a gate. It cracked open; someone took a look at him, and the two sides opened.

Bolek parked by a dirty Polonez. Everything like a building site: planks over mud. Under a lean-to, stacks of bricks, wheelbarrows, barrels of cement. At the far end of the yard was a house, half hidden by the pines. On the concrete steps he was greeted by a heavy man in a leather jacket.

"Go on in. He's waiting for you," the man said.

Bolek scraped the soles of his shoes on the edge of a step and pushed open the glass door. The man, following him in, flicked a switch in the hall and returned to his station. Bolek walked to the back of the house, his steps echoing on the cement floor. In places the walls were plastered, but half-heartedly. Another man in a doorway nodded to him. Behind him two others were playing cards on a small plastic table. A cartoon on TV. The room stank of socks. Somewhere at the other end of the house, a slow, hollow thumping, like someone beating his head against the wall. An overweight dachshund appeared, old, too tired to bark. It simply lifted its nose and sniffed.

At the end of the hall, a broad oak staircase with a carved balustrade and glass chandelier over the landing. A tin bowl with dog food. Bolek headed up the stairs. Halfway, the oak flooring turned to bare concrete, then a green rug covered with cigarette burns. Here the walls were white and had a few pictures: naked women with orange-brown skin against an ocean background. He reached a mahogany door and knocked.

"Unbefuckinglievable," said the fat man, and dropped into a leather armchair. "Who was taking care of it?"

"Waldek and his men," answered Bolek.

"I'll goddamn see to him," said the man. "Tell him that. On my territory I don't tolerate dipshits, motherfucking amateurs."

"He said he got away from them. They saw two. He said they chased them."

"You tell them I'll goddamn see to them. And stop standing around like that."

Bolek squatted on a low padded stool. The man in the silver pyjamas reached into a drawer of the desk and took out a bottle of white Absolut. He filled two glasses and motioned with his head:

"Here, Bolek. You're a good kid."

Three walls of the room panelled with oak, the fourth glass, letting in bright light.

"Fix it. Old Max is asking you."

"I'll fix it, boss," said Bolek, reaching for the glass.

"Tell him I'll see to him."

"I'll tell him."

Mr Max gulped the vodka, felt the pockets of his pyjamas, took out a cigarette. Bolek jumped up and gave him a light. Mr Max took a drag, stood, beckoned, put an arm around Bolek, and led him to the glass wall. Below, the glistening blue of a swimming pool, two women in swimming costumes waist-deep and talking.

"Any idea how much all this costs, Boluś? A goddamn fortune. The bitches alone are half your salary, without the extras." He hit the glass. The girls looked up, startled; they broke off their conversation and started splashing.

"I pay them to look nice, not talk. But you turn away for a second, and yadda yadda. They're all like that. You're my eyes, Boluś."

"Yes, boss."

"If you were my son, I'd say to you: One day all this will be yours. But you're not, and you have to come to terms with that. You can't complain, right?"

"No, boss."

"It'll never be yours, but when the time comes, you'll make your own. You know how I started."

"I know, boss."

"You don't know squat. When you started, you had me. I didn't have anyone. Ask the people who know me."

Mr Max leaned on Bolek's shoulder. He looked through the glass, but his gaze reached further, into days gone by. He sighed, pulled himself together, banged on the glass. The women smiled, waved.

"You want one of them? Or both? I won't watch."

"Thanks, boss, but I still have a little business today."

"You're a good kid, putting work first." He clapped Bolek on the back and went to the desk, his slippers flopping. He poured another shot; they clinked, and he asked:

"You got it?"

Bolek took out the package wrapped in black plastic. Mr Max weighed it in his hand, smiled, and put it away in the desk.

"You were alone?"

"Of course, boss. I know what I'm doing."

"You're a good kid."

Bored, scared, Iron Man flicked his lighter on and off in the hut not much bigger than an outhouse. One of its windows broken. Night had fallen. He wanted to read what was written on the walls, but there was hardly any fluid left in the lighter. He didn't like the dark and needed something to light a cigarette with. "The flint always lasts longer than the fluid," he thought. He tried to guess what the hut had been used for. One room, a hole where the window had been, the door. In the short flashes he read: *Mariusz reservist 92 did Dorota. Horses condoms. Patrycja sucks.* "I wouldn't be able to get it up in here," he thought. "I always have trouble in the cold."

He took a few steps along the wall. In the next flash, an upside-down cross, in charcoal. He wanted to read what was written underneath, but remembered about the fluid. A train rumbled along the embankment, heading east. Black people in yellow windows staring into the night towards Iron Man, but not knowing that he was there, that he existed. It was like that even in the daytime, in the middle of the city. He was invisible. If he had vanished one day, no one would go looking.

The red lights of the train disappeared. He took out a cigarette, tore off the filter, and lit up. The night on all sides. Visible in the little glow: the litter, the glass, graffiti, the cracks in the wall. He took a long drag and said into the darkness: "Don't think, Iron Man. Thinking is not for you." His fear eased. "A drink would be nice," he thought aloud. "Where did he go? So cautious lately. Before, when there was nothing to brag about, you couldn't shut him up. Now he's the man of mystery. The car, Marlboros, clothes that cost fifteen mill, a watch that's another fifteen. Shoes too. And five years ago he was bringing me a Zodiak radio and asking if I could fence it. Liked to fight but was always cautious in business. Never inside more than forty-eight hours. It takes all sorts. One guy likes flowers, another when his feet smell. One day he comes and says: Iron Man, there's a big job. I ask what kind, and he says it's a little risky, one or two guys may have to be blown away, but the take is big. And I say: Thanks but no. On TV it looks great, Boluś, but in real life I don't even like to see somebody getting an injection. So off he goes, and I stop seeing him, like he was iced or went abroad. But now he remembers his old buddy." He realized that he had been talking to himself. He stopped, listened carefully, but the silence stretched all the way to the city. Far off, a monotonous hum and a cold light, as if machines lived there, not people. He flicked his lighter on again, took a step, and read: "Fuck everybody." Angular, smeared letters. Must have written in shit.

Out of nowhere, a skinny guy stepped forwards and stood next to the desk. Wearing tight orange jeans and a yellow T-shirt. His mousy hair fell over his face, so Bolek was unable to tell how old he was.

"Dad, I need six hundred thousand," in a screechy voice, as if inside him was a cheap Chinese tape recorder.

Mr Max glanced at him, then looked up and far away. After a long pause:

"What else do you want?"

"Nothing. Just that."

"What do you need six hundred thousand for?"

"A cab. There and back."

"One of the guys can take you there. Three hundred will be enough."

"Dad . . ."

"I said three hundred."

Mr Max reached into the desk and took out a telephone. He pushed two keys and said:

"Get Hairless up here. He'll take the kid to the city and bring him back." To his son:

"You heard? Get dressed right now, or Hairless will chuck you in the car like you are."

The kid tried to say something, but Mr Max had lost interest. He filled his glass again, signalled to Bolek. The kid was gone, as suddenly as he had come.

"I thought he'd amount to something, but it doesn't look like it. He spends my money but won't touch the business. Disappears for two or three nights and comes home smashed. That's OK, but the guys have seen him with the kind of people . . ." Mr Max lowered his voice and leaned over:

"It's an awful thing to say about your own child but . . . well, I think he's a fairy."

Mr Max dropped his head.

"Maybe not, boss," Bolek said. "If he got a haircut . . ."

"Boluś, it's not the hair. You're smart, but sometimes not so. Did you see how he walks, moves? And to think I'll have to leave it all to him. And he'll piss it away on his man friend . . ."

Mr Max sighed, had another drink. Then he took a second mobile phone from the desk and gave it to Bolek.

"Here. Turn it on in two hours and take care of that arsehole."

Paweł was repeating Jacek's route of the day before. He counted the circuits from when he entered the underpass by the Forum. The crowd parted for him as you let a madman, tramp, or dope-head pass, but he didn't notice, because time was a tightening noose around his neck. The events of recent days converged, pressed out space and air, and spun. He counted from one to nine and added zero, but each digit could have been the beginning of the number. Backwards was a little better, but there was no certainty. To breathe, he went up to street level by the Metropol.

Jacek's window was still dark. He wondered if he was there but hadn't turned the light on. Holding on to this hope for an hour now, he'd been up there three times. The last time he hammered with his fist, then evened the door with a kick. Somewhere in the building, a voice shouted: "Who's making that racket? I'll call the police!" Paweł ran up the stairs into darkness, nothing. He felt along the wall and wooden shelves, then wall again or maybe a door, because it sounded hollow. His hand touched warm pipes. He leaned his back against them, squatted, listened, but there were only the usual building sounds, slamming, the diluted tumult of life, the trembling of the city's tarmac skin. "The prick," he whispered, and repeated it in his mind until the fear left. He touched the floor.

Grains of dirt stuck to his hand. He pulled his knees up to his chin and wrapped his arms around them. This was a good place to wait, nothing new would happen here, and above was only the cold black sky, where nothing needed to be done.

After a few minutes he went down the stairs and put his ear to the door. The noise of the street filled the apartment, circulated, brushed against the furniture, reached the door, returned to the windows, went back and forth without end. He searched his pockets but couldn't find a piece of paper. He stuck a used match in the door jamb to leave some kind of sign.

Now waiting at a bus stop pretending to be a regular person. Waiting for his 131 or 180 or for someone he knew. He lit a cigarette. The wind blew from Constitution Square and brought smells. He remembered that on the far side of the square were stalls with hot food, but he hesitated, mentally counted the money in his pocket.

A few hours before, the man in the tracksuit clapped him on the shoulder and said, "You know yourself how things are, right?" He'd started off in a random direction, but the man said, "I'm going downtown. I can give you a ride." So Paweł followed him towards the station. He hung back a couple of steps and watched the swagger, the white flashes of the trainers. At the cab line the man chose a dark blue Audi 100. The driver lowered his window. They talked for a moment, then the cab driver got out, took out his wallet, and gave the man his registration.

"We'll take Syreny Bridge," the man said as they drove in the shadow of the viaduct. An electric train waited overhead. Inside the car it was quiet and smelled of Wunderbaum air freshener. The needle of the speedo rose and fell. Paweł noticed a pair of leather slippers under his seat. The man was whistling some song, and when they turned into Zamojskiego, he hummed another. The gearstick had a leather cover; a silver key chain with a naked woman hung from the ignition key; a tin Saint Christopher dangled from the rearview mirror next to the Wunderbaum air freshener. No sound. To the left people were walking towards the bus station or coming back from the stadium. The rust-red tops of buses warmed themselves in the last sunshine. Something chirped in the glove compartment. The man stretched out his hand. Paweł reached in, felt cold metal, found the mobile phone, and handed it over. The man said, "Not now," and gave back the phone. They passed the tunnel and the port, the sky red between the bare trees. They turned left under the viaduct, drove along the embankment, then pulled into the parking lot in front of the stadium. The man looked around. The roofs of the cars gleaming in the slanted light from the river. People standing on the canopy. Some approached their car from behind. The man pushed a lever, and the lid of the boot hid the new man. Paweł started to turn but heard, "Keep out of it." The other man closed the boot, then they headed to Wybrzeże Szczecińskie and the bridge. Without speaking. Paweł remembered the empty stadium twenty years ago. He and Jacek jumped over the barbed wire surrounding the grass and went to the middle of the playing field. Late evening. Over the top of the stands, a silvery moon, and the grass bright with dew. He couldn't recall what they talked about.

At Świętokrzyska the man said, "I'm going to Central Station." "Fine," said Paweł. They had a string of green lights and in four minutes were at the main lobby, pulling up behind a white Merc. The neon lights of the Holiday Inn shone to the left, and it was dusk. Paweł held out his hand and said, "Thanks a lot."

The guy shook his hand with the same frozen smile. Paweł reached for the door but felt a strong grip.

"Don't thank, read," said the man, and looked down. Paweł followed his eyes and saw that the meter, which had been dark, now showed 450. He tried to pull away but knew it was hopeless.

"Are you crazy? I thought . . ." Nothing more came to him.

"You thought wrong."

Paweł tried to reach the door with his left hand, but the man twisted his wrist.

"That's no way to behave."

"Let go," said Paweł, because the man had his hand in both of his, twisting it down. Paweł slid off the seat and felt the gear-stick in his stomach.

"Half a mill, or I rip your hand off."

"Let go . . ."

The driver of the white Merc got out. Paweł tried to shout to him, but he came up to their car on the left.

"What's this? Some smart-arse?"

"One . . . Mundzio, stand on the other side and watch the door."

The cabbie walked around and leaned his back on the window. He was big. Paweł rubbed his freed hand.

"So out with the money."

"I don't have it."

"Everybody has something."

Paweł looked out, but black leather covered the window like night.

"I don't have it."

"If you want, I can ask him to come and join us."

———

So now he was mentally counting his cash, and his hunger slowly left. Cigarettes are cheaper than food. French fries with ketchup, salad, fried fish, burgers, and kebabs go quickly, but Sobieskis, a pack of twenty, can last for hours. He thought about this to keep from thinking what had happened. He remembered the nauseating smell of vegetables as they left the apartment. He took a deep drag, and the nausea passed. His legs hurt. The cold getting through his jacket. A ground frost setting in. The window still dark. Someone bumped into him and said sorry. I'm standing here like a royal dick, he thought.

"With what?" asked Iron Man.

"Dogs."

"You're shitting me, Bolek."

"Honest, he started with dogs. He'd stand on Targowa near the Różyckiego bazaar selling puppies out of a cardboard box. In the sixties. He told me himself."

"And he lived on that?"

"No, something else. But puppies was how he got started."

"Well, I don't see why not," mused Iron Man. "Puppies are nice."

They were standing in front of an open wardrobe, Iron Man trying on different outfits. The shirts OK, the jackets a problem: they hung on him like cloaks, as if he were on the run.

"You can pull the trousers up and tighten the belt," said Bolek, closing one eye, then the other.

"The crotch is at my knees."

"That's the fashion now."

"Don't make an idiot of me, Boluś."

"You have to look decent."

"There's nothing older? I mean, from before you got fat."

In the next room, Syl clicked the remote. Sheikh lay in his place and stared at the screen, waiting for a cartoon with a dog and a cat.

"I don't know. Maybe stored away."

They went into the hall. Bolek brought a chair. It creaked when he climbed up on it. Plastic sacks and bin bags spilled from the storage space. He got down and started rummaging: bell bottoms, handbags, light blue nylon jackets, well-worn cherry shoes with toe caps and crepe soles.

Iron Man regarded the mounds of garish colour, the Dacron and tricotine, the frotté and bouclé, and an odd fabric that jackets were made of twenty years ago—light as paper, rubbery to the touch, and so flimsy you could wrap the whole garment around your hand. He tossed it aside and examined, from sacks, sleeveless Wrangler jackets, black clogs, striped hip-huggers with horizontal pockets just big enough for a condom or an old hundred folded in four, padded trousers with a cyclist motif, jeans washed to purple, T-shirts with decals, but didn't find what he wanted. Ankle-deep in the stuff, they remembered the discotheques in the Chemik club, where they would hang out in the bushes drinking and smoking, their cheap jeans stretched tight across their arses. When the cops came by, you ran for it across vegetable gardens, fences, backyards, and the trousers would split from knee to crotch. Afterwards they would go to Iron Man's mother so she could sew them back together on her prewar pedal-operated Singer, which she did without a word and not asking any questions, even though the two of them stank of cheap wine and Sport cigarettes, and sometimes in their pockets she'd find money. In the dark of the movie house the girls would shine like twenty-zloty coins and have on the latest Hungarian deodorants. The boys stood in a circle of their own smells. They'd go out to dry the sweat from their bodies. That's how it was, the girls in their reptile blouses and bracelets in the strobe lighting. The boys desired them but knew they'd be able to see everything only by force or trickery, the way things are always taken into possession, also the girls would be used up soon and the boys would have to begin all over again, so as not to settle or come out a loser.

They found a pair of brown Radoskór trousers with four jagged stripes and rotten insoles; an imitation bear hat; green leather knee-length boots; a suede vest with tassels; a pendant with a picture of Sweet on a cord, and the lads had straight fringes and velvet chokers around their necks; a sweat-stained wristband; a dozen bundled-up plastic socks. Bolek said, "Got it," and took out a cornflower suit. He put it on a hanger next to his bomber jacket. Wide lapels, patch pockets, covered buttons, and a half belt in the back.

"My wedding suit," he said, feeling the material. "It's not crumpled at all."

"Because it's wrinkle-resistant. They don't make them like that any more," said Iron Man.

"I was a beanpole back then."

Iron Man put on the jacket, unconvinced, and looked at himself in the mirror. The sleeves were a little long and the shoulders drooped, but it looked good.

"A little like a hick?" asked Iron Man.

"No. People wear all sorts of things today. It's in one piece and doesn't have any stains. Get a shave and clean your fingernails, and no one will know the suit is twenty years old."

"I should have a wallet to go with this. It always looks nicer when you don't take money straight out of your pocket."

"What are you planning to take out?" asked Bolek.

"I mean just in case. And a decent lighter. Not a disposable."

"We'll find something."

They went through two rooms, to the living room, and sat by the coffee table, which had an open bottle. Iron Man asked:

"Did he seriously start with those dogs?"

"He had to start somewhere."

"I guess when you're starting, it doesn't matter with what."

"You're not wrong, Iron Man, you're not wrong."

A throbbing green light across the black sky, headed towards Okęcie. Bolek poured, and they clinked. The sound rang pure and high, and Iron Man thought, "Damn, this is crystal."

The Hoochie-Coochie was empty and warm. A stream of smoke, rising vertically over the bar, dissipated in the dimness beneath the ceiling. The owner was nowhere to be seen. Beata and Jacek sat in a corner, she touching his cheek, brushing his hair aside. He looked twice her age.

"It's dry," he said.

The bartender came from behind the counter, tall, skinny, unshaven, and didn't even look at them. Putting out his cigarette, as if it was by some miracle that he was still on his feet. He looked like Jacek, Jacek's brother.

"I'm sorry," said Beata.

"It was a nice day. The forecast was good."

"You're not hungry?"

"He was the hungry one."

"I have money."

"Where from?"

"I took it from my mother when I went up there."

"A lot?"

"Everything."

"That's not a lot." He smiled and touched her hand.

"She'll kill me when I get home." Smiling back.

They were calm. The evening wasn't over yet, they could touch each other, and no one would care. Not many came here. Those who did, did their business and left. Long hair, short hair, ordinary in jackets. They spoke briefly with the bartender, sat for a minute on the tall stools. If they ordered a beer, they didn't finish it. In their wake, the smell of cosmetics, dirt, insomnia. The place looked like it was open all night, though at some point they did close up.

"If we get bored, we can go to Wola," he said.

"Why Wola?" she asked.

"I haven't been there in ages. We could take a 26 or a 34 to the end. There are cemeteries and factories. At night everything's deserted." He told her how once he went on foot from downtown all the way to Grochów, then back again, not over the Poniatowskiego Bridge but the Śląsko-Dąbrowski Bridge, taking Świerczewskiego, Wolska, and Połczyńska. At sunrise he was outside the city, fields all around stretching green and flat to the misty horizon. He thought he'd keep walking and never return, but as in a fairy tale he looked back and saw a crimson glow in the east and the black silhouette of the city as heavy as a mountain. The Palace, the Marriott, the Terminal, the Forum, the Intraco building emerged from the sea or from inside the earth, and his strength abandoned him. He would never get anywhere, because there was nowhere to go. He left the highway, took some lane, dragged himself to bushes, curled up, and fell asleep like a dog. At noon the sun woke him.

She asked if he ever tried that again.

"No, it's not for me. People should stay where they were born. In another place you'd have to start from scratch, and your head gets screwed up. Here everything is shit. I envy people who spend their whole lives sitting on their arse."

"People travel," she said.

"Right. And they come back or they don't. You want another juice?"

"Orange, without ice."

He went up to the bar and, elbows on the counter, said something to the barman. Without looking up from his glasses, the bartender shook his head and answered out of the corner of his mouth. Jacek said something else, then the man leaned over and whispered in his ear. Beata watched his red eyes going from one empty table to the next. The bartender straightened and shook his head again. Jacek paid and came back to their table.

"You know him?" she asked.

"Storkie? Yeah."

"He doesn't look well."

"It's the work. Not enough movement and too much worry."

"He has worries?"

"Last month they smashed the place up."

"Who did?"

"Bad people, kiddo, bad people."

The passage had become less crowded. All those who had been hurrying home an hour ago were now home. Paweł stood by the public toilets watching people use the phones: inserting cards, punching numbers, speaking. Their faces blank before and after. Some took out a slip of paper or a notebook, but most knew the number. Hey, how's everything, I'll be back in an hour, I might not make it in time, see you, kiss my arse. He lip-read. A woman in a fur coat smiled at him, and for a moment he panicked. A tall man, closing his flies under his coat, went up to a blonde; she handed him a black case and they walked down the passage hand in hand. Paweł followed, having nothing else to do in this place, where everyone showed for a moment only, coming from all directions to intersect with the others and then vanish, their trails like a spider's web spreading, yet sooner or later they returned to the centre here, sooner or later everyone had to pass through this tunnel, though it held nothing special. Indifference, fake stone, glass, a few ordinary things to buy, tickets, matches, underwear, sanitary towels, razors, a few shop dummies, all the same as elsewhere, and soldiers buying only cigarettes.

He passed the steps to the roundhouse, afraid to go up to street level, though it was darker there. He heard the rumble of the trams arriving from Mokotów, Żoliborz, Praga, Ochota. People transferred, tangling themselves into a living knot like a great muscle beneath the black skin of the sky. Veined, supple, unvarying. Passing the steps up to the square, he wondered what was behind the wall to his left, concealed by that cement cylinder around which were clustered all the little stores, kiosks, booths selling odds and ends, trinkets, knick-knacks, rubbish, pottery marvels from the fairy world of the old 1001 Sundries. Because there had to be something there. A giant piece of machinery, the source of all movement, the axis of the city, a magnetic point, because otherwise everything—distant Wola, Żerań, Radość, Falenica, Chomiczówka, Tarchomin, Okęcie, Młociny—would fly off into space like shit thrown at a propeller.

He passed the exit for the Metropol and felt a pull, people in a spiral, because for all their will and business they couldn't break it, returning like moths to a flame, like carnival balls on elastic strings. When he passed the toilets and the exit for the Forum once again, he realized that his own life was no different, that from the beginning he'd wanted to be at the centre, in the navel, pupil, arsehole of the city, and that his imagination had raised a series of shining, supernatural images of downtown in which both the glow and the chill created a perfect mirage.

"Screw it," he thought, and again remembered the peeing girl and the bike he'd got for his first communion. Riding to the Vistula and seeing the skyscrapers. A long time ago, and the Palace had loomed over everything, but in his heart the handful of pathetic buildings were a glass mountain, castle, Everest, and consummation always had the taste of high floors, precipitous drops, and air trapped between geometric planes. Glitter, polish, sheen, and the ambiguity of a world that multiplied human phantoms and made them walk like angels. "Everyone wants to be there," he thought, "but there's not enough room. Most will suffocate, and only the ones on the surface will be left."

Fifteen minutes later, weak, he went out onto Marszałkowska, found a deli, and bought two rolls, a piece of sausage, and a bottle of mineral water. He went back up to the apartment but this time didn't even knock. He found his warm corner, sat down, and ate. Before he was done, he fell asleep and dreamed about his own life.

But it was early and most people were still up. Bolek and Iron Man couldn't tear themselves from the past. Syl kept them company, though she was too young to have memories. Bolek glanced now and then at the mobile phone Mr Max gave him, but it lay silent amid ham and smoked eel sandwiches. A little troubling. Then he would look across at Iron Man, who was pleased with himself, and at Syl smiling in a silver dress that came halfway up her thigh, and he stopped worrying, among friends and in a world that generally met his expectations. Iron Man stroked the leather upholstery of the sofa. He had taken off his jacket and rolled up the sleeves of his pink shirt and was trying not to swear. The Smirnoff inside smoothed out the present so the seductive past could show through. The television off. Warm smells drifted from the kitchen. Syl checked in there from time to time and returned with a mysterious look. The curtains drawn. Iron Man stopped tearing the filters off the Marlboros. He didn't have to look longingly at an empty glass, because his glass was always full. The frost on the bottle looked just like the frost in the ads. He could feel the carpet sink. A golden light from an unknown source. Iron Man was reminded of a tranquil merry-go-round. Even his thoughts were elegant. Syl took out the ashtrays when they were full and brought them back clean. She passed him mayonnaise, mustard, and beetroot salad with horseradish sauce. He handled them as comfortably as if they were cigarettes.

"More herring salad?" Syl looked him in the eye, because after a shave Iron Man was handsome. "Try some mussels?" she urged, but he turned his disgust into a joke:

"And no frogs either."

Then to Bolek:

"Remember when we went to Wileński station for sausage?"

"Sure. It cost seven fifty and the place was open after midnight. Does the 612 still run?"

"It does."

"Now that was a line."

"Still is. Remember when the Hindu got on, and you tried to swipe his watch and ended up dislocating the poor guy's arm?"

"There were Indians back then?" asked Syl with interest.

"A guy we knew. He looked like a Gypsy," explained Iron Man.

"I was clumsy, and he struggled," said Bolek. "I don't like it when people struggle."

"And the store?"

"Which one?"

"The one we did."

"Yeah, but which?"

"At the very beginning."

"The grocery store?"

"Three hundred zloty in change, six bottles of orangeade, and you pissed in the pickle barrel."

"Porkie! You did that?" Syl clapped her hands.

"Wasn't all," Iron Man said proudly. "But after that he couldn't eat cucumber soup, because his mother shopped there. He avoided salads, raw vegetables, everything. And any soup, because she made it in the same pot as the cucumber soup. In those days there were three kinds—cucumber, tomato, and vegetable. Except for broth. But broth isn't soup."

"Why?" Syl wondered.

"All tainted—the barrel, the cucumbers, the liquid they were in. And the jar that his mother brought the cucumbers home in, and the knife she cut them with, and the pot. Once something's tainted, it can't be touched."

"Those were the days," said Syl.

"The whole neighbourhood must have been tainted, because the whole barrel was eaten. All the pots and plates and knives and spoons and tables, all the kitchens. Bolek and I refused to shake hands with anybody. If they'd known, they would've—best not to say."

"I guess it's a little like AIDS," said Syl.

"Not really, because the doctor won't find out, but your pals know."

"I'd like to do something like that someday," said Syl, looking at Bolek.

"It doesn't count if it's a girl," said Iron Man. "You could go in there and piss for an hour, and the worst that would happen would be the taste would be different."

"That's not fair," said Syl with a pout.

"No one's saying it is," said Bolek.

And so they went on, and the light of innocence shone over their heads as they kept returning instinctively to childhood and their bodies grew free of the sediment of time, which accumulates in muscles and thoughts, fills bellies, heads, and veins, and makes things harder and harder to do.

But it wasn't so easy for Bolek. He tugged at Iron Man, back to the present. Syl cleared the table, laid out clean place settings, and in a few minutes brought in the main course, steaming, shimmering, and fragrant. The phone lay among the dishes. Sheikh approached the table and put his head in Iron Man's lap. Iron Man scratched him behind the ears. Bolek and Syl exchanged a look. The dog prodded Iron Man with its snout, for more. Iron Man ruffled the skin on the back of its neck. Bolek couldn't believe his eyes. Iron Man emptied his drink, pushed the dog away, and picked up his fork.

"Wow," he said, staring at the meat, the salads, the sauces, the piles of vegetables.

Bolek got up, opened the door to the hallway, and shouted: "Out! Onto the mat!"

"Leave him. He's not bothering me," said Iron Man.

They ate, with silences. Chewing, lifting their glasses. Iron Man sometimes sat back in his cushioned chair, looked furtively at the furniture, narrowed his eyes like a tomcat in the sun. He lit a cigarette and continued to eat and drink. "This is how things ought to be," he thought. Bolek watched him out of the corner of his eye and thought that most people are good for something, you just have to find the right thing. It was almost ten, so he took the phone and went into the next room, closing the door behind him.

On the other side of the river Zosia was closing the bathroom door. Today she had been able to eat. She'd tried yogurt with sliced banana, then two thin pieces of toast, and kept it down. She'd started to feel like coffee.

Now she sat in the armchair, her cat in her lap. "There's nothing we can do, Pankracy. We've done all we can, haven't we?" The cat didn't reply but was warm and soft and acted like a tranquillizer. She felt sleepy but put off the waiting bed in case she remembered some domestic chore, though in her tiny apartment the chores were few. She picked up a copy of *Four Corners* magazine and put it down again. "It's the fresh air, Pankracy. I did a lot of walking today. But I don't know those neighbourhoods at all. I was never there before. Isn't that funny?

"To live in the city for so many years and still not know it. If you were a dog, you'd have liked it there. Lots of space to run in. In the summer it must be very green. Not like here—wilder there. But a cat might like it too. Plenty of rooftops. To begin I took a 195 all the way to Gdańsk station. You could walk all day and not get there on those short little legs of yours. I got out at the viaduct and went down the steps to catch the tram. I had to ask which one goes to Żerań. Only one did, the 12. A nice old lady told me. We waited for a long time and talked. Finally one came, and it was almost empty. Then it crossed the bridge and there was so much water below. You'd have died with fright, Pankracy, to see all that water. For you it would be like the sea. You know, you have no idea what the world is like. You never go out anywhere. You sit on the windowsill, and that's it. After the bridge there was nothing but factories and factories. I finally learned where they make cars. It's horrid there. For miles you only see workers. A few were waiting at the stops. I'd hate to work in a factory. It's so odd. They lock you up then let you out. And nothing but men. The tram kept going, I thought it would never stop. Not a single house or a single woman. The old lady had got out before. I was all on my own and afraid, Pankracy. Buildings and cars everywhere, and everything so bright and empty. The cars whizzing by. At the last stop I got on a bus. There were chimneys that reached to the sky, and it really was the edge of the city. We crossed a bridge, and there were cottages and shacks, then real woods. You poor thing, you don't even know what woods are. But after a minute there were houses again. Old ones, probably from before the war; and we had to wait because the barrier was down at a level crossing."

The cat was asleep, but she continued her journey, and only now did it seem real to her. Ten hours before, fear had filled the air, and that was the brightness. It had entered her body and made her almost visible. All she wanted was a little sympathy. Deciding to track down Mr Paweł because there was no one else. She found his address in her papers, located the street on the map, right by the edge at the top and a little to the left. Beyond that, the city ended. She got out too soon, wandered about. People looked different, in their faces, in their clothes. Women sat in some of the windows watching white and ginger chickens in the yard. Flocks of pigeons wheeling against the blue like fast black rocks. She saw stray dogs. "You wouldn't have liked it, Pankracy." Crows cawed in overgrown gardens, motionless so it was hard to spot them. She found Mr Paweł's building; someone pointed it out to her, someone who knew his name. A two-storey apartment building, unusually big for the neighbourhood. On the dark stairs she had the urge to cry. Another person said, "Second floor, the door on the right." She started counting steps, thinking she would throw herself into his arms and sob out everything that had happened to her the day before, even though when she left her apartment, she'd decided, coolly and seriously, to warn him.

"Don't be jealous, Pankracy. Mr Paweł's a person and you're a cat." Interrupting her story for a moment, then going back to the dark stairs and the hope that in a minute, less, the door would open and in the bright stream of light she would see a blue denim shirt, the same that often appeared in the store and that she liked so much that one day she bought one like it, and alone in her apartment she would put it on to feel the touch of the blue cloth on her bare flesh. Like now.

She knocked loudly and for a long time, but no one opened. Since her knuckles hurt, she used her fist. Then a voice behind her:

"He's not there. He went out yesterday morning and hasn't been back since."

The tea was pale yellow and sweet. The old lady had added three spoonfuls and stirred. "It'll do you good, dear. It must be cold outside." On the wall, a large picture of Christ with a flaming heart. Dried palm leaves stuck behind the gilt frame. A smell of vanilla, warm air from the kitchen. On a walnut bookcase, lace napkins, a china shepherdess on each. Seven pink girls in dancing shoes and garlands striking poses beneath a green rhododendron. "And you know, Pankracy, there was a cat there too, a tabby. You would have liked her. Quite refined, with long hair, like a Persian, bluish with dark streaks." The woman removed the cat from the armchair and sat down. "I've known him since he was this high, my dear. I knew his mother. Such a religious woman. She would even go to church during the week, and on Sundays she never missed confession and Holy Communion. Though I can't imagine what sins she committed. They were poor people but decent. I've known him since he was this high and won't say a bad word about him. He always said good morning. She was an orderly in the hospital, the husband worked at the plant, and Paweł collected bottles—he was always so resourceful. He would follow the drunks and wait till the bottle was empty. He had two sisters, but they always stayed home. They had a little house. It was only a few years ago, when he started to do well for himself, that he bought the apartment. His parents got two rooms in a complex, because their house was bulldozed for a highway. His father worked all his life on that house; he was always building, patching, fixing, but it wasn't much of a place—maybe three small rooms. I don't know, I was never inside. I didn't know them well. Paweł was so resourceful and always did his best. He was an altar boy, and his clothes were clean, even if they were darned. They never had much money. Other kids loafed, but he would take a sack and pick grass for the rabbits. Back then people kept rabbits. Rabbits make good pâté. And in the autumn he'd pick mushrooms in the woods. They aren't as many nowadays. The family ate them at home, but he also used to dry and sell them. At fourteen he was already working part-time on construction jobs. People built, though not as much as today. In these parts everyone was putting things up, making extensions on their own. At most they'd hire a helper. The other boys would run about all summer long, but he'd be working. He worked at the greenhouses, growing carnations and gerbera, then freesias when they became popular; and on All Souls I'd see him outside the cemetery selling candles and chrysanthemums. When he was older, he delivered milk. At three or four in the morning he got on his bike and rode to Bródno, because there were no apartment buildings around here. He made it back in time for school at eight. He was starting to shave but didn't drink. With his schoolmates it was hello and good-bye. In the little garden at their house, he made a tunnel of plastic and sowed radishes and lettuce to sell. He bought an old motorcycle, made a sidecar for it, and took his produce out and sold it. But he went to church less, didn't have the time. He might have worked on Sundays too. The Lord will forgive him, because he's a good boy. Everyone wants a better life. There's nothing wrong with that. He always said good morning. Others stole. I know what they did. In the morning I'd see him from my window carrying his bags to the bus. One in each hand and one over his shoulder, like a refugee or a Russian. He'd stand on Marszałkowska in a transparent plastic raincoat. I saw him there one time. It was raining, and you couldn't even tell what he was selling, because it was covered up. He didn't recognize me. He was looking into the distance. The people walking by didn't stop, the wind flapped his raincoat, and there was a puddle, but he stood there all the same. The other merchants had packed up and left, and he was on his own out there. I remember it like yesterday."

The cat stirred. Music went on in the apartment below. The woman said she knew they were young people, but it was Lent after all. Zosia sipped her tea to make the time pass more slowly.

"You know, ma'am, I came because there was something wrong with the phone. A busy signal the whole time."

"Yes, the night before last. Someone was there. I was in bed, but you know old people, dear—I couldn't sleep. This house was built before the war and the walls are thick, so it must have been loud. Then I heard someone coming down the stairs, and a car or two drove away. I don't know, I didn't get up. But he must have still been there, because I didn't hear the door lock, and you can always hear that. He probably left in the morning. I'm always sound asleep then."

"Those kind of people?" asked Beata.

Two men came into the bar and went to the counter.

"More or less," said Jacek, and turned away from them.

One rested his foot on the crossbar of a stool. His sock was white. The other picked up an ashtray and tapped it on the counter.

"Storkie!" he called towards the bead curtain and spun the ashtray like a top. The bartender appeared with a glass in his hand. He came out slowly, dull, as in a black-and-white movie.

"Load us up, Storkie."

The bartender put the glass down, reached under the counter, and took out a box of balls.

"The cues are in the other room," he said.

"Bring us two beers," said the man with the socks, and both went into the dark room by the Gents. A white glare flooded the pool table, but they were in shadow.

"You know them too?" asked Beata.

"They're all the same," he said. "Like Chinamen."

"Chinamen smile."

"And those guys don't?"

"They give me the creeps. Their faces don't move, like animals. Dogs. As if they don't have face muscles."

"Dogs have face muscles."

"But they only use them for biting."

The bartender, passing with two beers on a tray, didn't even glance at them.

"He's pretending he doesn't know you," said Beata.

"Sometimes it's better that way."

"For who?"

"For everyone," said Jack, and rubbed his temples.

"The ears have the least blood supply of any part of the body," said Beata.

"They feel funny."

"Does it hurt?"

"Where there's little blood, little feeling."

The bartender came back and vanished behind his bead curtain.

In the garish light over the pool table, hands, cuffs, and cues. The players circled lazily. They took off their jackets. Their shirts as if cut from black paper. Smoke gathered and hung beneath the lamp. The balls scattered with a crack, and one man said: "Fucking Sarajevo." They moved slowly, prepared in an instant to leave on serious business. In their veins, not blood but images of actions. They were actors in a reality they had made up, because the time when sons repeated the gestures of their fathers was over. Cars went down Tamka. In the oxidized night the drivers gazed at the world and accepted it. Astras overtook Corsas, Corollas left Golfs behind, Nexias passed Twingos, Ibizas drove alongside Almeras. Darkness drifting in from the river. The cars dove into it like lemmings, only to reappear on the far bank in the stench of the port.

Green, yellow, red, blue, silver, and white, beads on a rosary in the fingers of the city.

"Shit," said one of the players and straightened. Two balls dropped into the pockets and rolled into the low belly of the table with a dull rumble. "Maybe an easy round of bar billiards?"

"My arse," said the other, and began to set up a new game. Three cigarettes burning down in the ashtray.

"Tell him to put something on," said the one who had lost.

"He'll only put on fag music," said the other.

"Whatever. Just so it's not quiet."

"Quiet bothers you?"

"When it's quiet, something can happen."

"And when the music's on, it can't?"

"It can, but you don't have to wait."

"Shut up and play, Waldek."

Jacek could see them out of the corner of his eye, could guess what they were talking about. The balls clicked on the table, like people who meet, do things for each other, go their separate ways, and meet different people, until the last one dies. He repeated to himself the telephone number that Paweł was supposed to call. A number useless to him, but to someone else wealth or salvation. The balls clicked less now. Then there was only the tap of the cue and the soft knock of a solitary ball against the cushions.

"Why are you smiling?" asked Beata.

"Nothing. Pool makes sense. Let's get out of here."

Sleep came and went. At times he was in the apartment with the throbbing red neon outside the window. The shop assistant in the deli had given him a look when Paweł said, "A hundred and fifty grams of sausage." It was Easter Friday, and he had dirty fingernails. He noticed that when he handed her the money. The fingernails returned with the rhythm of the red light, and other images, floating up from the past, places he'd been. The Kudamm in Berlin, two Turks and him. He was walking behind them and trying to feel at ease. Loud talk and gesticulating, like the Gypsies from Targowa. Inconspicuous on the pavement, he sniffed at the unfamiliar smells, the Germans leaving a trail of scent behind them. It was getting dark. He had thirty-four marks, and his Caro cigarettes were almost all gone. He took one out with a cupped hand, so it wouldn't give him away, because on the first day he'd noticed that in this country there was no brand with such a short filter. The guy at whose place he was supposed to spend the night didn't show. The Turks eventually disappeared. In the drizzle, his white trainers turned grey and shapeless. He was tempted by the shops but afraid of the light. All that he remembered about that night was that his feet hurt, he had a runny nose, he was cold. At dawn he met two Poles. Coming back from somewhere, they took up the whole pavement. He started telling them everything, quickly because he was afraid they'd sober up. They took him with them. He slept on the floor, woke at noon, the others still snoring. Then two more came and wanted to throw him out.

He tried to stop the images and rewind them like a movie, but they were fragile, kept breaking, and the darkness filled with noise. Someone sat down beside him. He tried to imagine a woman but was left on his own. He tried counting all the money he'd ever had, notes in wads, fans, piles, heaps of coins, his first ever five-zloty coin with the fisherman on it, but he couldn't recall whether it was really his, he might have stolen it from his mother's purse. But he remembered the taste of the moment when he put it on the counter and watched the shop lady take a bottle of orangeade out of a crate and a chocolate bar with pink filling from the shelf, and give it to him with complete indifference, and with thirty groszy in change. He remembered the warm feel of the low wall in front of the store and the smell of petrol from the blue moped that belonged to the postman, who sat nearby drinking a beer. The five-zloty coin probably wasn't stolen; in those days he often took money, but it was mostly twos. He could have got it for ten bottles from the old geezer in black who drove around the neighbourhood in a huge two-horse cart and bought empties. Only fifty groszy, but the empties didn't have to be rinsed. In the recycling centre they paid a zloty, but the bottles had to be clean and the dragon with the cigarette holder would take every tenth one for free. "This is chipped," she'd say, and no one would argue with her. In the bare yard, nothing but an awning of corrugated iron, boards for a tabletop, the steel box with the money, wooden crates filled with glass high as the sky. Cash without trouble, for nothing. All you had to do was know the corners where the drunks hung out, the bushes where the better-off ones threw their bottles. The old guy too. He cleaned out cellars, junk rooms, attics. His cart trailed the stink of vinegar, stale beer, cheap fruit wine. Everyone said he was rich but to disguise it dressed in rags and didn't wash. He lived in a tumbledown house behind a wooden fence. He hired boys to help him. The filthy bottles were soaked in tin tubs and barrels. You stirred and skimmed the greasy scum from the top. Then the bottles were taken out and washed with a drill that instead of a bit had a wire brush attached. One kid got an electric shock. After a couple of days working your hands were raw, from the lye.

He saw it clearly now: the old geezer smiling, telling him to come back in a few days to see if there was an opening. Paweł walked along the fence made of sawmill castoffs. Golden droplets of sap oozed from under brown bark. He rounded the fence and tried entering again, but now instead of piles of bottles there were cages of foxes. The animals paced and circled in their wire-covered runs. In the pit underneath them, hot, fresh droppings. A woman in an army jacket showed him what to do. A shovel, a wheelbarrow, a path through the bushes, and a heap of old shit in a stand of pines. He wheeled new loads away, could barely breathe. The foxes never quit their hypnotic walk. The shit stuck to the spade, to the wheelbarrow. He had to scrape it off. She said, "You'll get a thousand." Her hair dyed black. Later she showed him the cold storage room where the food was kept. The ground red meat smelled like a corpse. Each time the door was opened, green flies rushed. A bare lightbulb. She told him to wash the shovel, the wheelbarrow, which he then used to bring their food. The woman opened the little chain-link hatches and doled out the portions with a coal scoop. The only break in the animals' pacing. They ate on bent paws, their lowered tails quivering. Then he had to drag out a hose and pour water into the same bowls. "Not too much," she told him. "That way the bowls are licked and we don't need to wash them." It was summer, and he didn't have school. Sometimes an older man appeared. He'd put a small cage at the gate of a large one and prod the animal in. The new cage had a polished tin floor and was tight. The man would turn on the electricity and push a long spike up the animal's arse; the spike's handle was in-sulated. "A special order," the woman explained. "The middle of July, and she decides she wants a fur-lined jacket." The man did the skinning in the yard among the cages. The red body hung from a hook where all the animals could see, but they kept on pacing as if nothing had happened. The rest was Paweł's job. He had to take it down, wheel it away, and dig a hole. It was hard to find a place where the spade didn't hit bone. The green and blue flies never left him alone. At times he felt that everything, the trees, farm, house, stood on a thin layer of earth and in a moment would sink into the animal graveyard.

After a month the woman stood on the steps of the house and called him in. In the sitting room everything cool and dark. Cut glass shiny in a cabinet. She sat him down in front of a picture of a naked woman asleep on her back. Roses twined, and in the background a deer drank from a pond. The woman wore a kimono with yellow and black flowers, and her leather slippers were red and gold. A scent he couldn't put a name to. On a side table, a cage with an orange canary. On another, a lace napkin and a blue Virgin Mary with her foot on the head of a snake. He sat in a deep armchair and watched her open a cabinet and take out a white envelope. She had to stand on tiptoe. He could see her flexed calves and a yellowish raised heel. In the envelope, a thousand-zloty note with a picture of Copernicus. "I'm pleased with you," she said. She must have been as old as his mother but looked completely different. She lit up and pushed a hard pack of women's cigarettes towards him. He took one and lit it with a refillable lighter of the kind he dreamed about every time he passed a kiosk. It was enamel and decorated with pictures of birds of paradise. Cost sixty-five zloty and was made in China. He smoked and answered her few questions. Out of the corner of his eye, her crossed legs. He could feel his crotch growing warm, but didn't let it, because his mother kept appearing, as if standing in the door and watching. He didn't want tea or cookies, he wanted to leave as soon as possible, to get rid of this shame and take a good look at the note.

That same day he bought himself the Chinese lighter. He rode the bus for a few stops because he didn't want to do it at his neighbourhood kiosk. Then he walked back on foot and at a different kiosk bought a pack of Carmens. Eighteen zloty. He stopped for an orangeade, was tempted and bought a chocolate bar. Walking home, when the street was empty, he tried the lighter. A click, but no flame. The blue spark flared in the dusk and died. Then he realized there was no fuel, so he ran back to the kiosk where he bought the cigarettes. For eighty groszy, an egg-shaped capsule of soft plastic. It was then that he noticed the pack of cards. Thirty-six zloty. Hard, angular, pleasant to the touch. He also bought a tiny penknife on a chain for nineteen zloty. He cut the capsule with the knife and filled the lighter. It worked, and he was happy. As he walked, he touched the pockets in which he'd put his new things.

At night he had a dream. The woman in the kimono leaned over him and took out some notes, took them from her cleavage, waistband, between her legs, her arse, under her arms, and she handed them to him. He jammed the money into his pockets, but the notes wouldn't fit, they kept falling out, scattering. He gathered them, excited and embarrassed, and when he woke up his pyjamas were wet.

This dream inside his dream made him pull his knees up under his chin and wrap his arms tightly around them. Warmth swept over him. The sounds of the building, no longer grave-like, surrounded him like water. He was sinking to the bottom, convinced he would never emerge again, that time itself would yield to his weight.

On the last day of that summer he worked till sundown. The next day the job would end. From time to time he'd squat and take out a pack of twelve-zloty Albanian Arberias. In another pocket he had blue Caros that cost sixteen, but the Arberias had a stronger and stranger smell, so they did a better job of masking the stench of the cages. The glow of the cigarette red in the gathering darkness, he collected his tools, put them away, and went for his money. It was like before, but a lamp was on and the canary was gone. She handed him an envelope.

Inside, a thousand and two one-hundred notes. He looked at her. She said it was a bonus. "We should have a drink to celebrate the end of the job," she added, and brought in a bottle of Yugoslav vermouth and two cut-glass tumblers. He liked the taste of it, a little like medicine and a little like juice. Sticky, and it left a bitterness on the lips. The flounced red curtains were drawn. On the wall, gold lamp brackets with coloured shades. The rug a sheepskin. Hard to tell whether the flowers were real or not. He'd never seen so many expensive things and such a big living room. He sat in the same place as before. She stood in front of him. He didn't raise his eyes and could see only her hands.

Later, when he was on her and licking slowly and evenly, because that was what she told him to do, he learned that skin does not always smell like skin. It reminded him of an object that can be owned. He tried with his teeth, nibbling and tasting. She told him to do this, that. He followed her orders delicately. When by accident his mouth met the fabric of the armchair, he did not stop the caress and felt no difference. It was the same with the rug when they moved to the floor. The touch of the white fur was just as nice as her body. He nuzzled the rug, until she had to call him back. It went on for a long time, because from the other end of the house he heard a clock strike the half-hour, then the quarter, then eight and nine. She led him to the kitchen, to the bathroom, told him what she wanted, as if they were still at work. In the bright bathroom her nipples were the colour of raw meat and hundred-zloty notes. She examined him too, touching, choosing this part, that, using it however she wanted. The water could not wash from her the smell of furniture, clothing, perfume, the whole house. Her hands were rough, like those of other people. He was surprised there was no hair under her arms, and her arse was tanned all over. Her red toenails were like the playing pieces of a board game.

When their clothes were back on, she told him that whenever he came around, he'd get money. He asked how much. She said it depended, say two hundred, and he remembered the extra two notes in the envelope.

Iron Man stayed behind, as Bolek told him to. He had no desire to leave. The last thing he heard was: "I'll be back in two hours. Make yourself at home," and Bolek gestured at the littered table, the unfinished bottle. Syl didn't know what to make of it, so she pretended to sulk until the door closed behind Bolek. Then she smiled and said:

"Have another drink, Iron Man, and tell me more about those times."

He poured himself a drink, settled comfortably, lit a cigarette, almost as if he were stalling, but actually he just felt good and had no desire to talk.

"What's there to tell? Water under the bridge."

"It interests me. I was born in December eighty-one, and Porkie, I mean Bolek, doesn't tell me anything. He just comes and goes; he wants food on the table, and has only one thing on his mind. And I'm so ignorant."

"Don't you go to school?" asked Iron Man.

"I went to cooking school for a bit, but there's no future in that."

"I'm not so sure," he said pensively. "People need to eat. And they're eating more and more. In our day there were only three kinds of soup. And now? Or main dishes. We used to have pork chops, ribs, dumplings, fish on Fridays, and once in a while a roast on a Sunday. That was it. If you wanted extra, you went out. Bolek and I would go over to the milk bar on Targowa near Ząbkowska for lazy pierogi, Silesian pierogi with mushrooms, or *pyzy* in butter . . ."

"What was that?"

"*Pyzy*. Round dumplings. They sold them at the bazaar too, but I was fussy, could never eat off plastic, and there they served them on those little saucers you put under flowerpots."

"What else was there?"

"At the bazaar? Tripe soup. From a milk can. There was an old lady with a five-gallon can wrapped in a blanket or kid's clothes, the whole thing in a baby carriage. And it was good business, because there was nothing else at the bazaar, and you had thousands of people. Everyone was hungry. Not like now."

"And Bolek?"

"What about Bolek?"

"Did he eat that tripe soup?"

"Sure. He was never picky when it came to grub."

The guy on the floor was moving less. He lay on his side, as if trying to ride a child's bicycle, curled up, knees under his chin, turning his legs in a fading circular motion, his socks bright as bandages. The man in the purple tracksuit wondered what to do next. He was weighing options. He could keep kicking, but the guy was barely conscious and probably wouldn't feel it. He could pick him up and sit him somewhere. "Screw that," he thought. "He'd just fall down again. I'd have to keep putting him back like it was a potty." He took a deep breath. "If we were somewhere out of the way, I'd run him over. With one wheel. He'd survive, but he'd remember. Cars are useful." Holding the edge of the table, he jumped with both feet on the clenched hand of the man on the floor. He heard a crunch, but it wasn't much, so he did it again. Trainers were no good for work like this. Then his eye fell on a cue stick left on the pool table. He picked it up, hefted, tried to bend it, swept it through the air to hear the swish.

"Boss," he called, "I could stick this up his arse. A nice surprise when he wakes up."

Bolek was sitting on the edge of the table smoking a cigarette. He rubbed his chin with his hand and said no.

"Why not, boss? I can't leave him like this."

"You'll spoil the tool."

"What?"

"You heard. Didn't you ever do time?"

"No. And I don't plan to."

"Exactly. You're all like that these days. When something's spoiled, it's no good any more. You have to throw it out."

"So we throw it out. What's the problem?"

Bolek sighed, put the cigarette out, got up.

"The problem, son, is that things are divided into yours, other people's, and things I tell you to break. The cue isn't yours. It belongs to Mr Max. Like everything here," he said patiently, and headed for the door. He stopped in front of the man cowering in a corner.

"You saw?" he asked. "Go and tell who you need to tell it to. And take him away."

In the bar he went up to the counter. As usual Storkie stood still, his hands doing something. Bolek patted him on the cheek and said:

"Good boy. Now unlock the door for us."

The bartender took the key and went towards the exit.

"There's something I need to take care of," said Jacek, when the sliding doors from Emilii Plater opened automatically in front of him. In the main hall they were immediately immersed in figurines. He left her by the sandwich stand and went downstairs. The smell of coffee, perfume, subterranean air. She went up and asked for something without meat, was given a cheese sandwich, ordered tea as well, and sat down at a table. The poisonous white bread was surprisingly good. An unwavering light fell from above and made cadavers even of the clean and rested people. Though in motion, they were the dead from a sunken city. She went back for another sandwich, another tea, added three spoons of sugar. She tried reading the big timetable over the ticket counters: too far away. She realized she had never been anywhere. To the country near Siedlce a few times while her grandmother was alive, and once she visited her mother in the sanatorium for a couple of days. She hid in the room, and her mother sneaked food for her. She couldn't recall the name of the place, only remembered flowerbeds stretching out endlessly. They came back in a crowded train. They got out at East Station, crossed the street, and were home. Now she remembered that in her mother's bedroom a souvenir from the place still hung on the wall. Plastic, with the name of the town.

An elderly man in a dark blue overcoat came up to her. He inclined his head in her direction and sat down on the chair next to hers. He glanced, now at her, now at the people passing by. She swallowed and said:

"If you're wondering if I have a place to sleep, don't bother."

The man gave her a flustered look, got up, and left. She

went on eating and trying to remember the name. When Jacek returned ten minutes later, she said to him:

"Let's go away somewhere."

"Where?"

"Anywhere. Today. For instance to the mountains, Zakopane. I've never been."

He sat down opposite her and toyed with the empty Styrofoam cups from the tea. She smiled: as if she were asking him to go to the movies or for a walk.

"I have almost two million," she said.

"Not enough for Zakopane."

"I've never seen the sea either, Jacek. Honestly. We'll manage. We don't have to buy tickets."

"I'm too old for that kind of thing, kid. I need a ticket."

"Fine, we'll buy one. For you."

"And then? Where do we sleep? It's winter there."

"I know, you're old. You need a bed."

Both laughed. He set the cups aside, drummed his fingers on the table, and looked around the hall as if he were waiting for an answer.

"All right," he said. "There's one to Zakopane in an hour or so. I'm meeting a guy. He's not here yet but will be. If all goes well, we'll have some money."

"I didn't bring anything," she said, passing her hands over the pockets of her army jacket.

"You can buy yourself a toothbrush," he said. "I'll be back in fifteen minutes, OK?"

"OK. I'll buy a toothbrush."

The woman disappeared. Maybe she'd moved to someone else's dream. Now he was in an endless field, and it was much earlier, because he was wearing shorts with crossed braces. His knees bruised and sore. Kneeling on the hard, parched earth while others passed, overtaking him. When he reached the halfway point, they were already on their way back. Some paused by the edge of a wood to smoke a cigarette in the shade and talk, but even so they were always faster. The high sun didn't seem to be sinking. His shadow was a small patch at his feet. Sometimes he ate a strawberry to quench his thirst. The fruit was covered with dust. He chose the biggest, which were watery. In the middle of the field, a wooden shack, the stink of chemicals and fertilizer. The people took full baskets there and got empty ones in return. The man had a ruled notebook and put crosses against names. Paweł had the fewest. The deal was simple: for a full basket you got four zloty. That was a loaf of bread in those days. At church, you put two zloty on the collection tray. He got that much from his mother on Sundays. He would clutch the aluminum coin with the crossed sheaves of corn, making it hot and damp. One Sunday he didn't move as the sacristan in the surplice passed. Fear afterwards, but nothing happened: the heavens were indifferent, and the two-zloty coin didn't disappear from his pocket or burn up in the fire of a curse. From that time he didn't move. Bambino ice creams cost exactly two zloty. An old man in a white apron sold them outside the church. He looked like the twin brother of the sacristan, and with time the two men became a single person, so the money ended up where it was supposed to. Later the ice cream changed, to a double flavour, a stripe of vanilla and a stripe of pink fruit. It cost one zloty eighty, and when he got his twenty groszy in change, his conscience stirred, but then went back to sleep.

146

The pages of the notebook were old and stank of pesticide. The paper disintegrated as crosses were added. The man wore broad khaki shorts and a cycling cap sewn from coloured wedges. He didn't speak. On his finger, a death's-head signet ring. He smoked Wawels. One day Paweł swiped one of the small flat packs with the golden castle on the inner lid. He carried it in his shorts pocket till it fell apart. He used it as a purse, though the most he ever earned was ten zloty. The coin was big and heavy and had the profile of a man with an upturned nose. It rattled pleasantly inside the box. With it he bought a red plastic racing car shaped like a cigar. Underneath, the words INCO-VERITAS, and for a long time he thought that was the make of the car. He called it that during his solitary games. He sped the little car across the tarmac and shouted, "Inco Inco Veritas!" One day it broke in two, he cried, pressed the two halves together but they wouldn't hold.

In the evening a dusty Żuk lorry would come and take the crop. He would watch it from far off as he stood on a dyke between two ponds. Sweet marshy shade, cool and close. Wild ducks started up when he appeared, only to settle a few feet away. The dark water received the birds in utter stillness. Loud, contented voices from the shack. He couldn't quite see, but thought there was a woman or two inside. Giggles, squeals, shouts. Curious, he tried to get closer along the edge of the strawberry field. The trees gave cover, but the gathering dusk concealed things and magnified sounds. He'd never heard grown-ups so loud. At home it was always quiet. His mother never laughed, his father never spoke.

When they left, he sneaked across the open space, pressed himself against the wooden wall. The smell of petrol still in the air. He thought that money must be somewhere inside, hidden in a round metal tin, coins and dark green notes. A padlock on the door. He touched the windowpane, held in its frame by a few rusty nails. All around, quiet and deserted, the sky red between the trees. He picked up a piece of wood from the ground and smashed the glass.

"I was here earlier," the man in the purple tracksuit said to Bolek.

"Yes, people go in circles and get diddly," answered Bolek. The sliding doors closed behind them. They crossed the hall, went straight to the steps, not looking around, like travellers without luggage hurrying to catch the train. In the passage they turned left.

"I gave a ride to some bastard who wouldn't pay," continued the man in the tracksuit.

"So what happened?"

"Nothing. He paid in the end."

"That's how it is with people," said Bolek.

They turned left again.

"If it were up to me, I'd arrange things better," said the man.

"For now just go in there and get me that guy standing by the phone. The one in the light trousers," said Bolek, stepping back against the wall. The man went into the snack bar, into the red light, and clapped the pinball player on the shoulder. The player didn't look, just shrugged the hand away, so tracksuit grabbed his jacket, turned him to the window, and pointed at Bolek.

The three of them went out into an empty Jana Pawła. A sprinkling of light above, but on the ground, darkness, as if they could vanish at any moment. Cars hurtled overhead.

"Tell me what happened," said Bolek, and tracksuit stood

behind the kid.

"Well, this guy came yesterday and said he had a few grams."

"And what did you say?"

"Nothing." The kid shrugged. "What was I supposed to tell him? I know how things are. Rats saw him too."

"There you go. And Rats followed him and pointed him out to Waldek."

"I was waiting for a client."

Bolek took a step forwards; the kid retreated and bumped into tracksuit behind him.

"And Rats called and gave the information."

"Boss . . ."

The kid flew forwards. Bolek had to stop him from falling.

"Boss, Waldek chased him . . ."

"But didn't catch him. And he didn't say anything to anyone, and he never called."

The kid's head jerked left, right. On the overpass, the monotonous whizzing of the cars. A man in a drab Subaru changing cassettes. In four minutes he would turn into Wawelska, then Grójecka, and drive down Krakowska, out of the city, heading south. "Six Blade Knife" started from his speakers.

"Let him be for a moment," said Bolek, and tracksuit stopped what he was doing. Grabbed the kid by the hair and held him.

"He's supposed to come today—that's what he said. He said he'd bring the goods. Let go . . ."

"Did Waldek know about it? Talk!"

"Yes. Rats told him."

"So he knew and didn't say a word," Bolek murmured. "Wanted to keep it for himself."

"'That's right. He thought he had the goods on him, but the guy told me he'd bring it today. Let go . . .'"

"Fuck him," said Bolek. "And fuck you too. You thought you'd sell some stuff that wasn't ours?"

"I didn't think that . . ."

"You didn't? Then why is he coming today?"

"I'll show him to you," said the kid.

"Always the waiting," thought Jacek. At night the station became small and cramped. People brushed against one another. Darkness gathered, and the people hid from it, recouped, plunged back into the gloom. No one spoke. The passages filled with uneasy silence. The rustle of clothing, the whish of air, the echoes of a million insect footsteps. "Whether you're selling or buying, you always end up standing like a dick." At a kiosk he looked at naked women: beautiful, vulgar, glistening. "They're waiting too," he thought, and imagined the life of one of them. She'd get up in the morning, brush her teeth, get dressed, go out, and people would have no idea what her body looked like. Boring, like the rest of the world. Imagining the mountains in the south worked better—a sunny morning, the rails ending, then nothing but snow-covered ridges, the smell of smoke in the clear air, and golden glints on distant peaks. But he realized that he was looking at this image through a glass pane, that it was as lifeless as the naked women.

People kept coming, as if there would never be an end of them. He counted them, to shorten the time. He tried guessing their destination but couldn't. The human tide made him want to puke. "Fuck all of you to Gdańsk or Komańcza or whatever godforsaken suburb is at the end of the line. Where's that bastard?" His eyes sought a curly head and light trousers. He put his hand in his pocket and touched the box of tranquillizers. With him permanently now. For four months, since the time he crossed Poniatowskiego Bridge in the middle of the night and felt like jumping. The water black and viscous. Light scuttling across it like lizards. The hot hand of panic slid into him and felt for the tenderest spot. He hadn't slept for a week, had been walking the city, and then his mind broke free of his body. He ran, but the glow of downtown came no closer and the water beyond the railing was blacker than black. He ran, pushing away from the barrier, which shrank to his knees, to his ankles. Halfway across the bridge the cops stopped him. He gave them a story, didn't let them get a word in, but one cop whacked him on the head, so he started again from the beginning, politely, convincingly, but still too fast and making no sense. When they got to Nowy Świat, they told him to beat it. They probably saved his life. He forced himself to go home, locked the door, and paced between door and window till morning, when he dropped to the floor in his clothes and woke at midday in a pool of sweat. Later someone told him you need relanium or oxazepam, something like that.

Nothing much inside. He groped, knocked something over. A rattle of matches. He got down on his hands and knees and searched for them. The smell of chemicals, even from the packed earth beneath his fingers. Like smoke, as if the shack were on fire. It stung his eyes. Finding the matchbox, he was afraid but he lit one anyway. The flame went out. In the flare of the next, he saw an upturned crate littered with stuff. By the light of the third he found a votive lamp and lit it. An improvement, though everything was hazy, shaky. He put the light on the floor and rummaged on all fours like a dog: cardboard boxes, empty paper sacks. Rakes, spades, and hoes, all caked with old soil, rough and crumbly to the touch. The stink came from the plastic containers. He crawled into the next room. Living quarters: a low table, two stools, a rough bed made up with blankets. He found mustard, tumblers, a knife, tin utensils, but the box was nowhere to be seen. The corners all in shadow— only rubbish there, sweat-soaked overalls, rubber boots. The little wine left in a bottle was awful, he spat it out. A can full of cigarette butts. He put a thick purple wine glass into his pocket, but it was uncomfortable so he took it out again. It never occurred to him before that grown-ups didn't have anything interesting. Nothing to play with, to imagine over. Thinking they had everything, he had envied them. Shadows jumped across the wall. He found a bucket and a basin full of soapy water. He could hear the beating of his heart. He turned, crawled over to the bed, slipped his hand between the blankets, which were still warm, felt something smooth and soft, pulled it out: in the yellow light, knickers. A surprise, because only the owner of the farm slept here, but then the memory of women's voices ten, fifteen minutes ago. He spread out the knickers on the bed, lifted the lamp, pictured her body, hips, stomach, thighs, and for a moment he was not alone, caught red-handed. He looked around. Outside the window, the sky now dark blue. Through the thin walls he could hear the croaking of frogs. He put the lamp down and started rooting in the bed, not sure what he was looking for. Blankets, a thick sheet, some striped material. Nothing under the pillow. Crumbs, a flattened roll of newspaper. He threw it all on the floor. The mattress was torn. He ripped it open more, dug his hands into the coarse horsehair, pulled out handfuls, threw them behind him. Someone once told him that people hid their money in mattresses. He also remembered what other boys said about women having hair down there, there was even a dirty song about it they would scream out when no one was listening. The mattress sank inwards, and the floor was covered with tangled tufts. Finally he reached bare boards, got a splinter under a fingernail, felt a rage and strange excitement he had never known before, tipped the table over, with a clatter of glass and tin, pulled the overalls from their nail and tossed them on the pile of junk. He tried to move the bed frame, but it was fastened to the wall.

Unable to catch his breath after running, he took a few stumbling steps in the darkness, to the edge of the woods, turned back to see the fire now coming out of the broken window.

But not even the flames could wake him. Sweat ran down his back, it was from that distant summer, when he lay curled up at home, waiting for the morning so he could go there and see how the place looked.

"Really it's Lucyna," said Syl. "What about yours?" They were face to face and moving to the music. Iron Man put one foot forwards, then the other, thoroughly contented.

"Mirosław. But no one calls me that. As far back as I can remember, it's been Iron Man. Even my mum called me that."

"Iron Man's nice," said Syl. She was moving her hips in a lazy twist, from time to time rearranging the strap of her dress when it slipped off her shoulder. "Mirosław's nice too but kind of rare these days. You don't hear it much."

Iron Man tried to look away but without success, because Syl kept circling and staring into his eyes. Her shoulders rose and fell like anemones—that was how she imagined it. She often thought of herself as an exotic plant, growing in a warm room and not having to do a thing. Everyone admired her, and some tried to touch her.

"Right," said Iron Man. "It's hard to find a Mirosław. It used to be easier. Like with other things." He made a few foot motions, swung his elbows in a windmill, and to get out of that he sat down on the sofa. He rubbed his hands and poured himself a drink from a fresh bottle. Syl immediately sat next to him.

"And how about me, Mirosław?"

He tried to speak but hadn't finished swallowing. It went down the wrong way, and when he filled her glass, he had tears in his eyes and got some on the tablecloth.

"Looks like you've had enough," laughed Syl. "When Porkie starts spilling it like that, he goes off to bed."

Iron Man caught his breath and said:

"It always went to his head. We'd have to carry him."

"That must have been hard."

"No, he wasn't that big then. He could even borrow my trousers. They were a bit short on him."

Syl ran her fingers through her hair and sighed:

"I'd like to have known him then."

"You weren't alive then, kid. It wouldn't have come to anything."

She was still playing with her hair, her eyes fixed on something distant. She kicked her slippers off and pulled her feet up onto the sofa.

"I actually prefer slim guys," she said.

Iron Man sensed a problem, so he edged away, poured a drink, and looked at his watch.

"He said he'd be back in two hours," he said.

"He always says that," said Syl. "Then he comes home in

the middle of the night and tells me to run him a bath, make him something hot, and get the bed ready. He snores too."

"A man should snore. When my dad stopped, my mum would wake up to see if he was still alive. She couldn't sleep if he wasn't sawing away."

"He snores even on his stomach," said Syl.

"He was always that way."

"With the snoring?"

"He only slept on his stomach. And he liked to have his head covered but not his feet. The opposite of me. My feet always get cold," said Iron Man.

The music came to an end, and the CD player gave a click. On the floor above someone dropped something. Iron Man looked around. He took a cigarette, turned it a few times in his fingers, put it in his mouth.

"Light one for me too," said Syl.

He handed her the pack and the lighter. She lit up herself, pouting slightly.

"If we're not dancing, maybe we could put a film on?" she suggested after a while.

"We could, why not," answered Iron Man, and felt relief.

Beata waited. She walked in the hall, her hands in her jacket pockets, fingering the yellow toothbrushes and the tube of Colgate. Yellow were the most cheerful. She'd thought about buying soap but decided to ask Jacek. It occurred to her that they'd never bought things together. She was working out a plan: they'd also get a plastic bag, paper towels, something to drink, and sandwiches. For a start. And maybe newspapers, be-cause six or seven hours travelling in the dark would be boring, nothing to see out the window but lighted platforms and the names of the stations. She imagined an empty compartment with brown seats, a curtain, and a little rug on the floor. A little warm room gliding safely through the night. They'd choose a smoking car and open the window to let the wind in. She thought of going up to one of the windows to ask how much the ticket was, but there were people at every window. It was a little embarrassing. A woman was taking a pile of checked bags in a pram. She looked like Beata's mother. Three men with shaven heads wearing Flyers were walking like a patrol. They probably had nowhere to go to and just came to watch others setting off, because it was either that or the windblown streets. She tried to guess people's destinations but didn't know many places. People from the country were drabber or more colour-ful than those from cities. They looked around the hall furtively, like nonbelievers in church.

Dudes in short jackets stood along the wall, talking in a whisper and keeping an eye out. They weren't going anywhere either, condemned to remain in the endless cross draught of this station, which brought people together but rarely linked them. She recalled the huge aquarium in the biology lab at school: the fish swam within a hair's breadth of one another without pay-ing attention. Once, one died. It floated just above the floor of the aquarium, and the others swam by and nibbled at its red fins. She wondered how it would end, whether a little fish skeleton would be left, but someone removed the body.

"It can't be more than three or four hundred," she decided. "It's a regular express."

A wreath of men surrounded an automobile on a platform, leaning towards one another and exchanging comments in an undertone. She pictured herself on that platform, separated by a rope, with a sign that gave her date of birth, measurements, likes, and secret desires. They'd be standing just as they were now, talking to one another. There were two railwaymen too, their uniforms crumpled as if they'd just completed a journey.

It was then that she saw the three: a big thickset man, a curly haired kid, and a guy in a tracksuit—the one who'd thrown them out of the apartment earlier that day. They entered from the direction of the taxis and headed for the stairs leading down, the kid in the lead, the others a few steps behind.

There are times when the mind works faster than it can understand, so fast that afterwards, when everything's over, it's amazed at itself. Or perhaps it's just that the body takes charge for a moment, in its unerring, animal way.

Electronic bubbling sounds filled the terrarium as creatures passed across the screens taking one another's lives as boys leaned forward to take in the bloodless massacre. They looked a little like surgeons, and a little like their mothers making dinner on gas stoves. Jacek felt suffocated, so he stepped out into the passage. And the curly haired kid appeared. The two went off to the side, and Jacek said:

"About time. You have the money?"

The kid said yes.

"So where do we go?" asked Jacek.

The kid shrugged.

"Then who's supposed to know?" asked Jacek.

"Maybe the Gents," said the kid.

"No, somewhere else."

"Where then?"

"Think of something."

"I don't know," said the kid, looking down the passage, and Jacek sensed he was afraid and lying, because it was a straightforward matter. All they had to do was take a short walk towards the Palace or the Holiday Inn and settle it in the regular way, like giving someone a cigarette.

The kid said, "Maybe the platforms . . ."

Jacek followed his gaze and among the rapidly moving outlines of people he saw the big man, by the kiosk and the left luggage lockers, a motionless figure but coming towards them. Even at this distance he was certain the man was looking at them. He glanced to the right and saw the man in the tracksuit. Only a few steps away, but when their eyes met, the man recognized him and stupid surprise appeared on his face. The curly haired kid moved away: he had done his job.

"There's no one at the tram stops, no one on Emilii Plater, no one on Jan Pawła," Jacek was thinking, though they weren't so much thoughts as images against which he saw his solitary silhouette on the lit-up pavement. So he ran forwards, down the busy passage lined with kiosks. The big man quickened his pace to cut him off, but he was too heavy and his shoes too fancy, with thin and slippery soles. Behind Jacek someone shouted, and he was sure that the man in the purple tracksuit had bumped into someone or knocked him over. A moment later he ran into someone himself; instinctively he grabbed the person by the shoulders, spun him around, pushed him away. There was a commotion, someone on the ground, but out of the corner of his eye he saw that the purple tracksuit was forging through, knocking bodies aside as if pushing through underbrush.

Jacek ran in a zigzag, a nervous slalom, a jump left, right, a woman with a child, diagonally to two nuns in smart overcoats, a gap between them, perfume, then a rigid row of faces, then back into a jumbled crowd, a train had just arrived, a stream of passengers pouring up the escalator from the platform, bags and suitcases everywhere. Something hard hit his knee, but it occurred to him that this throng would slow the other two a little, so he stopped dodging and ploughed forward, because the more confusion the better.

He heard her calling. She stood on the steps leading up to the main hall. "Jacek!" Her hands at her side, shouting. He had never seen anything so frozen. He turned, forgot about her, ran.

Then he dreamed of an old hundred-zloty note. It glowed as if the steelworks on the back were real and in operation. Plumes of red smoke from the stacks. Though maybe it wasn't steelworks but a general factory, because he also dreamed of the smell of his father, who once a month would take notes from his wallet and place them in front of his mother on the kitchen table. His father's jacket smelled of dust and fatigue, and something else. Later, when Paweł started work himself, he found out what it was: the metal lockers in the changing room. Sweat gathered in those lockers, even when it was cold outside. Sticky air drifted in from the shop floor and got into the enamel, clothing, shoe leather, the plastic shoulder bags they brought their sandwiches in. The bread, meat, and cheese soaked it up like a sponge, so even at lunchtime it entered the body. But that was later. As a child he would touch the notes laid out on the table and feel their soft cloth texture, the black creases. They looked like his father's hands. His father washed them frequently, but something always remained: under his fingernails or in the cracks of his thumb. Once in a while there were new notes, stiff and crackly. Where the red faded out, the paper was creamy gold. But most of the notes were ragged, made no sound, smelled like his father's jacket and the black bag for carrying sandwiches, with the pocket where he always kept his time card. Once Paweł took it out and read it: 5:56, 5:58, 5:52, 6:00, 5:59, a rare 6:07 or 6:01 in red, the same colour as on the notes. Even the numbers smelled of the factory.

His mother would hand him a hundred zloty and a list and send him to buy groceries, and the coins he got in change had the same smell, and so did the food he brought home. He learned why years later, in a line of men just before six o'clock, crossing the road, ignoring the cars. They passed through the factory gate in a clatter of time-card punches and, more slowly now, headed for the damp changing rooms with the rows of grey lockers, only there exchanging a few words as they stood in their vests and long johns. Their underwear white as skeleton bones. They smoked, transferred money and watches to their overalls, padlocked their lockers, tossed their cigarette butts onto the tiled floor, walked down the hallways towards the shop floor. On the first day he didn't do much. Someone was supposed to show him everything, but after he was given his overalls, beret, and a wad of chits for tools, they left him on his own. He waited, walked, before long was lost among the throbbing, hot machines, so in winter he wouldn't be cold here. At the exits from the shop floor, instead of doors there were curtains of hot air. He went through a few times, to feel the blast on his trousers. He came on a metal shop, where pneumatic hammers several stories high pounded pieces of red-hot metal into discs, bulging cubes, long bars, the ground shaking as if about to cave in along with the deafening hiss and clatter of the blazing furnaces. The whole time, redness and smoke, rolled-up flannel sleeves, the stink of burning minerals from the welding and soldering shops, the hellish glow of white metal turning to yellow, orange, red, then slowly filming over with grey, until you saw rainbow stripes on the hardened surface.

When he left at two in the afternoon with all the others, he smelled the same as they. He had it in his hair, on his hands, in his throat, even his cigarette.

Half an hour later, in the bus, as they passed the huge power plant, he calculated that he'd earned a hundred-zloty note, even a little more.

Syl went to the cupboard with the TV and VCR and started flipping through the tapes. They were on the bottom shelf, so she bent over, and Iron Man could see the bright triangle of her knickers. Yellow, pink, he couldn't say. He decided it wasn't important and tried to look elsewhere. But nothing held his attention, the television was no different, and the arse stuck out at him and even swayed a little, because Syl was choosing. Her red fingernail ran over the boxes, sliding them aside, starting over. There were more than thirty tapes, but she knew them all by heart.

"What do you feel like, Iron Man?" she asked.

"An action movie," he said to her arse. "American."

Syl chose, and the VCR swallowed the tape. She picked up the remote and sat on the sofa.

"It needs rewinding," she said.

"We can't wait." Sleepiness came over Iron Man, so he made himself comfortable and slid down, his feet out. He took the bottle, ashtray, and smokes from the table and arranged them so they'd be in arm's reach. He liked movies but often fell asleep in the middle, because the days were long gone when he'd sit in the Syrena Theatre on Inżynierska and the start of the newsreel music would give him a shudder of excitement.

The VCR stopped whirring, Syl held out the remote, and there were two men on the screen talking in German.

"I thought we were watching an American movie," Iron Man objected.

"We are. It's just dubbed into German."

"Can't they dub stuff into Polish?" he muttered.

The men were walking down the street. One had blond hair, the other brown. They were in suits. Nothing was happening. The picture jerked a little.

"I don't think much of this," said Iron Man, and his eyelids drooped.

He dreamed about the Syrena, Godzilla knocking buildings down, then Rodan the Bird of Death and Mechagodzilla, Hedora, finally the Chimera Califa, all pleasant, small, and not at all frightening, so he wanted the dream to go on and tried to stretch out more on the sofa, but Syl's proximity prevented him. Through half-open eyes he noticed that it wasn't Chimera with three curved necks but three people having a party: the two men, the blond and the brown-haired one, having fun with a redheaded woman in stockings and high heels, on a couch and armchairs, doing one thing after another non-stop. "Well, that's action," Iron Man thought, waking up. But didn't move a muscle, feeling Syl press against his hip and side. He kept thinking, "Jesus, no . . ." and felt really stupid. Of course he'd watched this sort of thing in his day, but it had always been with his buddies, no women present. Iron Man was mortified. If only he could sleep through the whole thing, but he was afraid of what might happen during that real or pretend sleep, so he lay flatter and stiller, washing his hands of everything. Syl's body had become hot and heavy, even though he knew she was skin and bones.

The phone chirped. The pressure eased, and a moment later Iron Man saw her stand, turn down the German panting, and pick up the receiver.

"It's for you, Iron Man," she said, blocking the screen.

"For me?" In surprise.

"Like I said."

After the call, two minutes, he was wide awake and didn't give a damn about the action. He had his jacket on, standing in the middle of the room and putting cigarettes and lighter into his pockets.

"We need trousers, underwear, a plastic bag. And call a taxi, kid. Come on, get moving!"

First they ran through the crowd and hoped they'd be lucky. Looked through the windows of the little stores and kiosks. People looked back.

"Fuck," said Bolek. "We should check the tram stops." Tracksuit said, "OK," and in three bounds was outside by the tracks of the Praga to Ochota line, while Bolek went up to the stops to and from Mokotów. His stomach hurt. At this time of day, all the people were grey, indistinct. "He won't be standing here waiting, the prick," he thought, and ran down again. The other guy was already by the fountain searching the crowd, standing on tiptoe, looking like a complete idiot.

"Nothing, boss. Thin air."

"He was damn fast."

"He saw us too soon."

"If I were a couple of years younger . . ."

They talked like this, wandering, glancing at dozens of heads. Tracksuit kept clenching his hands, as if he had glue between his fingers. Bolek thrust his fists into his trouser pockets and placed one foot in front of the other, to steady himself.

"What now, boss?"

"You go back. The girl that shouted—she might still be around."

"I heard someone shout, but I didn't see who it was."

"A girl in an army jacket."

"All right, I'll take a look. And that bastard, I know him from somewhere, boss. It went fast, but I could swear . . ."

"All right, but go now. I'll stay here a bit."

And Bolek was left on his own. He watched the other guy, made sure he was going where he was supposed to, and carefully took a few steps. The pain in his stomach was sharper, knotting, twisting. He bent forwards and took a few more steps, pushed his hands into his pockets, tried to think about peaceful things that had happened to him in life, but he kept counting his steps, the distance separating him from the tiled passage where young boys stood with cigarettes in their mouths. He stopped for a moment, and the pain let up. Five more yards to go, but he could already smell it. Two good-looking kids with earrings were watching him. One even smiled and at the same time lowered his eyes. Heavy black boots with silver fittings. The other adjusted a salmon-pink scarf around his neck. They exchanged a few words and the first one smiled again, this time no longer turning his eyes away. "Jeez," Bolek thought, but realized he was helpless. "Any other time, you'd be dead." And the boys went on waiting, because they'd seen worse than him in their lives.

Just as he was about to go in—the boys sure that the better part of the day was starting—from inside, accompanied by the echo of flushing and the smell of toilet freshener and the mirage sheen of tiles, Jacek appeared. The two stood almost face to face, and it was only a question of in whose brain a spark would fire first.

He dashed into Nowogrodzka, but it no longer made sense. He was soaked, old, and had had enough. The fear that had sent him flying up the steps was gone, and the big man was bound to get him before they reached Lindleya. Behind him he could hear heavy footsteps, the tapping of cleats. "You either wait or get the fuck away," he thought. The buildings on either side barely moved as he went. Up ahead, someone walking a dog. Nothing but apartments here, curtains and flowers in the windows, the blinking red lights of car alarms. Everything simple, empty. "Cops and the military live here," he thought. "Some guy in pyjamas and slippers could put a bullet in you." Still that click of cleats behind him. He thought of Michael Jackson: If he wanted to buy Bemowo, he could buy this place too, since there was nothing here either. Then they'd be running through the amusement park, lights, flashes, idiotic flora and fauna, the two of them wearing caps with the initials MJ, and the other million and a half inhabitants of the city too would be in the service of Ferris wheels, merry-go-rounds, glass rollercoasters, laser galleries, halls of mirrors, and everything forever after would be make-believe. But Lindleya wasn't getting any closer. He stumbled over a paving stone but regained his balance. His mind racing. A bitter taste in his mouth, from sniffing the junk, in the Gents, all the way up into his brain. The air was bitter too. The big man neither closer nor further. They could just keep on running and running like this, across goddamn Lindleya, then Raszyńska, the Airman's Monument, towards Żwirki and Wigury—from there it was broad and straight, and by the Russian military cemetery autumn would begin, in September the trees bursting into red and yellow, and from the vegetable gardens the smell of burning leaves and grass. Old people going to their sheds with sandwich bags and flasks of tea, dogs running in a misty yet mild day. From the airport, blue buses with sophisticated people coming to take a look at our country. This was how he passed the time, but Nowogrodzka refused to end, a dream in which space had come unglued from time. If the big man was alone, if the other one was gone, he could turn and face the fatso, or do something else. What else? Nothing that he might pick up and use, a litter bin, a flattened cigarette pack, dog shit— no weapon. It wasn't courage, he was just tired of running, being trapped in this endless street. He thought of movies he had seen, things he had owned, counted them, named them, when suddenly he realized that he was running alone.

The big man had come to a stop. He was some distance away but under a street lamp, and it was plain that something was wrong, because he was oddly bent, his arms out, as if trying to creep up on something. Jacek looked one more time, then turned and left. The corner of Lindleya was a few steps away.

A clatter woke him, but he curled up even tighter, because it sounded like footsteps, as if a giant were striding from Żoliborz to Mokotów. Before he went back to sleep, he saw that the dream of his life made no sense. His first briefcase, which cost four hundred and fifty zloty, made of hard black plastic, with aluminum fittings. In those days everyone had one like it, and in the trams you could hear the click as they knocked together in the crush. But now it wasn't a tram but the stairwell of a tall apartment complex out in Gocław. He was coming down slowly, as if afraid, standing in front of each door in turn, then continuing, until he reached the first floor. At the next building, he waited until no one was near the lift before pushing the button. On the way to the top floor he swore to himself that he'd knock on the doors with numbers that had a lucky 3 and 7. Everything smelled of fresh grey paint. In his head he repeated the words he'd learned by heart and tried to smile. Good morning, we'd like to offer our services in interior finishing, good morning, we'd like . . .

He went one floor down, counted off, went to a door behind which were noises. It opened at once, and he found himself in a hallway surrounded by children who stared at him as if he were Santa. From the far end of the apartment a woman in a dressing gown asked what he wanted. He explained about wood panelling, but she didn't understand. He then gave her the presentation, rested his case on his knee and opened it: "These are some samples, ma'am. We can do the walls in ash, pine, or oak, and for the door the padding can be claret, brown, beige, or black." The children stood on tiptoe to see. One grabbed the edge of the case, and everything was on the floor. They threw themselves on the treasures, each picking up a piece, and the women smiled. "Give the man his things back," she said. "Mummy will find you something else to play with." To him she said, "We're only renting. Wait a moment, and I'll get the landlord's number for you. Maybe he'd like to have it done. Panelling would be good. The kids dirty the walls."

That day he sold nothing. Did not get beyond those few words. Did not stick his foot in any open door. Became confused, offered the wrong things. The next day too. He tried different apartment buildings, riding up, walking down. He met some men in overalls who were soundproofing doors and panelling hallways. A few times when someone opened a door, he said, "Sorry, wrong apartment." For four days, the same. His feet hurt. He thought about how much the briefcase cost. On Friday he ran out of clean shirts, put on the one from Monday. It was hot. He took more breaks. He did two complexes in Witolin, crossed Grochowska, sat in the square by Kwatery Głównej, smoked two cigarettes, thought of giving up, went back to the complexes. Outside a new building he was stopped by a short, skinny guy: "You do soundproofing for doors, right?" "I take orders." "I thought so. I need something like that. Come with me, I'll show you." They went into the stairwell, and the guy wouldn't stop talking. "It's an unusual job because it's in the cellar. My workshop is there and the neighbours complain about the noise. I need a layer of foam and something on top to make it look nice, but the door's an irregular size, it'll need to be measured. You don't have a tape measure? No problem, I do." It was dark on the stairs. The guy said he'd go first and turn on the light. Then someone pulled. There were two of them. They pushed him into a cramped place and hit him a few times, not particularly hard, and told him if he ever showed his face on their territory again, they'd knock the shit out of him. They took the case and smashed it against the wall or floor. Then it was quiet. He found the door, but it was locked. He stumbled over the broken case. After an hour he started to shout, and someone called the super. Later, in the park, he examined the briefcase carefully, but nothing could be done with it. In his dream, he saw the number 1985, bright over the city like a neon light, a significant date, the beginning of some age, yet worthless, like everything else. That was what he thought between waking and sleeping, and he dived again, hoping that somewhere at the bottom he'd find the true beginning.

———

"You didn't say it had to be uncarbonated," said Iron Man.

"Do I have to spell everything out?" said Bolek.

"What am I, the Holy Ghost? How was I to know? You told me to buy water on the way. When a person's been drinking, bubbles are good. We always used to buy it after drinking."

"What, I'm supposed to tell you over the phone?"

"What difference does the phone make?" asked Iron Man.

"Some things don't need discussing," said Bolek.

"Oh."

Practically in whispers as they stood in a dark courtyard off Nowogrodzka, but some of the windows were still lit.

"So how is it?" asked Iron Man.

"Stings, because of those damn bubbles," answered Bolek.

"I'll know next time, Boluś."

Despite the dark, Bolek was visible because he wasn't wearing anything, not even underwear. Pouring the water from the bottle on himself, washing. Iron Man stood nearby, sniffing.

"She must have put something in my food. When I get back . . ." whispered Bolek.

"Come on, Boluś, we were all eating from the same pot, weren't we? You overate, and that's all there is to it."

"I never overate in my life," said Bolek.

"Never say never."

"What's that supposed to mean?"

"Nothing. But you should ease up on the food, Boluś. We're not young any more."

"Now I'm supposed to ease up? When I can buy what I like? You remember how strapped we used to be? A roll and cheese, some milk. And now . . ."

"Food's just food."

"Why should I deny myself?"

Bolek tossed away the empty bottle, and Iron Man handed him a new one. Bolek rinsed front and back, bending like a dancer. Finally he decided it was enough.

"That should do it."

"I don't know," said Iron Man. "You still smell a little."

"Any more water?"

"I only brought that."

"You couldn't bring three bottles?" Raising his voice.

"Come on, Boluś. You call in the middle of the night, bring me this, that, I run like there's a fire or some accident, and you only shitted yourself, and then you get mad at me . . ."

"Let me tell you something, Iron Man," shouted Bolek, but didn't finish because a light went on in an apartment over their heads and a man appeared in an open window:

"Stop that noise or I call the police! And get out of the courtyard, you fags! Now!"

Without another word Bolek put on the clothes that Iron Man had brought, the underwear, the trousers, hopping. Iron Man squirmed: he didn't like people saying "police" when he was around.

Of course she could have run after them, after Jacek and the big man and the blond guy. Her heart was pure, noble, a stranger to fear. But she had hesitated, and they were separated by the crowd, the people walking up the steps. The men were gone. She followed, but felt herself going slower and slower, and in the end she stopped. And turned back. Her strength failed her. On the departures board the black letters formed ZAKOPANE. Everyone around was busy with his own business, as if her shout and the men's pursuit was nothing, a hallucination. It occurred to her that everything happened this way: it ended, broke off without a trace, and the world immediately healed over in that place. She touched the toothbrushes in her pocket, and tears welled. She walked in that direction again, because it was darker below and people wouldn't notice. There was the same dull yellow light. An army patrol passed her, officers with solemn, childlike faces. They too knew nothing. Solitude on all sides, endless. The glass doors slid open, slid shut, mingling the dark night with the station light. At the tram stop she tipped back her head to check exactly where the Marriott melted into the sky.

"What do I care?" Jacek thought. Cars drove along the Aleje as if there were no problem. "You can't even do a lousy little business deal without getting chased." A train rumbled down the other side of the street. "Looks like that holiday will never happen," he said aloud. "There's no justice." The station to his right enticed with its glow. He ought to go back there, put an end to it. The curly haired kid had once walked him all the way to his building. "One more bit of business screwed. The world's become too small. You meet someone and don't know what it'll lead to. Things used to be easier. Maybe he remembers, maybe he doesn't feel like remembering. I'm not a good person for him to know right now." A number 7 moved from the stop, scattering sparks, as if the street might catch fire. He cut across the Aleje, into Żelazna. The old apartment buildings absorbed the light, their windows flickering, from oil lamps or candles. The people were probably afraid that the city would come and reclaim their old cave and force them out, and then they'd go blind. At Złota he turned right. Jana Pawła was deserted. He ran, hopped over the fence, and was on Emilii Plater. No lights from the Palace. "Great fucking centre of the universe," he thought. "A few watchmen on the first floor, and not a soul in the bushes because it's too cold." But the place was as good as any, so he crossed the road and went among the trees. The first night buses revving their diesel engines. He watched them head towards the Aleje and disperse. It looked like some great calamity or plague, because the streets and bridges were empty now, and the people in the buses were prisoners or refugees packed in and hurrying to the distant cliffs of Natolin, Wawrzyszew, Targówek, Kabaty. A 601, a 602, a 605. "Three sixes, the devil already," he laughed. "Or eighteen, that's adulthood, the right to vote and buy alcohol. Everything falls into place so nicely, a person can't see the join." The world sped along but offered no hope, left no memory. Its content entirely of now: without consequence or continuation, like a television image. He decided against a bench in the dark and a cigarette, because it would have looked like an interruption in the transmission, a power cut, please stand by. He went at an angle to Świętokrzyska, where the shining cars, the window displays, and the endless details were food for the soul. The brain needed something to occupy it, so it didn't have to occupy itself—the horror of the vacuum. An orange road sweeper moving with an insect hiss. In the glare of the intersection, its top glistened with sweat, then it entered the black ravine of Świętokrzyska. He waited for the green light, crossed, made for the roundabout. From the right, night rolled in and broke against the silver department stores. One long arm of it reached deep into Złota and didn't end till the lights of Nowy Świat. "When it used to be Kniewskiego here," he thought, "the shop dummies weren't as sexy." He tried to hold on to that thread to the past, but it snapped and again he was alone on a long, bright, straight line past the charade of empty clothes for the rich. He went down into the underpass. By the phones it occurred to him that he ought to call Beata, to tell her or warn her, but he didn't have a card or token, and that calmed him.

"I had a dog too, but it ran away," said the blond guy.

"What kind of dog runs away?" Bolek sipped his drink.

"It happens," said Iron Man. "We had a cat once, and it wouldn't stay in the house either. It would come when it felt like it, then it stopped coming altogether."

"Cats are awful," put in the blond guy.

"A cat's not a dog," said Bolek. "Cats don't get attached."

"I don't know," Iron Man said thoughtfully. "We had one once that never went anywhere. It would lie around all day and only get up to eat."

"With cats you can never be sure," said the blond guy.

"But can you be sure with dogs? You said your dog ran away." Iron Man was annoyed.

They were sitting in the closed Hoochie-Coochie, each drinking something different. Bolek had a beer, Iron Man a vodka, and the blond guy rum and cola, because he was driving and Bolek had told him to go easy. Behind the bar Storkie wiped glasses. It was dark in the pool room. Iron Man straightened the blue jacket he had on. Bolek's bomber jacket was on the back of a chair. The blond guy had hung his up along with the top of his tracksuit, and from time to time he looked at his biceps.

"My Sheikh never goes a step away," said Bolek. "When I'm out, he won't eat or drink. He lies there or stares out of the window, though he can't see anything because he's too short."

"He's not short," said Iron Man.

"For a dog he's big," agreed Bolek, "but too short to see out."

It was almost two in the morning, and the smoke circled over their heads. Bolek was smoking Marlboros, the blond guy

Camels, and Iron Man both. Storkie kept polishing glasses, to handle time. Even though the glasses were all polished, he took them to the back room and started washing them. Looked in the mirror over the sink and thought: "This is what I'll look like in ten years, if I'm still alive."

The men at the table watched the street through the blinds. Through the narrow slats the night was a television out of focus.

"Maybe I could call for some babes, boss," the blond guy suggested.

"No," said Bolek. "We have work tomorrow."

"Then let Storkie put some music on; we're sitting here as if something bad happened. Don't worry, boss, it'll all be fine. I'll take care of it."

"All right, he can put music on," agreed Bolek. "But something quiet."

"He's got this neat song about a mother and a bike," said the blond guy, pleased. He called towards the bar. Storkie came through the bead curtain with a glass in his hand.

"Put on the thing that was on before, Storkie. The one about the motorbike."

Storkie nodded and started flipping through the CDs. He found it, put it in.

"What's the name of them?" asked the blond guy.

"The Fireflies," said Storkie.

They listened, and Iron Man even tried to tap his foot to the rhythm. Bolek finished his beer, played with his glass, pushed it aside, and said:

"I can't say I know this kind of music."

"Right, it's not Boney M," said Iron Man.

"Better take us back. We have work in the morning," Bolek concluded.

They walked out into the dark. From below, from the Vistula, came a cold, odourless wind, and distant car horns called out like the frozen souls of the damned.

He was in Berlin again, riding the U-bahn, counting the stops and clutching the ticket in his pocket. Sometimes people looked at him, but it was just after the unification, so maybe they took him for an Ossi. Everything he owned was in a plastic bag labelled USA from the Różyckiego bazaar. Above him, the city that he hated and desired. He felt the touch of its immense feet. A crappy job: three days of hammering, dust, and rubble, and nothing but a cold-water tap, so he stank for sure, even though he'd taken his Polish *Wars* deodorant with him. The guy was surprised to see him. A month before, in the middle of the night on Targowa they'd hugged like brothers and swore they'd never forget each other. Now he had three hundred marks in a pocket fastened with a button and safety pin. He counted the stops. At Oskar-Helene-Heim two black men got on. Afraid to lift his eyes, he stared at their new white Nikes. His moccasins were cracked and grey from the dust. The tassel missing on one of them. He hid his feet under the seat. The cut on his hand hurt. Thielplatz, Dahlem-Dorf, and in his pockets shreds of tobacco and a handerkerchief stiff with dirt. But he could have gone on riding for ever—this wasn't at all bad. There was nothing he had to do. He didn't have to elbow his way through the crowd around the station or point to which sandwich he wanted, or drink beer slow to make it last. It was fine here. His imagination filled with angular, martial German women trying on gold jewellry and black lingerie in the big department stores on the Kudamm, he watching through a window, unseen by the naked women, as if he were not there. The light bounced off their bodies as it did off varnish. They walked from floor to floor of the towers of glass, trying on overcoats, garter belts, tossing them aside and moving on to the next display or hanger or shelf for more shoes, perfumes, gloves, rings, discarding these in turn, finally wading ankle-deep in a heap of things scarcely touched, in an infinitely mirrored series of rooms, a labyrinth, like paradise or eternity. He too tried to enter, but the glass walls were smooth, without the tiniest chink or crack. More and more women came, appearing on the street where he stood, passing through the glass and, once inside, immediately casting off their old clothes, and on the gleaming floors rose piles of fragrant garments.

Green and white lights went on and off in the shadows, reminiscent of Christmas. A chill blew from far Krakowska, and she felt a prickling on her cheeks. Some white already gathering in the seams of the pavement. The wind drove bits of ice and formed them into flakes. A booming sound to the right, lower, and the earth shook. Her hands numb in her pockets. The plane landed. In a movie once she had seen a landing strip like black water. It seemed as if the plane would keep falling, to the centre of the earth, but it didn't.

She was calm now. What she had run from floated slowly back to her, cooled, transparent. The fear no longer rattled in her body, it settled in her throat like a pellet. The driver told her that this was the last bus, that she could catch a night bus back. The trams had all left too. She walked a little, just to hear the sound of her footsteps, it was so deserted. Cars passed the concrete island, some headed for the wide world, others returning. She felt something in the lining of her jacket, found the hole and fished out her old leopard lighter. The flame didn't last. "The fuel must have evaporated," she thought. In the cigarette receptacle of a litter bin she found a long butt with a white filter. She warmed the lighter in her hand and managed to light up. The smoke had a minty taste. A limo sped by. A rumbling, pulsing bass came from inside even though all the windows were up. The glow over downtown was so bright that she couldn't tell where the sky began and where the air of the city left off. Somewhere over Mokotów the moon occasionally appeared, white as mercury and almost a circle. It never completely disappeared in the clouds, as if that cold, sightless eye couldn't leave her. Another booming of a plane. Those people up there were happy as angels, sitting in comfortable seats, being served colourful drinks by beautiful young women, the city below like a crystal palace, but the glow of her cigarette they couldn't see, it was too tiny. Green and white flashing signals again, now from the south, from the depths of the darkness. "That's where Zakopane is," she thought, and at that exact moment tasted the burned filter. "But they're coming from some far, hot country." She pictured palm trees, sun, blue water. She tossed the butt away. The roar descended, covered her, but this too was a kind of shelter.

Something went wrong with the mechanism. There were slips, breaks, blanks, as when a film snaps, the screen goes white, and the audience starts whistling and stamping. Strangers appeared and wanted something from him. They spoke directly to him, like the people on TV who read the news. Berlin vanished. The past gone, its place taken by a present that made no sense. That's always the way when the mind has had enough and wants out. Terrified, he couldn't breathe, he opened his eyes, felt around, knocked over the bottle of mineral water. *"Ich entschuldige,"* he said, to see if what he had dreamed was true. The words came easily. *"Zug nach Braunschweig.* I'm fucking nuts. Next minute I'll start speaking Russian," he finished in Polish. He found the bottle, took a swallow, said, *"Danke,"* in a whisper, beginning to enjoy the game.

"Autobahn, Strasse, bitte," giggling, short of breath. *"Hände hoch, schnell, schnell,"* breaking out in a sweat. "Hands, hands, Hans," trying not to burst into laughter in the darkness. He dozed again and saw Zosia in an apartment he didn't know. She was walking from room to room, but the rooms were endless. He followed her, not to pursue but in a kind of game, because she looked around from time to time, to see if he was keeping up. Everything in order: beds made, tables cleared, chairs arranged, vases on shelves, heavy curtains drawn across the windows so you didn't know if it was night or day. The light from an unknown source, because as he walked he saw no chandeliers or lamps. Completely quiet. Zosia wore high heels. He was certain that she was leading him somewhere, showing him the way, taking him to a safe place deep in the labyrinth, where no one would find him. There were sofas, padded footstools, couches, bookcases filled with objects. At times he came within arm's reach of her and could see the double swell of her backside under her short dress, the back of her neck with a visible line of backbone, the outline of her shoulder blades beneath the bright, colourful fabric of her dress. She opened door after door, but he couldn't grasp any handles, couldn't touch any piece of furniture, he was too distant. He trusted her, loved her. Tears welled. He broke into a run, saw her profile, her smile. She quickened her pace lightly, her hair flowing as in a wind. He was happy, sure that he would catch her in the end and that she wanted him to. Mahogany shelves left and right, red and gold

cushions piled on leather sofas, mirrors in carved frames, black televisions on low silver tables beneath papered walls, unlit candles in ornate candlesticks. She pushed open a double door, and they were in a huge kitchen. The metallic surfaces gave off a cosmic light of luxury and desire. The floor was warm, and he was aroused. Since no more doors led anywhere, he understood that the chase was over. Zosia had her back to him, her hands on an immense sink. The memory of a porno flick, but it wasn't like that, from now on everything would be different and he wouldn't think about such things. He went up and put his arms around her, felt sweetness and trembling, slipped to his knees and embraced her hips. She turned to face him but was no longer wearing the flowing dress, it had turned into a purple tracksuit, and above him, legs planted apart, stood the blond man. Paweł tried to move away, but the man grabbed him by the hair.

The light blinded. It went off, then on again. He felt the wall at his back and another flash. He raised an arm to shield himself. The light went out again, and a woman said quietly:

"I thought it was Jacek. Someone was moaning, and I thought it was him."

Beata put the lighter in her pocket and knelt by Paweł in the dark.

"He's not in the apartment. I knocked. I thought something had happened to him, that it was him hiding."

"Is that you?" asked Paweł.

"It's me," she said.

"Why isn't he there?" he asked. "I knocked too, then I came up here and I've been waiting."

"You were yelling in your sleep, having a dream."

"Where is he?"

"He ran away. I saw them chasing him."

"At Central Station," he said.

"How did you know?"

"I didn't. I was guessing." He curled into a ball, put his arms around his knees. He couldn't see her but felt her warm breath on his face.

She touched his knee, his jacket, as if looking for something, then grabbed him by the shoulder.

"Tell me, you have to tell me."

He tried to pull away. "They chased him before, so they could chase him again," he answered, so she'd leave him alone. He had a bad taste in his mouth. He turned and spat into the darkness.

"Who was chasing him?"

"How should I know? Listen: I came here yesterday. I don't even know him. I used to, now I don't. I don't know anything. I'm waiting till he gets back, because he has a phone number I need. Not written down but in his head, an important number. I'm here by chance. Nothing connects us. I had nowhere else to go. Some business of his is going badly, but it has nothing to do with me." All this in a whisper, quickly, but when he felt the girl's grip relax, he stopped.

"I'm afraid," she said.

"Everyone's afraid."

"Afraid for him."

"He'll be fine," Paweł said. "He always lands on his feet. He makes no effort, but it comes out OK."

"We were going away."

"He would always laugh at me when I tried to do something."

"I even bought toothbrushes. See?"

She moved, and he felt cold air.

"They're yellow," she said.

"When were you going away?" he asked.

"This evening. I've never seen the mountains. He said he had something to take care of and we could go. He left, then I saw him running."

"Ran off with my phone number," Paweł muttered.

"He said he'd be right back and bring more money. We only had two million. Not that we needed to buy tickets, right? At worst they take down your names and addresses. Like in the tram. I don't know how many times that's happened to me . . ."

His turn to move. She heard the swish of his clothes, the crackle of cellophane.

"Give me one too," she said, reaching.

Their hands tried to find each other in the dark like a game with a blindfold. He caught her wrist, held it, put the cigarette between her fingers. They were dry and warm.

"Ever been to Zakopane?" she asked.

"Yes."

"Are the mountains nice?"

"I don't know. We always got there in the evening, loaded the goods, and had to go back."

"What goods?"

"Leather, sheepskins. When they went out of fashion, the trips stopped."

"You never saw the mountains?"

"Once we were there in the daytime, but it was foggy."

The tips of their cigarettes made slow red lines in the dark. In the silence, they could hear the smoke leaving their mouths. The beating of their hearts. They were completely alone. The

181

city crouching in wait below. A copper glow over the round-about. The bodies of people in their beds were reddish, as if moulded from clay and baked in an oven. Refrigerators hummed quietly; clocks showed the hours and minutes; thermostats turned on the central heating. In the old-fashioned cold-storage plants in remote spots, freon condensed and vaporized in turn. Current flowed, maintaining essential operations. The girls in the purchasing office dozed off for a moment. In concrete tunnels, the stream of sewage slowed and at times stopped entirely.

She crushed out her cigarette and said:

"I have to go."

"Where to?" he asked.

"Home. He might call."

"It's up to you," he said.

He heard her knock at the door on the floor below, then the silence fell again.

People dreamed different things that night. Everyone dreams. The worst people and the best. Iron Man fell asleep in the back seat and dreamed he was a watchmaker. He was sitting in a warm place on a soft chair, and people kept bringing him their watches. A lamp was on, and a large table held hundreds of timepieces. Some were ticking, some only lit up, and some had quartz hearts to push the hands around. He listened to the gentle ticking, studied the straps and bracelets, unscrewed or prised open the casings to check that dust hadn't gathered inside and to gaze at the little red jewels. The modern ones he set aside, though some were expensive. With clockwork there was no trickery, but with electronics you never knew. When a real watch stopped, there was something wrong you could fix; when an electronic watch stopped, it was dead. A clockwork Atlantik, sometimes it was enough to blow on it to start the tick tock again, and the little silver bird chirp. Polyots, Vostoks, Raketas, each had its own sound, but those Casios—a boring flow of electrons like everything else in nature, nothing there to admire. This was Iron Man's dream. He sat, wearing black sleeves over a white shirt, reaching for a magnifying glass to look deeper. Beside him, a fresh bottle of Królewskie beer and a full pack of Caros.

Bolek and the blond man were not asleep. The blond man drove, and Bolek stared into the emptiness of Łazienkowska. They came to the bridge. To the right, the dark Torwar skating rink. Bolek thought about Irina, compared her to Syl. They were a little like mother and daughter. It resembled a dream, because he couldn't stop one from turning into the other. He was going to Syl but would have preferred Irina. A man needs a woman who understands him. What could Syl understand? He tried to remember what he understood when he was sixteen: things happened, that was all. He wanted someone to understand him without words. Also, Irina was bigger. The silver street lamps reminded him of her earrings, the night of her black brassiere. Syl, on the other hand, was a sparrow, nothing to hold. Syl and Irina, Irina and Syl. At some point he lost the "a," and it was Irin. It sounded nice. He'd call her that when they next met.

The blond man had his eyes open, but he never woke up. Life took whatever shape it wanted, and there was no point in thinking about that. People did one thing or another, for different reasons. Dreams were dreams, and you couldn't back out of one. Things were a little more even than people, since they didn't change as quickly, because people always wanted something. He knew what he wanted and wasn't afraid to take it. As they crossed Paryska, he clapped both hands on the wheel and said:

"Don't worry, boss. We'll get him."

"I'm not worried. I was just thinking," said Bolek.

Zosia dreamed of Pankracy. He was bigger than a dog—almost as big as a lion. They walked down a dark alley with a confident step. By his side she was nimble, strong, and pleasantly empty. He was leading her, not she him. She touched the fur of his neck. Muscles rippling under skin. The road was wet and glistening, and the buildings they passed grew smaller and smaller. No lights on in the windows, and the cars all old and shabby. She'd never been here before and wouldn't have come on her own, but now her eyes pierced the dark. She was all in black. But this also wasn't a dream, because she could see it as she lay with eyes open. Pankracy was asleep, curled in a ball on the pillow. The curtains were drawn, and all the lights were on.

Outside, it was as bright as a stage. The world went further, no doubt, but here it resembled a blue box. Friday morning, and the usual stream of cars from Ochota to Praga, from Żoliborz to Mokotów and back again, bringing to mind geometry. The planes of the buildings superimposed on one another, all coming to rest against the plane of the sky. The eastern light crumbled against the straight edges of the roofs. Below, shadow, the puddles not yet thawed, ice reflected in glass, multiplied and magnified images. What he saw was only the sum, resultant, of an incalculable number of reflections, a satisfying thought. He could simply stand there, knowing no formula to make sense of a million random events. The roundabout a convex mirror. He imagined images gliding across its shining surface and disappearing, while the view from the window was infinity. Except he could not make out what lay beyond the blue sky, which hindered a precise grasp. When he stopped thinking, things returned to their places. But his thoughts had come to an end anyway. The ribbon of impressions was now a blank tape that passed through his head with a rustle.

"Have you remembered it yet?" he heard behind him but didn't turn, because it was too dark back there, too cramped and complicated.

"You don't even have a towel." Paweł raked his fingers through his wet hair. "Or a fucking lightbulb, or toilet paper. I need that number, OK?"

He moved towards Jacek, but Jacek's immobility took his courage away. He stopped in the middle of the room and looked at his wet hands. He shouted: "The number! Don't play games! You said you'd remember it. You've been standing there like a prick for the last hour and staring out of the window at nothing." He kicked the chair, startling himself. Jacek, not moving, said:

"If you don't stop, I won't remember. I have to concentrate."

"You've been concentrating for an hour. You've lost your goddamn mind. Anyone can see that."

"Call the first number again."

"I can't. He told me not to. He said he'd only say it once, and that was it."

"So? Do you have to do what he says? Go and make the call."

"Remember it."

"I'm trying. I can't."

"You can't remember it, and in the night you couldn't let me in . . ."

"I couldn't."

"Out of fear! You were so afraid, you shat in your pants!" He moved towards Jacek again, his hands dry now and clenched into fists.

"Don't shout. You'd better leave if you're going to shout."

"And where am I supposed to go? I need that phone number. You're in deep shit yourself."

"I'm not in anything." Jacek's voice a tone higher.

"They're coming to kill you. They'll find you, because you're as stupid as I am, even more, and then you'll really shit yourself, and they won't knock, all you'll be able to do is jump out of the window, but first you'll stand at the door for hours listening. Like me. You'll walk around asking people to remember a phone number or let you in, but no one will, because bums like you have to stand at the door and listen."

Jacek jumped and sank his fingers into Paweł's face. The two careened across the room, knocked over the table, fell to the floor. The bookshelf rocked, and books tumbled down on their wrestling bodies. Rubble and ruins, each trying to strangle the other or tear off a limb, but they were too weak, could only tug at clothing, hair, thrashing like clowns or death throes, floundering among broken plates from the table, crunching things into smaller pieces, slipping in the soup smeared across the floor. At times they lay side by side or one on top of the other gasping, then resumed the struggle, which was not mortal, merely desperate, like drunken love or a hysterical fit. They rose to their knees, put their arms around each other, fell back down, but more slowly, because now even the weight of their own bodies was too much. They climbed as if the floor had no air and they were trying to reach the surface. Then simply looking for a body to lean on. Someone hammered. They froze, listened, clinging to each other. It was only the neighbour below banging on the ceiling. They slipped to the floor, panting like dogs. Jacek crawled to a corner, turned his back, curled.

Paweł pushed himself higher with his hands a few times, but finally gave up: it was better to lie and listen to the new silence. His nose was bleeding. A red drop on his lip. He tried to touch it with his tongue. "We can't even fight right," he thought. "There was no one to teach us. Always being pushed around—bring this in, take this out, sweep it up, carry the suitcase down the platform. Now it's too late." He put his hand in his pocket to find something familiar. He took out a small amount of money and started counting: he always did that when he had time. He smoothed the notes, put them in order, folded the wad in two and put it back in his pocket. That calmed him. His breath had settled, his muscles had stopped twitching. He got up, went over to Jacek, and squatted down.

"All right, easy," he said as naturally as he could. No response. He patted him on the shoulder, but that had no effect either, so he shook him a little, then more. Slowly, heavily, Jacek rolled over on his back, full length, his arms out.

"Asleep," Paweł said.

Jacek was actually snoring. He lay like one shot, but he snored. The sleeve of his jacket was ripped, something spilling from it. He slept like an empty shell, cold air entering and leaving. The clocks in the city showed seven. Not a cloud in the blue sky. Mothers entered rooms and woke children. People sat in their cars listening to the morning news, or glancing through newspapers at red lights. Everything in place, fifteen channels, ten news programmes, no surprises, everything matching. Express trains set out in all four directions. A long-distance train pulled into Central Station after an overnight journey. Nothing needed to be added or subtracted. There was no wind. The flags over the petrol stations hanging motionless. It was promising to be a nice day.

"Porkie's pissed," said Syl, rolling back to her warm spot. "He doesn't like anything, though this is his best time."

"I didn't get enough sleep," said Bolek.

"Couldn't you have come home sooner? I thought something happened."

"What could happen?" Bolek grunted.

"You never tell me anything. I know you have a lot on your mind, important stuff, but you could tell me sometimes."

"Uh," said Bolek, and turned his back on her. Syl took the corner of the blanket and held it to her cheek.

"And you haven't bought me anything for ages. When we first me, you said you'd buy me things."

"And what, I didn't?"

"But not recently. I can't keep going out in the same clothes."

"You never go out at all." Surprise in Bolek's voice.

"Exactly. You don't take me anywhere. I have to stay here and clean and cook."

"The cooking hasn't been great lately."

"What do you mean?"

"Iron Man had a stomach ache yesterday."

"He kept taking seconds and didn't say anything."

"It didn't hurt then. Later."

"It was from all those seconds. Not everyone can eat like you, Porkie." Syl tried to put her arms around Bolek. Against his huge white back she looked like a doll. "You know what I mean. A scrawny little guy can't compare with you. You could pack away half a dozen seconds with no problem." She moved her hand lower, murmured:

"Porkie, I saw these really neat shoes . . ."

He rose on his elbow and cocked an ear.

"Where did you see them?"

"On TV, silly. Where could I have seen them?"

He fell back, reassured.

"What were they like?" he asked.

Syl perked up.

"You know, really smart, all black with little stuff here . . ." She threw the blanket aside and lifted a foot to show him. He watched her quick, precise gestures.

"And here they had . . ."

Sunlight began entering the room, through a crack in the curtains. Gold fell across their bodies like an eerie mist. The world was telling them something, but, like all lost souls, they saw only themselves, in their simplicity believing that only they were beautiful. Syl's pale skin took on the hue of honey, and Bolek reached out. The whirl of sunlight came to the centre of the room. Particles of dust rose and spread in a trembling fan. The light submerged them, and a moving edge of shadow passed like a razor over Syl's breasts, then passed on.

"All right," said Bolek, "we'll figure something out." Syl clapped her hands, scrambed onto his belly, slapped it with her bare arse, hugged it with her knees.

"Porkie, you're great! When are we figuring it out?"

"Maybe today," Bolek mused. "We'll see."

"Today, today!" exclaimed Syl. "We'll go and find them."

She started to knead and mould him between her skinny

thighs but didn't hear the groan that always started it. He lay and stared at the ceiling, from which Irina was descending. She wore gold stiletto heels and a black brassiere. Chunky earrings dangling. Her figure, half flesh and half balloon, wore a precious stone in its navel, and Bolek knew it was no fake, just as Irina was no fake, an incarnation of the ideal woman. She swayed, enticing, hovering near the chandelier. Her French perfume tumbled down like silk and covered his face. He closed his eyes, sighed, and hope stirred in Syl's heart. He took her by the scruff like a kitten and moved her. Now the smell of fish and chips was added to the perfume. Irina did a somersault, and now he saw her from behind, swaying from side to side as if teasing. He moved his head to the same rhythm, but she avoided his eyes. He remembered a joke about two sailors in a whorehouse, but this time it wasn't funny. He tried to concentrate, to regain control, but Irina had put on some clothes and now was sitting in her dress with the silver threads, legs crossed, ignoring him completely, which made him angry. He liked people to do what he told them. He put his arm under his head and snapped:

"Cut it out and bring me a cigarette." In his thoughts adding: "I'll get you those shoes, and then it's good-bye. I'm not living with a woman who doesn't do anything for me any more. And you're not much of a woman. We learn from our mistakes."

When Syl came back with a lit cigarette, he took a long drag and blew smoke at the ceiling, but nothing happened. He tried again, but this time he coughed so hard, he had to get out of bed.

"Poor Porkie," said Syl.

"Go to the kitchen and fix breakfast. Feed Sheikh, wake Iron Man and tell him to get in here."

She went without a word, unaware that she was going back.

She knocked on Iron Man's door, waited a moment, opened the door a crack, and said that Bolek wanted to see him. She put the coffee on and started examining the contents of the refrigerator. She was always surprised at its size: standing in front of it was like being at the entrance to an additional room. She did all the things she did every morning, but her time and space had frozen. In a dirty courtyard four kilometres away, a bench, at this time of day still unoccupied. On the wall of the apartment building, in black spray paint, her name and something else besides. The writing partly rubbed off, because she'd worked at it all night. Learning that spray paint was more enduring than memory. They sat and drank wine till late at night. When it ran out, they were bored, did things, but the dark covered them so well that the next night they could start again. So the bench was waiting, with the wall of the apartment building and the other walls that had windows with the faces of grown-ups and her father, who never came downstairs but always waited for her to come up. He would shout, like all old men who have no strength or money and can't cry because no one taught them how. The courtyard was waiting for her, and the windows with the women in rollers and the men in undershirts. Nothing had changed. The dustbins, the carpet-beating frame, the hard earth. She put Sheikh's food in his bowl and changed his water. He sniffed at it and walked away. People did the same. One day she went down to the courtyard and saw a cat hanging from the frame and some boys shooting at it with an air gun. She was going to say something, but they might write her name in black spray paint again. The cat moved, tried to reach its rear legs, where it was tied. With the next shot, she heard the smack, and the cat jerked. She understood it was a game. They called her over and put the heavy gun in her hand. She pulled the trigger,

191

the shot rattled in the bin, and they laughed. One held her hands to help her aim. She tried to close her eyes but couldn't. Shouting, applause. She giggled and wanted to do it again, but they were low on pellets. They forgot about her, but the giggling wouldn't stop, it was deep inside. She went to the sandpit and threw up. No one noticed. Now she had to go back there.

It's eight in the morning. Shadows shorten, and a breeze begins from the east, cold but driving no clouds. A grey Ford Fiesta circles the Starzyński roundabout and exits towards Targówek. A woman in a light-coloured jacket glances in the rear-view mirror to check her make-up. She overtakes a 176 bus and turns on 11 Listopada. On the seat beside her, sunglasses and a handbag containing a lighter and a pack of Davidoff lights. She's crisscrossing the city because today she decided to be unfaithful to her husband and is putting off the moment. Probably to remember it better.

A yellow baby Fiat with a customized exhaust pipe pulls up outside Ruy Barbosa High School and parks on the pavement. A kid with a ponytail gets out, slams the door, checks the inside pocket of his jacket, glances quickly to either side, and enters the school. A kid in a similar jacket but with a shaved head is waiting for him at the gateway. They stand together, talking and watching the street, then disappear behind a rusty white delivery van that says ROWOHLT GMBH BERLIN and moves slowly. When it passes, the shaved kid is gone and the one with the ponytail is getting into his car, turning on the music. He drives off, catches up with the van at Stalingradzka. From Gdański Bridge you can see the skyscrapers. An old man in the back seat of an Opel Vectra doesn't recognize the buildings. He asks his son, who's driving, but the son only shrugs. In a moment they'll turn on Okopowa, drive as far as Wolska, and half an hour later go in the direction of Poznań to settle a complicated family matter concerning an inheritance. On the far side of Kutno they'll be hit by a lorry, and the young man, dying, will think that he's been unkind to his father all his life and now has no time to tell him he loves him. The father will survive, but the rest of his days will be poisoned by guilt.

On Profesorska a woman wakes up and, lying in bed, goes through all the French names she can think of. First the names of film directors, actors, writers, then perfumes, fashion designers, producers of lingerie. She makes sure she hasn't forgotten anything, that "Picardie" is as firmly in her memory as "cinéma vérité" and "bois de Boulogne." Then she gets up and tiptoes to the refrigerator.

At ten past eight the blond man emerges from a gateway on Białostocka, which is deserted. He presses a button on his remote key, and the car responds with a joyful beep. He presses again, and the vehicle flashes submissively. He puts the key in his pocket and walks towards the Wileński station. Passes long-distance bus stops, turns right. By a stand selling sausages three buddies are polishing off a bottle, drinking from a plastic beaker. They call him over, but he just nods. He buys cigarettes at the kiosk, goes out onto one of the platforms. A blue and yellow local from Tłuszcz is opening its doors, and passengers pour out. Hands in pockets, feet slightly apart, the blond man is taller than all the people arriving. They part in front of him, merge again behind his back. He looks at their cheap clothing, counterfeit shoes, fake gold, plastic briefcases, watches from Hong Kong, the girls' worn high heels and the boys' imitation leather jackets, the plastic bags, generic Popularne cigarettes lit with matches, dyed fringes. When they all pass, stooped figures hurrying for the underpass to catch trams and buses, he spits. He returns the same way. The three buddies have finished their bottle, and one comes up sheepishly, but the blond man reaches into his pocket, takes out loose change, and says, "Here, now beat it." With the money he took out his key chain, but doesn't put it back. He twirls it on his finger until he sees his Audi.

"It began with 7 and 6," said Jacek, at the window. "That makes 13, an unlucky number. Not a good start."

"But if you add the next numbers," said Paweł, "it's not 13 any more."

"Right. The last one was a 6, maybe a 9. The one before it . . ."

"Either you remember or you don't." Paweł's hands were wet again. He waved them in the air.

"If I could get a little more sleep."

"We have 7, 6, then a 6 or 9 at the end. What about the middle?"

"A 4, maybe, a 5? It wasn't a zero. A zero I would remember. I notice them. Empty inside. With a zero you can draw around things. Remember when we played amoeba?"

"Yes."

"You think and think, but in the end it can be drawn around and made a circle. That was the point of the game."

"You've lost your mind," said Paweł. He looked through his jacket pockets, found a pack, took out a cigarette.

"Give me one," said Jacek.

"The pack's almost empty," said Paweł.

Jacek took the cigarette, lit it, continued pacing. "Empty like a zero."

Paweł felt the world slipping away, from the chair beneath him, from the apartment. The two of them would go on sitting there until their lives were completely used up.

"She's waiting for you to call," he said, trying to create a thread of meaning.

"Where?"

"At home. She said she was going home to wait."

Jacek paced.

"All right. I'll call."

"You remember her number?" The joke was weak.

"It adds up to 10. Divided into three parts, and each starts with a 1."

Paweł got up to block Jacek. Jacek passed him, brushed against the wall, went into the dark kitchen, where he said:

"What's your problem? You count money, I count numbers. Each to his own."

Something dropped, shattered. "I see no contradiction," Jacek went on, and something else fell, something tin. "If you thought about numbers once instead of money, you wouldn't be standing here now like a complete idiot." Another object hit the floor. "If you relaxed a little, went to bed without knowing what you would do in the morning, didn't give a flying fuck about tomorrow, you wouldn't be in such shit today." He appeared in the doorway, his face cold. Paweł stepped aside to let him pace again, but Jacek said: "OK. I'll try one more time. We'll go find a phone. Seeing the dial may work. Visual memory."

In the living room, he picked up his coat from the floor, examined the torn sleeve. "While we're there," he said, "I'll call her."

They stood for a moment, patting their pockets though there was nothing to pat. A knock at the door: regular, calm, not especially loud. Three times. It stopped, then repeated. They both counted, and the air grew colder.

They left her. The rattle of the glass pane in the door, a hum from the street. She still saw the faces from ten minutes before. The woman with long, almost white hair, carrying something under her arm, wearing perfume that was too strong. Women shouldn't smell like that: men start sniffing like animals. Under her arm, a red leather handbag with a gold clasp. The memory of the smell like a lemon drop dissolving on the tongue. Now she lay on her stomach, her face in the fake fur bedspread. A tram bell so close, as if the tram were brushing the wall. She wanted to shout but gasped instead, like waking from a bad dream. She knew the tram was distant, but the quiet of the room brought everything near: the cars, people, children going to class, a ruddy spaniel with a collar made of silver links. When the blond man struck her, she spun around and hid her face in her hands. He did it lightly, in an almost friendly way. Came into the room, smiled, and said, "How's it going?" Then she felt the pain and realized it was from being hit. She looked at him through her hands as a child spies on adults through a crack in the door. She saw only his back, a denim shirt. He was putting a cassette in the tape deck. Music came on. He turned and said:

"I just want to know where he lives."

"Who?"

He tipped his head to one side and smiled as if listening to some distant, pleasant sound. This time the blow was harder. She came to on the couch. The pain so deep, she felt only fear.

"I'm going out now," he said. "I'll be back in five minutes, and then you'll call him."

"He doesn't have a phone," she whispered.

"Whatever."

He turned the music off. The girl in black opened the door for him, but she didn't see the door, only heard the rattle of the pane. Counted the seconds, whispered, chose concrete things— the perfume, the spaniel, hoping they would carry her into the heart of the day. "No one ever hit me," she thought. "Not really." Her mother's slaps had been impulsive, weak. Occasionally her face stung, that was all. The blond man hit her as one hits a man. Again the terrible fear, so she tried to remember an event, but the events were all dust and useless. A dull shooting in her stomach. Skaryszewski Park, the women archers in their white uniforms. When they drew their bows, their bodies became light, as if lifting off the ground. The arrows flew, and the feet in white trainers touched the green grass again. Slowly she pulled her knees up, felt the air move over her.

"It'd be better if you told him," she heard. "Don't be foolish."

The girl was looking down at her, a cigarette in her hand.

"Why did you call me here? Why did you tell me to come?"

"He'd have done the same to me . . ."

"Not to you, Luśka."

"You don't know him."

"I know you. He told you to talk to me now?"

"What difference does it make? Tell him. Don't be foolish."

The girl knelt, put the cigarette in Beata's mouth. Beata took a drag, took the cigarette from Luśka's fingers.

"What will he do to me?" she asked.

"He's not a bad guy, just persistent." Luśka took the butt, looked around for an ashtray. Far off, a train hoot.

"I feel sick," Beata said.

"Don't be afraid," said Luśka. "If you tell him, you won't need to be afraid."

"It's the cigarette, not the fear." Beata curled up.

Iron Man sniffed. The scent of Fahrenheit aftershave in the cab made him sad. To cheer himself, he touched the wallet in his pocket, fat with notes. On his feet he had a pair of Bolek's new socks straight from the packet. He'd even taken sunglasses with him: they dangled casually from the breast pocket of the blue jacket. On his finger, a Mercedes Benz signet ring.

"Take Poniatowskiego Bridge," he told the driver.

"It was supposed to be Łazienkowski Bridge," the cab driver said.

"I took the Łazienkowski yesterday. I don't like going the same way twice."

They turned on Grenadierów. The car's upholstery, warmed in the sun, had an elegant smell. Iron Man stretched his legs and gazed at the world outside. A blue sky over boring Grochów. They sped across Stanów Zjednoczonych on the tail end of a green light. The apartment complexes on Wiatraczna rose white like an immense pueblo. He read the names of streets and wondered who came up with them. For example, Cyraneczki. All he could think of was President Józef Cyrankiewicz and his bald head. He wanted to ask the driver, but the guy didn't look more than thirty, so forget about history. Waszyngtona deserted. A golden light from downtown. "In this kind of weather everything looks foreign," he thought. They came to Skaryszewski

Park on the right. Dogs scampering among bare trees. Before they reached Zieleniecka, he slapped his knee and said:

"Maybe we could go through Praga. Over Dąbrowski Bridge?"

"We could even take the Grota-Roweckiego," the driver said with a shrug. "Or via Nowy Dwór. I tanked up this morning."

Syl leaned forward, asked:

"Why Praga? It's out of our way."

"It doesn't matter. The stores aren't open yet anyway. No harm in going for a ride once in a while, is there?"

"I guess not." She dropped back in her seat.

The Wedel factory reflected in the silver surface of Kamionkowskie Lake. White plumes over stacked buildings. Through the window she could smell chocolate and marshmallow. A watering lorry came towards them, making the black tarmac glisten. She thought again about the shoes waiting for her somewhere in the city, in some store, on some shelf, or on display behind glass, surrounded by huge eggs and rabbits and chicks. She imagined herself going inside. A refined salesman places before her a box lined with tissue paper and takes out a gorgeous pair of black shoes, silver buckles tinkling, and she tries them on in front of a low, broad mirror. Excited, she leaves the store and looks for an entranceway or corner where she can quickly and discreetly take off her old shoes and step into the new ones. The high, clear tap of the heels on the pavement makes men turn to look at her, because she has become an entirely different woman. The shoes had to be there somewhere in the labyrinth of downtown department stores, somewhere in those thousand mysteries of style that could change your life, let you be born over and over again after the tedium of early morning, the sorrow of midday, the hopelessness of night.

A dull green train on the viaduct above Targowa. People stuffing packages onto racks, into compartments, a few of them looking down Grochowska. A jungle of antennas sprouted from the roofs of the grey apartment buildings. In the distance, an impassable wall of black tendrils, naked scrub. Syl could see the faces of the passengers in the windows, but no longing stirred in her. "I won't throw the old ones away," she decided. "They're not that old."

They stopped at a pedestrian crossing. A platinum blonde with long hair carrying a red handbag. Syl took a close look at the woman's red pumps. Gold heels. A 13 tram emerged from Kijowska, pulled up at the stop. Three teenagers tossed away their cigarettes and got in.

Fear makes a body tender. They lay on the floor, motionless so as not to stir the air or block the light. On the floor below, someone was sweetening tea: they could hear the rustle of the sugar poured in, the soft sound of the crystals breaking the surface of the liquid, the ring of the spoon against the glass. The tea must not have been hot, because the swallowing continued for a long time. Dogs yapped at the shelter out on Paluch, throwing themselves against the chain-link fence. In the church of Saint Barbara on Emilii Plater, complete silence, which they could hear, like all the other sounds of the city. The sounds melted into one and filled the apartment, driving out the air, so it was hard to breathe. The tea drinker got up from his chair and took three steps to the window. A male voice: "Their enemies and prey have no chance, for they are too slow and their killer instinct is undeveloped. The struggle for territory or survival must end in death for them, at best in injury." The voice stopped; singing began. The person on the floor below now went into the kitchen, and over the song he could be heard opening the refrigerator, taking something out, doing something with it. Then fat hissed in a frying pan, and eggshells were broken. He must have been heavy, because the walls and floor shook with every step. His slippers slapped. The singing turned into a monologue in German. The chair creaked again; a fork clicked against china. The ringing of a tram from the street. Two floors below, a toilet flushing and children shouting. The Cartoon Network came on, went off. The man beneath them must have finished, because the fork clicking stopped. A belch, then a long fart.

"Who?" Paweł moved his lips, pointed to the floor. Jacek shook his head. Again they were still, staring at the door. Hundreds of sounds from behind the door, from behind the walls, from the ceiling, the city: the rumble of the steelworks, the hiss of steam from the power plant, the jets at Okęcie, the crash of buffers in the engine sheds, everything mixed up.

Paweł tried to get up on all fours, but Jacek grabbed him and pulled him back down. Paweł submitted and lay flat. "How much longer?" he asked soundlessly. The man downstairs snoring. Outside the door, something moved, brushed against something else, fell silent. The peephole gleamed. Jacek loosened his grip. Paweł turned onto his back and lay with outflung arms. He could feel the whole building vibrate to the rhythm of the radio and television waves, the vacuum cleaners, mixers, refrigerators, and washing machines, the gas flames of burners. Heat rose up the walls and swept over his exhausted body, dissolving it, turning it into useless energy that dissipated for ever into the sky. Jacek stirred. Very slowly he crawled towards the hallway, his face sliding along the floor, his breath stirring the dust. At the door, he froze and listened. The soles of his shoes worn and cracked. Forty-four TV channels brought comfort to the inhabitants of the city, but there was no news, only silence, the sounds of life and time coming to a stop like blood in the veins of a corpse. Paweł stared at the ceiling. Something was going on above too. A fleck of plaster fell on his face. Jacek turned to him and placed a finger on his lips. The beating of their hearts filled the apartment.

Bolek waited for the door to close behind Iron Man and Syl, turned on his other side, dozed, woke, yawned, and let his feet drop to the carpet. He scratched under his arm and examined what he possessed. A pleasure for his eyes to move from one object to the next. He never did that when someone else was in the apartment. He liked people but didn't like them to touch what was his. As if touching diminished a thing. Now, in the quiet and solitude, there seemed more. He rose naked, went to the window, and opened the curtains—indifferent to the view, but it was from his window, so he devoted a moment to it. He found his leather slippers and walked slowly, so nothing would escape him: the artificial flowers in their plastic pots, the pictures in their spiral frames, the crimson footstools, the sword on the wall, the brass vent cover on the ceiling in the shape of a bouquet of lilies, the gold lion's-paw door handles, the oval mirror with the tulip sconce, the smooth wallpaper, the rough wallpaper, the red night-lights, the couches covered with shaggy white throws, the black nightstands with copper knobs, in their drawers old sports papers, girlie magazines, and combs, the wardrobes with suits, the chests with the rest of his clothes, custom-ordered marble windowsills, plaster rosettes in the ceiling and stucco mouldings over the fireplace where tin logs were lit by a flickering bulb beside a set of silver-plated fire irons, the sky-blue rococo clock that played seven different tunes, three cheerful, three melancholy, and happy birthday, the electronic calendar with a motion sensor that spoke in English in a woman's voice whenever you walked by, the revolving armchair, on it a pile of freshly laundered white socks rolled into balls, a computer and monitor he'd lost interest in after losing five games of Exterminator in a row, the nickel-plated gadget to tie neckties, the shoe polisher, the stationary bike, the massager, a copy of a Fragonard, a standing ashtray in the shape of a Corinthian column—then he was in the living room. He sat in the wicker chair. As usual Syl had prepared his vitamins for him. He tore open the packets, poured them into a glass of water, stirred, drank, and pressed the remote. Two animals devouring a third. Disgusted, he changed the channel. A woman with her head shaved was walking down the street and singing. The people ignored her. He went to the kitchen. On the table, under a glass dome, sandwiches. "She didn't make much of an effort today," he thought: ham, salmon, salami, cheese. "Couldn't be bothered to cut up pickles." He put a frying pan on the stove, opened the refrigerator, took out the bacon, counted out six eggs. After a moment added two. "Why not," he said out loud. He took the food into the living room. The woman was gone; two men in suits were talking. He settled down comfortably and started eating. A mouthful of scrambled egg, a mouthful of sandwich, and so on, alternating the sandwiches according to mayonnaise, ketchup, tartar sauce, mustard, still naked except for his slippers. He saved the fried bacon for dessert but added a few slices of it to a cheese sandwich with mustard. He wiped his plate with a piece of bread. He hiccuped and let out a fart.

Sheikh raised his head and cast him a wary glance. "Every day should start like this," Bolek thought. He shifted to the sofa and stretched out full length. The black leather creaked under his massive white flesh. Languidly he reviewed all the things he had to do. The phone was near, he could reach it easily, but he put off the moment, because Irina entered his thoughts again. Or had he entered hers? He yielded, closed his eyes, and she stood in the doorway in a flimsy nightgown with gold sequins. Her smile enigmatic. In her hands, a samovar, shining, steaming.

The platforms visible from the window: bulging checked bags piled on baggage carts. The women from Zielonka and Ząbki never left their sewing machines—if they did, they were immediately replaced by others, and the rattle of needles and the clatter of spools went on day and night. Every train to Minsk, every freight car to Moscow was filled with cheap denim, nylon, cotton, imitation leather, cut and fashioned into garments decorated with fake gold buttons, silver fasteners. The endless ribbon of fabric from the Far East flowed into basements along the Wołomin line and, turned into clothes, travelled east again, but a closer east, ever hungry for the fashions of the West, the cuts, colours, glittering imitations, as if the people there had been naked for centuries, in all those Shepetivkas and Homlas and Bobruyskas, and their eyes finally opened, and they sought to cover themselves, ashamed in front of the dressed world. Women in tracksuits stood guard, circled the checked bags, watched like sentries protecting burial mounds filled not with the treasures of the past but with the future and insatiable human longing.

The blond man gazed at the platforms of East Station, his hips swaying a little. Wearing jeans that cost three mill, he was contented. In his mind he added the shoes, another four, and the shirt, two, so it came to nine. In the hall hung a jacket for ten, and in the jacket was a phone that was three and a half and a wallet holding twelve in different denominations. Thirty-odd not counting the watch, the gold chain, the underwear, and other stuff he had in his pockets. "Not bad, though it could be better," he thought. He was worth something with his two hundred pounds and not an ounce of fat. Everything in working order. Reflexes perfect. Skin smooth, chest big, neck thick, biceps and abs clearly defined. That was why he didn't like crowds on the street, people coming into contact without his permission. Sometimes he would pick someone out, walk towards him, wait for the guy to bump into him, then he would flex his muscles and watch the guy bounce off, spin from the force of it, mouth open. And he kept on walking, because weakness disgusted him. One day he'd leave it all, Białostocka, Za̦bkowska, Brzeska, leave Wileński station and East Station, and the waiting for phone calls, because it would be him calling first, from some place far from the stink of people, his body safe from all chance meeting, physical decay, the commonness of tram stops and underground walkways, where he would send those weaker than himself but who tried to compete though they would never succeed.

"Garbage," he thought, seeing a man add more bags to the pile at the far end of the platform. "And they're out of cash, all they have are those worthless rags. Mr Max is stupid, doesn't do anything about them." The blond man smiled: a few days ago they tied a guy's hands with wire, wrapped the end around the steering wheel. Shut the door and poured petrol over the back of the car. Threw a match. Three seconds, and the guy started screaming. They could see his open mouth. When they opened the door and cut the wire, he told them everything. The blond man was going to lock him in the car again, but the others went on about Mr Max this, Mr Max that. Pissed him off. He liked fire and didn't like cowards. He kicked the guy in the chest, and they drove away. The guy ran for the fire extinguisher, but when they were a way off, a column of tarry smoke rose among the trees. He smiled at the thought that the yellow train was headed in that direction. He placed a hand on Luśka's head.

"Not this time, I don't think," he said.

The girl stopped and lifted her face. She took a deep breath and sat back on her heels.

"It's not your fault." He patted her on the cheek.

"You take something?" she asked.

"I don't use that shit."

"I know. I was just asking. I'll make some coffee." She got up and went to the kitchen. Lit the gas, put the kettle on. The blond man leaned against the windowsill, staring out.

"Too much on my mind lately," he explained.

"Relax."

"Right now I can't."

The kettle whistled, and Luśka took out glasses. The blond man zipped up his trousers. His thoughts were quick, touching on things and people with an animal sureness. Luśka put the coffee on the windowsill.

"Maybe you can with her," she said, her eyes following his. "Women talk more afterwards. You know, willing to confide."

A train pulled up at the platform and blocked everything.

The brown bear stood on its hind legs and rocked from side to side. Its red tongue lolled between its yellow teeth. Crows flew to its feet. It paid no attention to them, staring at the brick spires of Saint Florian's. At least it seemed to. Its fur was the same colour as the church. Syl threw it a cookie. The crows flapped, but the bear was faster. It dropped to all fours in a second and took the cookie.

"Its nose is like a dog's," she said.

"Kind of," said Iron Man.

Stooping, the collar of his jacket up, his hands in his pockets, he looked a little like a bear himself. He was rocking from side to side too, partly as a joke, partly from the cold, because the wind from the river was bitter. He was starting to regret his idea. "We should have kept driving," he thought. "Gone and sat down somewhere warm and had a drink." The April sun was cold as ice. He looked at Syl's legs in their tights and shivered. He could never understand how women managed like that. He wore long johns until the first of May.

"Do they sleep in the winter?" she asked.

"I doubt it. Too much traffic. The noise of the trams."

A second bear emerged from the concrete cave.

"That must be his wife," said Syl.

"Not necessarily. It could be his brother or just someone from the family."

She tossed cookie after cookie. The bears moved among the yellow discs, confused by the sudden bounty and making no effort to drive away the crows.

"Do you have family, Iron Man?"

"Not really, not any more. I used to. Sometimes I go to the cemetery," he added without thinking, because he was troubled: the Japanese, a watch he couldn't identify, and Bolek's words that morning—"Go downtown with her"—made him dread the coming day. "Shit, I haven't been downtown for two years," he thought. "That cab ride yesterday in the dark doesn't count." The Asians moved off to the other end of the zoo, and the two of them were alone again in the wind. Syl's nose was blue.

"We could go to the Biedronka," he suggested, pointing to Świerczewski.

"What for?" she asked.

"We could have some pancakes. They used to be good there."

"And the shops?"

"There'll be time for that, kid. We saw the bears, now let's get a bite to eat. You said yourself that you never go out."

"All right," agreed Syl. "But just for a short while."

"It takes five minutes to eat a pancake," said Iron Man, and felt relief.

Dust hung in the air. The cooing of pigeons. No light to speak of. They were hunched over, going practically on all fours. Jacek was in the lead. Paweł could hear him feeling his way. Their footsteps strangely resonant on the wood. Then there was light.

"They never put a new padlock on," said Jacek. "Last autumn I pulled the old one off, and it stayed that way."

He was up to his chest in the trapdoor leading to the roof. At his feet, Paweł said:

"What the fuck are we doing?"

"If they weren't outside the door, they're waiting downstairs by the entrance."

"So? You think we can fly away?"

"We can cross the roofs and go a few buildings over," said Jacek. He pulled himself up and disappeared. A blue rectangle of sky. Paweł squinted, gripped the rim of the opening, and entered the wind.

In the great air, the Marriott, the Terminal, the Sucomi Tower, and the shining obelisk of the Eurobank building were close enough to touch. The roof sloped. They grabbed the edge of a ventilation shaft. The sun was behind their backs, over Praga, but its reflection in the glass walls blinded like a magnesium flare. They sheltered in the shadow of the concrete cube from which came the smells of all the apartments. The roof fell inexorably towards the nothingness of the street.

"It's only hard at first," said Jacek. "You get used to it."

"You want to sit here till you get used to it?" Paweł wiped his nose on his sleeve, dropped to one knee.

"If you stay in the middle, you can't see how far down it is. And don't look up. Keep your eyes on the ground in front of you."

"You really think they're downstairs?" Paweł was now down on both knees and feeling for something to hold on to, something that stuck out, anything.

"They're waiting by the entrance. Smoking. Two, maybe three of them."

"What do they look like?"

"Ordinary. Like you, except neater and clean-shaven."

"How do you know?"

"They like shaving. They buy Gillettes or Wilkinson Swords, and shave twice a day."

"I used to do that when I still had the time."

"There you go. They talk about which shaving cream is best."

"Two or three of them? Like when they came to my place."

"Right. They never go around alone."

"Are they afraid?"

"It's not that. They like to talk about old times. In the evenings they drink beer and do that."

"Everyone does that."

"Exactly. That's why they're normal. That gun would have come in handy."

"What gun?"

"Yours, from two days ago."

"Oh . . . You know guns?"

"First we had a Nagan and a Colt, one time one, then the other, so there were mix-ups. We were young and didn't care about the difference. The main thing, both were revolvers. Then the Mauser came out. Comrade Mauser, the one with the magazine in front of the trigger. Loaded with a clip from the top—funny, huh? Because it made the grip like the handle of a file. Churchill had one in the Sudan when he was young. Then Lugers, in other words Parabellums, Walther PPKs, that was James Bond's gun in the seventies before the fashion for the nine mills, and of course the Uzis, all over, Uzis everywhere you looked. Now people use Heckler-Kochs, MP5Ks, because they're small, they fit under your jacket and look nice. Glocks too, because they're futuristic with all that plastic. I'm behind, because I had to sell my TV—"

"There was no gun."

"No gun?"

"I just said it. For something to say."

A red blimp in the distance, beyond the skyscrapers, pulling a long banner, but the words were too far away to read. The gold star atop the Eurobank building faced Mokotów. The reflection of the sun dazzled even in the shade. Jacek stood and set off along the middle of the roof. "Come on," he said. "It's only three or four buildings over."

So it's all settled. The key is turned in the lock and drops into an overcoat pocket, and the lift is setting off from the first floor. The smell of cakes baking comes from the doors of the apartments. Vanilla, cinnamon, and rum fill the stairwell. It's quiet, even with the clatter of pans down the hall and the children's voices. Silence swathes the body and head, makes thoughts audible. On the lift wall, a light patch is all that's left of the mirror. Check once that the key is in its place, and the metal door can be closed. For a moment, the old fear that, instead of descending, the lift will shoot upwards and smash to pieces against the roof, the grease-blackened cables whishing. It's better to shut your eyes and pretend it's just a game of peekaboo, till the car finally stops and someone on the other side opens the door obligingly. Just a few more steps, and daylight should drive away all bad dreams, Pankracy. That's why I wore white, so no one would see. At night, black's the thing; in the day, white is invisible. Now the pavement, grass, corner store, and not a living soul, as if everyone has left, though the cars are still there gleaming after they were washed for the holiday, and it's so bright, your eyes hurt, and the sky is so blue, Pankracy. Pass the kiosk and the café, turn right, straight to the crossing, then the bus, the tram, another bus. I'm not going into the darkness of the metro, never. Everything's memorized. You just recite the stops and bus numbers. I'll sit outside the door, on the stairs, or on the street. The weather is so nice, and the trees will blossom soon, but why is it so empty here, as if people are hiding, peeking from behind the curtains on all the floors, from every building, from everywhere, but I have to keep going, cross the road, reach the pavement, turn left, the stop's there, and the bus will pull in empty, shining, its windows all washed so you can see better. That's the reason for the white outfit, Pankracy, the white coat, dress, shoes, scarf, and underneath too everything is white as the air, so it should work, because he's completely alone, I've known that for a long time, he was just pretending when he made all those phone calls, hardly anyone ever called *him,* and I must stop being bad like yesterday when I left him as if he was never going to come again.

Shirt, underwear, socks. Bolek turned in the bathroom like a fleshy top. From the toilet to the mirror, from the mirror to the gold and white cabinet with an even larger mirror on the door, to the glass shelves and back again. The sound of running water in the sink, the toilet flushing, the whirr of the hair drier. He wiped the condensation off one mirror, the other, and couldn't decide which deodorant to use. "Underwear, underwear," he hummed. He chose briefs. "In a light suit, boxer shorts show," he reasoned. He sprayed Elements under his right arm, Cool Water under his left. Pleased, he buttoned his salmon shirt. "A man has to have a bit of mystery. A bit of romance. That's what women go for. And he has to be quick, decisive." He turned off the taps. The vision of Irina had left and wouldn't return, though he closed his eyes tightly. Only the samovar appeared, and it was cold and barely visible. It didn't even look much like a samovar. Reality is better, he decided, so he had to get ready, get dressed, go while there was still time. It was so easy for lovers to miss each other in this world and never meet again, especially in his line of work. He quaked at the thought of the vast East, where his happiness could be lost for ever. You could travel for a week without stopping, get out anywhere, and there would be nothing. He hurried to the closet and took out his suit, the colour of unripe plums, loose, glossy, rustling softly like crisp new notes. He bustled, chose which cuff links, thought about the tie, considered the question of socks going with braided moccasins. He thought about an ascot but remembered the men outside the public toilets the night before and their scorn. The big mirror on the cabinet door caught the scorn in his face, which he examined from the front and in profile. "It has to be a tie," he said. "Or nothing. It's warm today; I could undo two buttons to show the chain." He smiled. "A tie's not bad, but gold is gold." He pulled on his trousers and was ready. His clothes all perfect, as if he'd been born in them. But at the door his courage abandoned him. His knees weak, his mouth dry. "She's only a Russian," he told himself, but it occurred to him that she wasn't all that Russian. He would go down to his car, call on the way, say he had something important to see her about. His hand on the door handle, he turned and looked at Sheikh, who was saying good-bye. The dog loved him but couldn't help. He went back to the living room and poured himself a shot of Johnny Walker. He drank it down, grimaced, and poured another. His courage gradually returned.

Her mind went back. She no longer recognized people or places. The things she remembered, she wasn't sure if they had really happened to her. Can you remember what happened to another person? She didn't know. But she let herself be swept away by the tide of images. It was better to accept them. They were all blurry, and slow, as if underwater. She became aware of the cold. Her hands were tied behind her back. She tried to crawl under the bedding, but it was twisted. She pressed into the bedspread with her knees, squeezing, and felt a little warmer. The sun was over Saska Kępa, but the curtains were drawn and the room was dark. The golden circle climbed as it moved south, and the black roofs of Skaryszewska, Nowińska, and Bliska gave off the smell of tar. An articulated 115 bus, almost empty, turned into Chodakowska, passed the warehouses and the wretched city outskirts, the windswept fields and the chain-link fences, emerged on Stanisławowska, passed the velodrome and Wiatraczna, went through the roundabout, and headed east down Grochowska between the lower and fewer houses, to the Trakt Lubelski, a row of single cottages, shacks, unfinished apartment buildings, eventually ending at the edge of the woods. She tried to imagine what lay beyond, but the big green signs saying LUBLIN and TERESPOL returned her to the dark room.

Again she sank into the past. She was very small, and someone was leading her by the hand. They were walking down a quiet, snow-covered street in Radość or Międzylesie. Coal smoke in the air. She tried to slide on the pavement ice. Clumps of snow on the branches of the trees. A dog barked, a train rumbled. The far end of the narrow street was a grey-white point. Everything at arm's length. Icicles dangled from the eaves and gutters of single-storey houses, and the tops of the chimneys had curious little tin figures, human silhouettes. She wasn't sure it was her own memory, but the pain eased, so maybe she had been that little girl sliding on the soles of her shoes while someone held her firmly by the hand. A lull in the sounds of the street, and the distorted echo of the station loudspeakers. The metallic voice smacking the stone platforms. "You can't hear whether it's an arrival or a departure," she whispered. The people outside the door were talking. Someone put something on the stove. The lights must have changed at the Targowa intersection, because a tram squealed by. She felt the cold again. The fabric between her thighs was rough and foreign. Then suddenly she felt that all this had happened long ago and would never happen again, and now only a solitude awaited her that stretched from one end of the world to the other and would continue for ever. Fear entered her naked body: it wasn't the pain, it was the void consuming Kijowska like a flame, the station, trains, cars, people, stores, everything she had seen in her life up to this moment. All that was left was herself curled into a ball on a twisted bed that spun like a paper boat in blackness. She wanted them to come back, to open the door and talk to her and touch her, because human pain is better than inhuman fear.

When it finally happened, when they were resting, when she heard their double breath above her and felt their heat, and the smell of cooking drifted into the room, she huddled into the tightest ball possible and began to mouth words that came into her head from somewhere: "Angel of God, guardian mine . . ."

"Maybe Rutkowskiego," Iron Man said, hope in his voice.

"Where?"

"Rutkowskiego. I mean Chmielna . . ."

"No," Syl said firmly. "Marszałkowska."

"They always had shoes on Rutkowskiego."

"They still do. But not that kind."

"What kind then?"

"It's better here. There'll be more here."

They came to a stop outside the Metropol, and Iron Man gazed into the abyss of downtown.

"Sure," he said, half to himself, half to Syl.

People passed, smelling of different perfumes. His Fahrenheit had evaporated long ago, and he felt uncomfortable. The electronic billboard outside the Forum went too quickly to read. The ads stylish and mysterious.

"It's changed," he said.

"What's changed?" asked Syl.

"Everything. Now you can't tell where anything is."

"Let's go to Konstytucji Square; there's bound to be something there."

They went. Syl studied the window displays, while Iron Man reflected on time, which used to crawl but now rushed like mad. He thought about electronic watches, which you didn't mind losing and never missed when you threw them away. The time they kept was second-rate. Once, when you got a watch for your first communion, you'd wear it till your wedding and even longer. All you had to do was wind it up. Now what could a father leave his son? A shitty little plastic Casio with a supply of batteries? Iron Man had grown old. Marszałkowska was running on ahead, dragging Nowogrodzka and Żurawia and Wspólna with it, while he was going nowhere in his imitation leather shoes from the suburbs.

Syl stopped in front of tinted glass and silver letters that read BOOTICELLI.

"I'll look in here," she said.

"I'll wait," he said. "I'll have a smoke."

Remembering, he gave a start, patted his pockets, and took out his wallet.

"Four should do," he said uncertainly, counting out the notes.

"I'm not sure." She took the money, and the glass slid open noiselessly in front of her. He stepped aside and put his nose to the window. He could see some movement but nothing specific.

Syl's pale calves flashed for a moment. "You'd think they have miracles in there," he muttered. He went to the kerb to watch the cars. Fortunately you could still understand cars: they were shinier, more colourful, went faster, and braked better, but they were cars, not fakes of cars. He tried to guess the makes, but the logos meant nothing to him. He did manage to spot two Mercs and a Ford, but the rest was a puzzle, all silver hieroglyphs. He shrugged and thought about his neighbourhood and the men poking along in their baby Fiats, Polonezes, and Zastavas. The abandoned frames became overgrown with nettles, but the engine parts lived on in other vehicles.

"Iron Man, two hundred more," he heard behind his back.

"Six hundred for a pair of boots?" He turned, his face sad and resigned. "Even women's?"

"They're knee-length, and this is the best store," Syl said.

He reached for his wallet again and started to regret the cab ride that morning. Only one more hundred-zloty note, and some small change left in the compartment. Syl skipped back inside the store, while Iron Man raised his eyes to the heavens as if seeking a sign. On the roof of one of the buildings he saw a figure. It appeared then withdrew, no doubt frightened by the drop. "They're probably repairing a leak from the winter," he thought. The sun rose higher, and the ravine of Marszałkowska began to stink.

That was how it was. Events that took place at the same time confirm it. The driver of a 19 tram was approaching the terminus at Broniewskiego. For two months haunted by the thought of suicide. He would smoke one cigarette after another and draw up a careful plan: methods, places, times. He was forty-three. Smiling just then, because 4 and 3 made a lucky 7. At the terminus his replacement was waiting for him, a woman. He decided to do it after the holiday, discreetly and quietly, to spare his family.

A twelve-year-old boy was riding a bike on the footpath of the Grota-Roweckiego Bridge. He had run away from home, left in the morning without a word to anyone. By evening he would reach Zegrze and there go to the police, because he forgot his own phone number and his strength had completely abandoned him. His father would come and pick him up in his baby Fiat, happy and angry, because he'd have to unbolt the wheels of the bike and remove the front seat from the car. The boy wore a cap saying NIKE. The river was blinding and smelled of sludge and warm willow thickets.

The boy is eighteen, the girl seventeen. They walk in a hug down Kamienne Schodki. She is blonde and beautiful, he brown-haired and handsome. They talk about movies, marijuana, and love. They reach the Gdańskie Wybrzeże, run across the road, and find themselves on the large concrete steps leading down to the river. The girl points at the zoo and says she'd like to set all the animals free. The boy, overcome with affection, holds her tight and kisses her. At the beginning of May they'll learn that she's pregnant. They'll meet a few more times, then never again. He's in Levi jeans and jacket, she's in no particular brand, in pastels, in low-heeled shoes.

"All the signs are, it won't get cold," says a fifty-year-old man as he puts a wicker basket in the boot of a red Passat. His wife passes him a travelling bag and another basket. The dog, a ruddy spaniel, is already in the car, watching its master restlessly. The man closes the boot, opens the passenger door for the woman, shuts it gently, and takes his seat behind the wheel. Foksal is one-way, so they drive down Kopernika to Tamka, then take the Wybrzeże Kościuszkowskie, and in four hours they're at their summer house on the lake. They'll come back Tuesday afternoon, rested and a little tanned. The dog with them. It will yelp in its sleep and move its paws as it chases visions of ducks and grebes.

All this happens and will happen, since the world has no gaps or cracks. When something disappears, a new thing takes its place. In the afternoon Mr Max will start to worry about his son. There'll be only one bodyguard in the house. Or rather, Mr Max won't be worried so much as angry.

They were trying the third trapdoor, while their shadows grew shorter. The clock atop the Metropol said twelve fifteen. Jacek tugged at the flap. It opened a few centimetres, then was held in place.

"A padlock," he said. "If only we had a jimmy."

Paweł pointed to the forest of TV antennas.

"No, if you take one of those, someone will come running," Jacek said.

"If the roof were lower, we could find something to open it with. Things get lobbed up by kids . . ."

"If, if. Just give me a hand."

They both took hold of the flap and pulled. Jacek put his hand in. "I was right, a padlock. The bastards. Who are they trying to keep out? Unbelievable."

They were sweaty, filthy; the sun was overhead now, and there was nowhere to take shelter. The roof stuck to their shoes and fingers.

"At least we won't slip," said Paweł. He was gradually ceasing to be afraid. He thought that actually he might stay here: he wasn't going to find any place better, it was shit everywhere. Jacek gave up, sat, wrapped his arms around his knees, and stared into the distance between Wola and Ochota. Paweł sat beside him.

"Let's wait a while. No one's coming up here," he said.

"Fine. Maybe I'll remember that phone number." Jacek started to laugh.

Paweł laughed too.

"And I don't have my mobile with me."

"You should, without a mobile—"

"Someone stamped on it a couple of days ago. All I have left is my jacket, because they took my car too." Paweł straightened the jacket. It was dirty. Thin at the elbows.

"And the car wasn't enough?"

"For the interest maybe. It was a five-year-old Polonez."

"I was right all along," said Jacek, shaking his head.

"About what?"

"About not going into business."

They laughed again. The red blimp was now coming towards them over Mokotów. Its nose a little sun that gave no light.

"And what was that?" asked Paweł, pointing down at the street.

"Just a swipe. At most a couple hundred."

"Oh."

The shadow of the blimp passed behind them, but they didn't notice, recalling their lives. What else did they have to do? As the shadow drifted over Żurawia, they reminisced about the apartment on Syreny, Agawy, Patrice Lumumby. A five-storey building, weeping willows in the courtyard. They would watch the branches swaying. The apartment was on the first floor. The whole building, walls, stairwell, half-dead light—permeated with the smell of old food. People had cooked there for ages, and no one ever went into town for a meal. The same on the second, third, fourth, and fifth floors. They remembered the smell of boiling and frying and the rattling of the hand rails sheathed in hard green plastic. Permanently dark in the room that looked onto the courtyard. A palm in the corner, its crown pressed against the ceiling. Someone smoking Silesias. A blue pack of them lay on the table, and a black-and-white film was on TV. "A French serial," said Paweł. "No, there weren't any French serials," said Jacek. "There probably aren't any now either." But they couldn't remember what they'd been doing there or whose place it was. The living room window to the kitchen was broken, its frame discoloured, and the paint had begun to flake. Tea was passed through it in glasses with metal holders. The glasses stood on the tablecloth by the pack of Silesias. Outside, children shouted to one another, and a train rumbling. "It must have been Syreny," said Jacek. "You couldn't have heard it on Lumumby. It's too far, and there's the noise of the traffic." In any case they drank their tea and left. Rain, the tree branches shining, the smell of low-octane petrol from old petrol, the archaic clatter of the diesel buses. They got as far as the Pedet department store and couldn't remember any more. A visit ten years ago, and it may have been important. At any moment, life can lead in any direction. "So you think it's because of that half-hour in some shit hole in Wola that we're sitting on this roof right now?" asked Paweł. "You have to think something," said Jacek.

The oval shadow of the blimp cut across Nowy Świat towards Krakowskie Przedmieście. The street was too narrow for the shadow. On the long purple banner that streamed behind, nothing was written. No one paid attention to it. Only Syl clapped her hands, almost dropping her large box.

"Look, Iron Man! A balloon!"

"Not exactly," said Iron Man. "It's got an engine and a propeller and can go in any direction."

"How do you know all that?"

Iron Man was embarrassed by his knowledge.

"A person used to know a few things."

They'd had a burger and Coke then doughnuts, and now Iron Man was steering them towards the Skarpa cinema, but Syl wasn't interested in a movie. She wanted to find a place where she could put her new boots on, but there was nowhere right. "I can't do it in a gateway!" she said, indignant, when Iron Man pointed to a courtyard by Gałczyńskiego. "What, changing my clothes in front of people?"

"Then let's go down to the river," he said. "There's only the fish there."

He dropped the idea of a movie: the place did look like a hangout for local punks. He had a thirst, but none of the bars they passed deserved consideration. He doubted that any of them served regular Królewskie beer. Most had tinted windows, like the stores where they sold shoes for six hundred a pop.

A soft breeze blowing from the river. Syl called to tell him not to turn around. He had no intention. He was sitting by the water's edge, smoking and watching the white foam mushroom from the brown mouth of his bottle. On the far bank, Praga, as always. He caught the marshy odour of the port, the smell of burned sugar from the Różyckiego bazaar, mingled with musk, manure, hay from the zoo, coal dust from the power plant, heated metal from the FSO plant, horse sweat, and the rain-soaked pavement of Ząbkowska years ago but just as clearly as the fug of cigarettes and beer wafting from entranceways and the smell of cheap kiosk-bought fragrances—white lilac, lily of the valley, Seven Blossoms soap—in the trams on Stalingradzka, the mulch of vegetable gardens and the candle smoke from the cemetery. He smelled it all as an animal does, and his reddish nose twitched happily, restlessly. "Jesus," he thought, "how can people move away? Especially abroad?" He took a swallow and sighed: "Another five years, Mirosław Iron Man, and even here it'll be like abroad."

"Ready!" called Syl.

He looked and saw her against the sky. She stamped a foot. His eyes had to adjust, because the sun was dropping towards Wola. In the boots she looked even skinnier. The black leather to her knees, the heavy silver buckles like silverware on a Sunday table. She walked from side to side, theatrical. She looked like a child's spidery drawing.

"Well?" she asked.

He tossed his cigarette away, squinted, scratched his chin.

"Fancy. They're not too big?"

"I need to put some cotton wool in the toes, and they'll be perfect."

"They should fit," he said. "They shouldn't pinch, and they shouldn't wobble."

Syl twirled on an imaginary runway.

"The size doesn't matter. The important thing is that they're the kind I wanted."

"I guess too big is better than too small."

"It's a pity there's no mirror here. I must look cool. I'll wait a bit, and then ask Porkie to buy me a leather overcoat. In black, like the boots. I've seen ones like that."

As they went back up, by Tamka, Syl took Iron Man by the arm. Embarrassed, he walked with his elbow elegantly stiff.

"It's just to begin with," she said. "I'll get used to it soon." They turned on Dobra, and she looked for a cab. At the stand a white Tempra came by. Syl waved; the cab pulled over, and the girl pulled Iron Man.

"Come on. We're going back, aren't we?"

He gestured to the cabbie to drive on. He freed his arm and started patting his pockets for cigarettes, but instead of a pack he took out the bottle top from the Królewskie. He examined it, turned it in his fingers like a coin, put it away again.

"We're not going back," he said finally.

He reached into his pocket again and pulled out his wallet. Took from it everything that was left. Thought for a moment, kept the small change, gave Syl the hundred-zloty note. She took it unthinkingly, crumpled it in her hand.

"What?" she said.

"That's what Bolek said. I mean, he told me to tell you that you should go home."

In the distance, a local crossed the railway bridge into Praga. The sound reached them with an unreal delay.

"That's how it is sometimes." He wanted to add something, but his head was empty, so he just raised a hand. She moved to the side, helpless. He turned and set off towards Old Town, but he didn't take Dobra, instead turning on Tamka and then into Topiel, as if he were covering his tracks. A wind had started up, and now there were clouds over Żerań.

This time he took the Wybrzeże Helskie and for a moment saw the red humps of the camels over the fence. Again he thought it was time to have a son. He saw Irina's broad hips. "Her breasts too," he said to himself with a smile. To the left, the Vistula sparkled like brocade. Out of the corner of his eye, the brick spire of Our Lady's. "I'll take her to Old Town," he decided. "Lots of culture, monuments, the royal castle—they don't have those things where she's from." He wondered if they ever had a king. He remembered the Kremlin, recently on television. It looked like a high-security prison. "Not like here—everything's flashy, turrets, a clock with gold hands. We'll go to Old Town, leave the car, take a walk, some nice place to eat, not a bar, with tablecloths and candles, and a menu in Polish and English."

Approaching Gdański station, he recalled Winniczek and his tin shack in the middle of a field by the river, selling only beer and sausage. "How could anyone live like that?" he wondered, turning. "Going to work, leaving work, a beer on a windy patch of bare earth, and on top of that the cops checking ID like everyone was a tramp." The Beamer exited the curve with an agreeable swish. He lowered the driver's window and spat in the direction of the Golędzinów barracks. The water cannon idle. "Pricks," he thought but without hatred. Since he'd begun working for Mr Max, he stopped taking them into account. "Don't you worry about them," Mr Max would repeat, "worry about the work." A few young guys in T-shirts and combats playing volleyball. At Stalingradzka he let an 18 tram pass, waited politely till the light was amber, turned left. He was in a hurry but at the same time no hurry. In the left lane, but the needle settling at seventy. A red Twingo honked. At any other time, he would have raged, but now didn't even look in the mirror. The little car overtook him with disdain. He checked to the right, changed lanes. Kotsisa came up right away, so he pulled off, found a spot between a baby Fiat and a Skoda, and parked. He took out his mobile, dialled the first three numbers of the hotel, and lost his nerve. A teenager on a skateboard went past. He reached into his inside pocket and took out a hip flask. He sat with the phone in one hand, the flask in the other. "I'll have a drink, then make the call. No, I'll call first, then have a drink." He went with the tried and true: had a drink, waited for it to kick in, dialled the number, closed his eyes.

Five minutes later, the Beamer shot out on Stalingradzka in a squeal of tyres. He heard horns but didn't bother to look. Second and floor it, third and floor it, and in the distance, the viaducts already. The first drops of rain on the windscreen. He whistled a mixture of Kalinka and Katyusha, entered the shade of the viaduct doing well over sixty. The way ahead was empty, smooth, and straight. He could see the road like metal as it climbed to the bridge over the canal.

The woman appeared out of nowhere. Dressed in white, walking at the pedestrian crossing by the bus stop, carrying a little plastic basket with a handle. He honked, but she must have been deaf, she didn't even turn her head. He hit the brake, obscenities spilling from his lips like prayer. He felt the Beamer fishtail, so he took his foot off the pedal and straightened a little, but had to brake again, because the white figure loomed, larger than the car now, like a cloud about to engulf.

He felt nothing, merely saw the red plastic basket high in the air, and as he watched, the car gave a jolt, a network of cracks appeared on the windscreen, and everything stopped. Except the basket, which rolled across the tarmac and bounced on the kerb. A striped cat came out of it, tried to walk, but couldn't move its hind legs.

———

It seemed to be greenery. Vegetable gardens, Skaryszewski Park, Praski Park, or the bushes along the riverbank. It moved with a rustle, was moist, and glistened as if after rain. Crossings, passageways, paths led into a safe labyrinth of meadows repeatedly surrounded by trees. The grass swayed in the wind, making the whole picture sway like a reflection in water. She tried to breathe evenly and deeply. Outlines again filled the blackness, and they were followed by colours. She feared that her strength would fail her and the dark would sweep her into a well. The dark, dense, came from the walls, furniture, floor; the mattress was soaked with it, and it left a cold slick on her palm. Sometimes the greenery opened up and covered all the places she knew and could remember. Kijowska disappeared, Targowa disappeared, so did the dirty river, and downtown with all its skyscrapers and its endless streams of cars, people mad for lack of sleep, the underground whine of the metro, the apocalyptic jets and the electric horizon, as if none of it had ever existed. She felt the rough bedding and was overcome, because she couldn't remember a thing. At least the two were still there, she could hear their conversation and the everyday bustle in the kitchen. "It means they don't know where to go," she told herself. Relief swept over her like sleep, and the kitchen sounds recalled the morning noise at home when her mother was getting ready to leave for work and she could spend another hour in bed. She would curl up and doze before the alarm went off. From time to time opening her eyes to check the minute hand. The ticking loud and distinct. Morning slipped in through the half-open window: the clatter of crates, the rattle of bottles. Delivery vans driving up to the stores. The banter of the drivers and shopgirls. In the early, clear air, the sounds were resonant, and it seemed to her that the world was so large, it had room for everything. She would close her eyes to make the clock disappear. She would move her hand in the bedding to find a pocket of cold. When she found one, she would press her shoulder into it, her chest, trying to fit her entire body in it, until the cold was gone and she could start the game all over again.

Rain began to fall on Marszałkowska. Big drops hit the black roof and broke with a dry crack. They smiled at each other and shrugged, because everything around them was a joke they didn't get. A moment later, the downpour, and they crawled in search of shelter, but there was nothing but antennas, ventilation ducts, superstructures for lifts.

"Is there anything electrical up here?" asked Paweł.

"I don't think so. In the city it's all done with cables, underground."

"There could be lightning."

"Not in April."

"I didn't know that," said Paweł, and heard the city below go silent. He leaned back against a concrete wall. The rain penetrated his clothes, ran down his skin. The skyscrapers had disappeared behind a grey curtain of rain, and it was like being stuck on a strange, black, gleaming island. The rain intensified and blinded them completely. They moved closer to feel each other's touch.

At exactly this time the blond man came into the kitchen. Luśka closed the door behind him, then went to the sink and turned on the tap. She took the dishwashing liquid, squeezed some onto his hands. He washed them for a long time, thoroughly, almost to the elbows, rinsed them off, put more liquid on, and rinsed again. She handed him a tea towel. He dried his hands and reached for the phone. He looked out the window towards East Station, which was not visible, and patiently dialled.

"Maybe it's because of the rain," said Luśka.

"That has nothing to do with it."

He tried again, and again, then put the phone back on the windowsill. Kijowska was hazy, deserted, cut in two by the tram tracks like a fish along its spine. Beyond, nothing but the quivering grey of the rain.

"The fat bastard," said the blond man. "He's never there when you need him." He put the mobile phone in his pocket, turned from the window, looked at Luśka.

"She doesn't weigh much. The car's right outside."

"I'll look for something for the rain," she replied.

"Find something for her too. For appearances."

The girl went into the hall, and the blond man looked at the station again. Thoughts came, and they fitted perfectly. He checked that his keys were in his pocket. He pressed the button on the remote and wondered if his wet car had responded.

"OK. We can go," he heard from the door.

In the late afternoon it stopped raining, and the sun came out above the overpasses around the bus terminus. The shadows below were black, but the light was the purest gold. The power plant shone, the tarmac gleamed, the façade of the drab church was aflame, its iron railing too. The priest in his black jacket and black shirt locked the church door, walked down the steps, and closed the gate behind him. He was carrying a briefcase. Tiny bits of glass crunched under his feet. He slowed and looked around, but there was nothing. It was only when the cars pulled up at the light that he heard a faint noise. On the wet earth next to the pavement, in last year's grass, a dull-coloured cat. Trying to move. The priest put his briefcase on the ground and went to the animal. He took it gingerly in his arms, picked up the briefcase, and headed back to the church.

www.vintage-books.co.uk